The Wrong

Choice

Tasha, your attention to detail as a BETA reader is extraordinary. Thank goodness I benefitted from that expertise! Thank you!

Sherlynn A. Muckelroy

Novels by Sherlynn A. Muckelroy

The "Quest of the Ages" Series:

The Wrong Choice

SHERLYNN A. MUCKELROY

Sherlynn A. Muckelroy

Visit my website at www.sherlynnmuckelroy.com

Printed in the United States of America

First printing : November 2020

Self-Published

ISBN: 9798551065166

Acknowledgements

The inspiration for this book came from personal experience while growing up in El Paso, Texas. My mother reminded me of Lucille Ball with funny escapades and mishaps in the kitchen. A couple of the botched meals in my novel came from memory of how my mother explained their reality. Back then, the kitchen was the hub of the home where the family shared their meals and spoke of their day. A few of those humorous stories found their way into my novel. I am thankful for my family and how they molded me into the person I am today.

I am grateful for the two writing groups—The Las Cruces Writer's Group, and The Pens of the West Writer's Group, both in Las Cruces, NM. Talented writers of genres across the board have barreled through my manuscript, offering valuable advice and critiques. I am indebted to Lorraine Garcia, Steve Eiserling, Quincey Burkhalter, Linda Aragon, Joy Jones, Rachel Christiansen, Sarah Sayles, Marlena Fraune, Natasha Smith, and David McArthur.

To my BETA readers, Candy Slover, Marchelle Gebhardt, Patty Danley, Gwen McClure, Sarah Sayles, Rachel Christiansen, Marlena Fraune, Natasha Smith, thank you for taking the time out of your busy lives to read my book. Your suggestions opened my eyes to details I missed or those needing work. You are awesome!

I would also like to thank the photographers from Pixabay.com who graciously granted me permission to use their images for my covers: Jerzy Gorecki, Valentin Tikhonov, and Krish Shillode.—

Sherlynn A. Muckelroy

Do you know you're kisses
are warm and tender?
Do you know their touch
is soft and sweet?
And do you know they
fill me with wonder?
And leave me all breathless
and weak?

Do you know you're kisses
are fiery?
Do you know they are
thrilling too?
Do you know you're arms feel
strong about me?
Do you know I feel
something new?

Do you know of the turmoil
inside me?
Do you know of the thrill of
your cheek on mine?
Do you know that inside I'm
all starry?
Do you know that's what
makes my eyes shine?

June Loretta Murray

$\mathscr{P}$rologue

The Year Is 2017 in Golden Spires Assisted Living Facility

$\mathcal{M}$y stars and garters, whoever thought an old woman like me could jot down her life story, and a year later, turn it into a whole cotton-pickin' book? I did! kind of; I only wrote five-years-worth because my fingers wore out. But within those five years are the best and worst times of my life.

I'm not sure why I created such a manuscript in the first place, other than it's the diary I never made as a youth. Besides, now as a resident in the Golden Spires Assisted Living facility, I will need reading material when my brain goes south. It will be like reading a romantic story whose main character's name is the same as mine. I will relive the shock and awe all over again from a reader's point of view, not as the one who experienced it.

So that explains that.

Now, I suspect you are chomping at the bit to know what happened to a sassy hip chick like me that caused me to move to Golden Spires. Two things. One had to do with ineptness. Not my own, you understand, but that of the nitwit bagger at the grocery store who packed three delicate artichokes at the tippy top of my paper grocery bag. Her failure to secure the vegetables caused one to pop out, and while lunging to save it, I lost my balance and fell flat on my face. And just so you know, carrying three bags to my car on my own instead of using a shopping cart had *nothing* to do with my unfortunate circumstance. Nothing at all.

Then some asshole called an ambulance.

Since entering the age of wizards and Methuselah, I have tried my best to avoid hospitals. All those people wearing color-coded outfits, uniforms, or whatever they're called, running in and out all day and night poking and prodding nearly drove me crazy. Especially that one lady who had a silk rose pinned to her pocket. It was red, and you know what that color means, don't you? Yes, indeedy. It's the color of blood, and all she wanted to do was stab needles into my arm for no other reason than to lust for that life-sustaining fluid.

Damn vampire.

To add insult to injury, doctors couldn't speak simple English. Oh, no. They used jargon filled with unintelligible terminologies. They told me I had a femoral fracture that occurred in the proximal end of my femur. What the hell? I had a broken hip, for God's sake. How hard was that to say?

After weeks of rehabilitation, I returned to my home where two flights of stairs greeted me. In going up and down them, I might as well have been climbing Mt. Everest. With each step, my hip *and* pride hurt in knowing my body was falling apart.

The second reason I moved was the fault of the Department of Motor Vehicles. They revoked my driver's license just because I did not read the teeny-weeny letters correctly in the eye machine. If they had made the letters bigger, I could have read them. It must be a government ploy to get old people off the roads.

Anyway, I couldn't drive my candy-apple red Mercedes, and I faced the exhaustive and painful climb of Mt. Everest within my home. I stressed my brain to come up with a solution around this fiasco, and this was the only choice I came up with: sell my car, put the house I had lived in for sixty years on the market, and move to Golden Spires.

And now you know the two reasons why I moved to an assisted living facility. Oh, by the way, I am prone to swearing from time to time. I try to keep the words incarcerated in my mind like my mother (adopted mother, but just mother to me) taught me to do, but sometimes circumstances dictate my using them with voracity. I apologize in advance if it offends you.

Now here are the two perks to living here. One is I don't have to cook any more. Good thing, too. At home I was a terrible cook. Whatever entree I had in the oven or on the stove ended up charred, creating eye-burning, nose prickling, throat gagging smoke that hung thick against the ceiling.

The second perk is the four o'clock happy hour every afternoon except Sunday. On *that* day, I invite a few "neighbors" to my all-inclusive single room apartment where we drink red wine I have hidden in the far back of a cabinet or white wine tucked behind the orange juice bottle in my small refrigerator.

Oh, listen to me ramble on about how good it is living at Golden Spires instead of telling you about writing my memoir. So, back to the task at hand.

A year ago, at the ripe old age of eighty-six, I started this massive project while still in my home. By the date they occurred, I organized the age-old, written memories that ended up covering my formal dining table and two card tables. My gnarly fingers prevented me from using a pencil to formulate the pieces into a cohesive manuscript, so I used a computer. Two hundred pages later, I nearly dropped dead from exhaustion, so I put the story away.

It wasn't until I moved to my current residence that I decided to see the real thing on paper. I pressed the PRINT button then joined my friends in the game room at the other end of the hall for a riveting round or two of Rummikub. An hour later, I returned to my apartment to find a disorganized mass of white pages littering the carpet. It was my manuscript! What happened, you ask? I forgot to pull out the page extender on the printer.

My mother's antique cedar chest lay a few steps away, so I plopped my tush on it to think about how to pick up the mess without having a heart attack. With the choice clear, I bent over a million times and snatched the pages off the floor.

What kind of idiot forgets to pull out the paper tray? Only a goddamned old, forgetful one, that's what!

If that wasn't bad enough, the scrawny scarecrow in the apartment next door heard my un-ladylike language and peeked in my door. "Is everything all right in there, dearie?" she asked me.

"Oh, sure!" I barked, smart aleck that I am. "I wanted to play 'Fifty-Two Pick Up,' so I threw a stack of papers into the air to see how long it would take me to pick them up!"

"Oh, and how long did it take?" she asked with sweet abandon.

In my rage, I slammed the door in her face, fished out the bottle of cabernet from its hiding place and took a swig. Forget the glass.

That day nearly killed me, but I've been through much worse as you will discover if you choose to read what I have written here.

Speaking of which, the events in this memoir are important to me. I even gave it a title: "The Life of Riley." Yes, I took the name of the 1950s television situation comedy, but it fits here, too. My name is Riley—Riley O'Keefe—and this is *my* story.

"The Life of Riley"

Chapter One

*I*n 1957, Dwight D. Eisenhower sat in the Oval Office as President of the United States. The housing boom exploded as did the baby population. Boys of all ages gathered around electric train sets. Little girls played tea party, drinking Kool-Aid from miniature china teacups. Marilyn Monroe (my personal idol) owned the title, "Queen of Hollywood," along with James Dean as the designated bad boy heartthrob. Even so, Humphrey Bogart held my favor in that position, minus the bad boy status. Elvis Presley claimed the crown of "King of Rock 'n' Roll," and Lucille Ball rose above all others as the "Queen of Comedy." How could anyone say the United States had no royalty.

In that same year, I turned twenty-seven-years-old. I lived and breathed love for my husband of two years who was more than a mere mortal. Sherman was my Adonis.

Even though I created an image of Sherman as a Greek god, he fell short of the myth. He did not boast of youth or a six-foot-five-inch stature bearing six-pack abs. At age thirty-seven, he displayed a five-foot-eleven, rugged and masculine physique with the beginnings of a potbelly from sucking down too much alcohol and not enough exercise. His calves lacked shape and muscle like the Greek god. If painted pink all over, Sherman would make a perfect flamingo lawn ornament. He lacked the chiseled jaw and piercing blue eyes. His jawline was soft and rounded, his eyes the color of my morning coffee. They twinkled as they peered through the smudges on the lenses of his black-rimmed glasses. Boyish curls spun of golden strands covered the crown of the Greek god. Not Sherman's. His black, short hair revealed premature hints of gray at the temples, giving him a sophisticated appearance. Both god and the opposite of one, however, shared the ability to make a woman swoon with a beguiling smile. Even if Sherman never physically resembled the Greek god of beauty and fertility, he was everything I hoped for in a husband, lover, and future father of our children.

Sherman kissed me goodbye and left for another day at the office. While changing the bed where I had given my husband a hand job earlier that morning, a strange thought came to me. A very strange thought. I recalled a conversation I had with my mother two days before tying the knot with Sherman. She had wanted to talk to me about a wife's duties and her place in the home.

"Riley, when you take Sherman as your husband, you must take excellent care of him. He is your top priority."

"In what way, mother?"

"Well, dear, you must provide him with a hearty breakfast every morning and a hot meal every night. He deserves a tidy house and beautiful wife to come home to after a hard day's work. So, before he gets home, you put on a fresh dress, make up, and jewelry.

"That's easy, mother. I love Sherman and want to be a good wife to him."

"Good. And to ensure you are a good wife, you must also…"

"Yes, mother, go on. What else must I do?"

Her face turned bright red, and she swallowed hard, which confused me. "You must…well, there are expectations of a wife that happen…um…in the bedroom."

"Oh," I giggled, waving my hand, "you mean making the bed every morning. Don't you worry one iota, mother. I am an excellent bed maker."

"That is a must, of course, but," her voice softened, "it's what happens **in** the bed."

It took me a moment, but I finally understood. "You mean having sex with him? Is that what you're getting at?"

Her eyes popped open with my candid response. "Yes, exactly. You must meet his needs in the bedroom as well as out of it."

"All right, mother. Can you give me some examples as to what those sexual expectations are?"

The telephone rang at that moment, prompting my mother to jump out of her chair and rush to answer it. I waited for her to return, but she never came back to finish our conversation. By her not pursuing the topic later, I assumed she had no intent on answering my question. Oh, well. Guess I'd find out on my wedding night.

Another thing I never received from my mother's *book of womanly knowledge* was how to cook. I relied on my cookbook to teach me. However, there weren't too many people who defined my culinary skills as legitimate cooking. Neither did Sherman, but he learned to politely smile through those moments. If he didn't, I'd get angry and stomp away, leaving him hungry *and* horny.

At the end of our second year of marital bliss, Sherman received the sought-after promotion of Vice President of Finance with the company he worked for—Unified Automobile Company. The bad part was the location of the new job. All VPs worked out of the company's headquarters miles away from our current residence.

When my mother found out we were leaving town, she shed a river of tears. "Riley, you will be so far away. How will I manage without you coming over to my house every week for our mother-daughter talks?"

"Mother, there's a little thing called a telephone, remember? All you have to do is pick up its receiver and dial my number."

My mother giggled. "Yes, of course. How silly of me. I'll call you every day." She could, too. My parents were quite wealthy, so the cost of long-distance calls would not bother her a bit.

Great.

Arriving at our new destination of Detroit, Michigan, we bought a charming, three-story home on the Northwest end of town. Being that the house was a 1923 fixer-upper, it needed a lot of tender loving care.

I made an extensive list of items to repair on the outside of the house such as replacing decayed facia boards, scraping stucco, and removing built-up oil stains from the driveway to name a few. The interior of the house required our attention just as much.

Good God Almighty!

I stopped writing at page three and started over with a more positive list when I heard Sherman cry for help in hanging a picture. In my haste to ensure the picture hung at a height where no one required a neck brace, I left the list unfinished and hurried to Sherman's side.

"That's too high," I told him.

"No, it's not," he replied.

"Yes, it is."

For ten minutes he raised and lowered the frame. I stood back and cocked my head. "Shift it to the right…no, no that's too much, now left. Sherman don't go so far. Back it up. There. Perfect."

He smiled. I could tell it was fake.

Since we were still speaking to one another, we moved to the brown brick fireplace that begged for a decorative mirror over the mantel. That's when I discovered my husband either needed an appointment with the optometrist, or his eyes were down-right crooked. Nothing I said convinced him my measurements were correct and his were off kilter. But I bowed out of the argument and allowed him to take the lead.

"There, now. You have to admit I did a great job," he crowed.

That was his opinion, not mine. "Yes, you did darling," I agreed. I'd straighten the mirror when he wasn't home.

"Sherman, two weeks is not enough to transform this mess into a gorgeous home whose picture will soon grace the cover of House Beautiful magazine. You have to ask your boss for more time so we can get everything done here."

"We could do it, Riley, if you wouldn't be so picky."

"Picky! I am not picky! Restoring a house takes a keen eye and time. I provide the eye, and you should get the time, Sherman. We want our house to shine inside and out, don't we?"

Taking my rant to heart, he requested and received, one week of vacation on top of what the company had previously granted. Nearing the end of the third week, we had fixed what we could before calling in the professionals to repair our handywork.

On the twenty-first evening, we collapsed onto the floral cushions of our metal swing. I held my mixed drink and made a toast. "Sherman," I clinked his glass of straight whiskey, "here's to a job well done," followed by, "and if I see one more putty knife, paint roller, or screwdriver, I will spit nails, adding to those left over from re-building the pergola."

My body ached for days. The way to solve the issue was to give myself a long, luxurious soak in the deepest cast iron bathtub that existed on earth. In a relaxed state, I had an epiphany. Sherman would not be the only one who monetarily contributed to our household. To hell with my mother's advice of staying home forever. I intended to become an integral part of the workforce and make a difference in the world doing something, somewhere, for someone. As a result, I planned a date with the job-wanted ads in the local newspaper.

Chapter Two

As a new executive, Sherman made sure he was the first one in his department sitting at his desk. To do this, he rose at five-thirty a.m. and flew out the door by six to make the half-hour drive to the office.

It amazed me how he got out of bed, showered, dressed, and ate breakfast without my feeling or hearing him. I figured he did this so as not to disturb my sleep.

What a gem.

As the sun rose, the rays shone through the space between the panels of the bedroom curtains where they didn't meet. To avoid the blinding light, I slipped out of bed and into my sheer baby-blue peignoir that covered the matching color translucent negligee. Yawning, I went downstairs to kick-start my energy with a pot of coffee.

No sooner had I entered the kitchen my eyes caught the sight of the remains of what must have been a whirlwind that forced its way into the house. Half the pages of the newspaper lay scattered over the glass-topped breakfast table, and the other half lay piecemeal on the floor.

Exasperated, I snatched up the papers. "The day I want to peruse the job ads, Sherman decides to wreak havoc with my resource. How is it that he can be thoughtful one minute and a pea-brain the next?"

Before arranging the newspaper in its proper sequence, I put on the well-needed pot of coffee. While the percolator perked, I re-organized the pages of the paper and flipped to the employment ads. It only took five minutes to find the perfect job.

It took a week to secure it.

Before the alarm split the morning with its announcement to get my lazy ass out of bed, I was up and preparing for the day. My new job as Office Manager for an employment agency didn't start until eight o'clock, but I would get there early to show management what a dedicated employee looked like.

The congested traffic during the one-hour drive to my new workplace tested my patience. "Why aren't people still polishing off stale donuts or gulping down frozen waffles?" I scoffed aloud.

And *slow?* Every one of them drove like they were on a leisurely jaunt, leaf peeping at the changing of colors in autumn on a Sunday morning.

Finally, I pulled off the crowded street onto the road leading to the covered parking garage that served the office building where my job awaited. Now to find the specific space the company's receptionist issued when she called me yesterday.

Once my eyes adjusted to the dim lighting within the multi-level concrete structure, I craned my neck at every empty space, hoping to be on the first floor. It was ridiculous to have thought that because my parking spot was number six-hundred-fifty-two. Even still, with high hopes, I moved up the ramp to the second floor, finding it vacant of cars. None on three, four, or five. Up one more and voilà!

the sixth floor—THE ROOF—with only the sky as its ceiling and again, no cars.

"Well isn't this just peachy, Bluebell," I had affectionately named my brilliant, blue-colored Nash Rambler, "you are the only car NOT under the *covered*, parking. I suppose the agency's receptionist didn't find it important to inform me my spot was closest to the sun. No wonder there aren't any cars; a solar flare disintegrated them all!"

I pulled into my assigned space and turned off the purr of my beloved car. With scrutiny, I admired my attractive reflection in the rearview mirror. My blue-gray eyes looked bluer somehow. The rose blush highlighted my cheeks. The dark pink color (dark pink, never red; red reminded me of blood) of my lipstick accentuated plump lips.

Perfection was the name of the game. If Marilyn Monroe stood next to me, *I* wanted to be the one who got the attention. Speaking of my Hollywood idol, I cut and styled my red hair to recreate the feminine glamor waves Marilyn wore so well.

The world was my oyster. With my knock-off Hermes handbag, and one of my father's discarded leather briefcases, I headed to the elevator. Toting a briefcase made me feel like a real career woman. Only having my lunch in it made me feel like an imposter. No matter. Image was everything.

In front of the elevator door and after pressing the "DOWN" button, I glanced at my wristwatch that revealed the time as seven fifteen. "Where is everybody? With so many floors empty, am I the only early bird?"

When the elevator made a snapping pop announcing its arrival, the metal door crept apart a third of the way then froze. I tried to help it along by pushing, but it did not budge. "Great, just great. Today of all days."

I looked around the spacious level, found the door to a stairwell and decided to walk down the zillion steps. Finding the door locked infuriated me. "Son of a bitch! How do I get off this roof?!"

I could move Bluebell to a lower floor except for all the signs stating parking violators would have their vehicles towed away. There went option one, and I wasn't keen on option two: walking down numerous car ramps in high heels. Back to taking the malfunctioning steel trap.

Once again in front of the partially opened elevator, I poked the button several more times, which resulted in the chip of a fingernail.

My efforts got the elevator to move, but in the wrong direction. It began *closing*, so I shoved my briefcase in the opening to coax the door to alter its direction. It did, but not before taking a crushing toll on my case. I stepped into the rusty, brushed-steel-lined box and pressed the "Level One" button. "God, please get me down and out of this hellhole in one piece." Talking to myself (and God) took the edge off my rising temper.

The elevator doors closed evenly and left the roof in its descent to the bottom until coming to an abrupt halt. The door crept open half-way to allow a view of the second floor at the level of my upper thigh. "Really?! You left me between floors?!"

In frustration, I planted both purse and crimped briefcase on top of the concrete floor and hiked my pencil-style skirt above my garter belt. I used my knee to get out of the elevator, but the pressure on my sheer hose when bending my leg, triggered a pop. "No! I just bought these!"

As I pulled myself up and out, I brushed against the metal panel with my left ankle, resulting in a snag in the other stocking that ran from ankle to thigh. "Shit, shit, SHIT!" I instantly clamped my hand over my mouth to prevent any more mannish expressions from spilling forth.

There I stood in all my glory with my skirt above my garter belt and my hair loose from its arranged coif. "Thank you, God, for making this floor empty so no one can see me. Wait...oh my God...security chose this moment to make rounds? Sure, why not?"

I couldn't get my skirt down fast enough before the guard's vehicle stopped. He leaned over and rolled down the passenger window. "Are you all right, miss?" He acted concerned, but his eyes popping out while drooling over the sight of my legs led me to believe it had nothing to do with my welfare.

"Yes, yes," I muttered while shimmying my dress down. "Don't distress over me, I'm one hundred percent fine. But thank you for asking." *Please go away.* "Have a good day, sir," I proposed as I flung my hair off my face and waved him farewell. He sat gaping at me. "Go on now, officer," I urged, "don't let me keep you from your duty. You have an important job to do."

"If you're sure you're okay miss."

"Oh, yes, nothing wrong here. Thank you again, officer. Buh-bye, now."

He gave me some advice I wished I'd had ten minutes ago. "Oh, by the way," he lifted his chin toward the half-open contraption, "steer clear of that elevator. It doesn't work properly."

I glanced back. "Oh, that one? Thank you for the warning."

He tipped his hat and inched forward. As he slowly pulled away, I saw him staring in his rearview mirror, so I kept waving until he disappeared up the ramp.

The rising fury that shot my pulse to the one-hundred-sixty range, found its peak. I growled and slammed my purse full force into the elevator door. "God damn you son of a bitch elevator!" The act did nothing to the metal panel, but it ripped one side of the purse's handle from its body, leaving it dangling in my hand. "I don't believe it! Why do you hate me, God?!"

The fact that Lucifer possessed the elevator did not completely dampen my enthusiasm. With my disfigured belongings in hand, I walked down the car ramp to the first floor. Like Marilyn Monroe herself, I held my chin high when strolling regally out of the garage.

Before entering the building complex, I smoothed the creases in my dress, gave my hair a last pat-down, tucked my crippled purse under my arm, noticed a scratch across one of my brand new shoes—*damn!*—then pulled on the door's handle. Acting as if owning the place, I marched across the marble-floored lobby and nodded at the building secretary sitting behind a massive desk.

I stopped in front of a glass wall with a door to match. Above the door, the agency's name shone in gold letters: "Employment Opportunities for Tomorrow." The way I figured it, if my disheveled appearance caused my new boss to fire me on the spot, at least I was in the right place to find another job.

Chapter Three

The first thing I intended to do upon entering the agency was to ask the receptionist about my non-covered parking space. However, when I crossed the threshold, my thoughts faded from aggravation to surprise. I stood in what looked like a sitting room in someone's home instead of the company's reception area. At one end sat a sofa with a peanut-shaped, shell and stone coffee table with inlaid copper swirls. It was too beautiful (and no doubt too expensive) to have any magazines covering its design. Placed on the sofa's right sat an end table with a real-deal Tiffany lamp: bronze base and confetti glass shade with specks of different colors. On the left stood a well-developed ficus tree nestled in a hammered brass planter. The only thing making it look like a reception area was the receptionist desk *minus* the target to whom I would make my complaint.

Alone in the room, I scrutinized the color choice of sofa and the largest wall. "Whoever decorated this space," I mumbled to myself, "has to be either colorblind or eccentric." The sofa and the accent wall behind the desk were a bright shade of lime green. I practically needed sunglasses to look at them.

The "un-womaned" wooden desk was contemporary in an upside down "U" shape. A narrow glass shelf held up by tiny metal cylinders graced the outside edge of the desk. To complete the room's décor, a companion ficus tree rested next to a closed door leading to the main office section.

I put the strange furnishings aside and closed my eyes. A smile crossed my lips as my senses absorbed the pungent scent of recently installed wall-to-wall carpeting mingling with the fresh lemony fragrance of polished wood.

In my reverie, I didn't notice the connecting door open, but that changed when I heard a female voice practically scream at me. "Well, wouldn't you know!" she barked. "What do you want and be quick about it."

With a start, I opened my eyes and saw a woman approaching. Her skin was olive, hair brunette, figure rotund, outfit outdated, and age somewhere in the mid-to-late forty range. By the less than amicable expression on her face and an empty storage box dangling in her hand, I sensed she was preparing to perform an unpleasant task. My assumption proved correct when she removed the lid and slammed the box on the desktop.

I took a step forward. "Uh, good morning," I replied in my most affable tone, hoping my friendliness would counter her uncongenial disposition. "My name is Riley O'Keefe, and I'm reporting for my first day as Office Manager."

The grouch narrowed her almond-shaped brown eyes and gave me the once-over. "Looks like you crawled out from under a rock, Riley O'Keefe," she scoffed while bearing a taunting grin. "Did you look in the mirror before leaving your house? Do you not own an iron? Tsk, tsk, tsk, tsk, tsk."

I defended my topsy-turvy appearance. "I assume you are the receptionist, and if so, you gave me a parking space on the top floor and—"

"And what? Did it hurt your little feet to walk down a few flights?" she mocked.

How dare she speak to me like that? My buried ire once again climbed to the top. "I didn't walk, I took the elevator."

She laughed. "Did you now? It looks like it chewed you up and spit you out!" she curtly teased.

I opened my mouth to speak, only to have her hand fly up. "Stop right there," she demanded, her scowl returning as she looked me up and down. "You came out no worse for the wear, so stop sniveling."

Before I could say another word, which I couldn't find one, the woman took her attention away from me. She snatched up a bulky stapler and threw it in the box followed by several cartons of staples.

"The elevator," she giggled to herself, "isn't that rich." She added an assortment of colored pencils to the box.

"Excuse me," I stressed, "I can see you're busy, but is Coral Stevens available? She told me to ask for her when I got here." This mongrel would not bully me.

She stopped her quest of scooping up all the writing implements and contracted her brow. "Is that so? Well, it may look like I work here, but as of five minutes ago, that witch fired me. With that said, your highness, you'll have to find someone else to announce your arrival." One by one, the woman forced the removal of the drawers from their encasements in the desk and dumped the contents into the storage box.

When the irate woman pilfered enough of the company's supplies, she forced the lid onto the stuffed box and removed her purse from under the desk. The weight of the treasure trove should have posed a problem, but the animosity she exuded provided enough power for her to fling the carton's bottom edge on her hip and whip by me as if I were one of those ficus trees.

"Enjoy your time at the agency!" she bellowed with disdain dripping from her lips. In her haste to vacate the office, she threw the glass door open so hard, it seemed it would come back on itself and shatter into a million pieces. I had never witnessed such an episode of hostility from a person in their place of employment.

Alone once more, I recalled the disturbing dialog. With indignation, the woman mentioned "the witch" whom I assumed she meant to be Coral. The Wizard of Oz came to mind. Was Coral a *good witch*, or a *bad witch*? It's obvious this woman thought the latter. But thinking back to Coral's interview with me, she seemed very congenial and good-natured.

I nibbled my thumbnail (there went the polish). Time ticked by. If I didn't do something soon, I'd be late in reporting to the boss on my first day. I knocked on the closed door out of which the female version of Attila the Hun had exited earlier.

It required knocking three times before someone opened the door, and when they did, it surprised me. There in front of me stood a young boy of about four years old who looked like a cherub with chubby cheeks ripe enough to pinch. Curls of dark brown hair framed his face and piercing green eyes sparkled under eyelashes that only a mature woman should own.

"Hi," he clasped onto the edge of the door and brimmed with a broad grin, "aw you heuh to see my mommy?"

"Uh, well hello there. And what is *your* name, little man?"

His brows furrowed with visible anger as he backed up against the door to keep it open, then placed his hands on his hips and scowled at my question. "I am NOT a little man," he exclaimed. When he wrinkled his nose, the countless freckles scattered over its bridge seemed closer and fewer. "I am a little BOY." He rolled his eyes at me and shook his head in disgust. "Yo a gwonup. You should know that."

When someone is serious and says something hysterical, how can you keep from laughing? Believe me, it was hard. "I *do* know the difference, and I am sorry I made such a bad mistake. Do you accept my apology?"

He crossed his arms and cocked his head. "Okay," he shrugged, "I accept yo polology."

"Thank you," I said with great humility and, again, trying not to laugh. "Now, little *boy*, can you tell me your name?"

"It's Beauwegard Fitzgewald Kingston the Thud!" he shouted with much ease.

My eyes widened at his pronunciation of such a difficult name. "My goodness that is a *wonderful* name. Do you go by Beauregard or Beau?"

He gave me a blank stare, whereby I rephrased my question. "What does your mommy call you?"

His little lips curled up. "Beau!"

"May I call you Beau, too?" I asked with the same enthusiasm.

"You can if you tell me yo name fust."

"It's Mrs. O'Keefe," I responded with as much gusto as he did.

He furrowed his brows a second time. "That's too long. Do you have a littleler name?"

He was so adorable. "How about Riley?"

He pressed his lips together and shook his head. "No, that's my doggie's name, and he's a boy. Yo a gul."

With that, I turned my head to hide a grin. To regain composure, I cleared my throat. "Well," I started in defense of my name, "Riley can be for people, too; a boy *and* a girl."

He shrugged again. "Why are you heuh, Wiley?"

"I'm meeting with Coral Stevens. Is that your mommy?" I asked, knowing the last names did not match.

The little boy covered his mouth with both his pudgy hands and giggled. "Who's that?" Then, puffing out his chest, he took on a committed stance as he looked me square in the eye. "My mommy's name is, *mommy*," he pronounced with a commanding air.

This young sprite tickled my funny bone at the pride he projected toward his mother. "You love your mommy very much, don't you?" I asked in a soothing tone.

"I do. She hangs on the moon. That's what my daddy says. She's vewy pwetty. Do you want to see how pwetty my mommy is?"

I could not take my eyes off Beau who agreed with his father that his mother *hung* the moon. "I would love to see how pretty your mommy is. Will you take me to her?"

He gripped the edge of the door. "I'll let you in if you can tell me the secwet wud."

Ah, it's a game now, is it? "Um," I remembered the secret word I learned as a child, "please?"

"That's not it." He moved to the back side of the door and pushed it shut.

I knocked on the door again. This time a woman in her mid-thirties opened it. Coral. She had a tall, hourglass frame, flawless complexion with high cheekbones, and lips to entice any man. Shiny, dark hair favored a wave at the front, and turned under in a soft roll falling below the collar of the ivory cream dress that hugged her curvaceous body. Her face beamed, revealing perfect white teeth made brighter by a deep red shade of lipstick. I frowned upon that intense color choice. It reminded me of a hungry vampire draining blood from a victim's neck.

Too many Dracula movies, I guess.

But back to this beautiful creature standing in front of me. I noticed her eyes were the same exquisite green as Beau's, which led me to believe they belonged to the same family.

Right before she spoke, two pint-sized arms reached around from behind her knees and encircled her legs. A headful of curls appeared, followed by two small eyes peering from around her hip.

"I am so sorry, Riley," Coral shook her head. "When presented an opportunity to meet someone new, Beau is first in line. How silly of me to think I had corralled him in my office. It's obvious he got away when I took a phone call." Steadying herself against the clamp her son had on her legs, she reached out a hand. "Welcome. It's nice to see you again. This is my little boy."

So, she was Beau's mother. Why didn't she take her husband's last name? Hmmm.

I put my best foot forward and shook her hand. "Yes, he made the little *boy* part quite clear."

"Oh, dear, yes, well," she stuttered, then pushing the door open, she took Beau's hand and stepped aside to let me pass into the hall.

"Wait, mommy!" Beau jumped in front of me with an outstretched arm which brought me to an abrupt halt. "She can't go in! She diddent tell you the secwet wud!"

Coral looked at her son with perplexity. "What secret word, honey?" she asked.

His palms faced up, his head cocked sideways, and his eyes flew open as wide as saucers. "Doodlebug!" he blasted out as if we were complete imbeciles. Coral pressed her lips together trying not to laugh at her son.

"Beau," I stated with the utmost sincerity, "the secret word is doodlebug. Now, may I come in?"

Not realizing he had disclosed the word, he gaped at me as though I had fallen from that moon his mother hung on. He pulled his mother's hand and allowed me entry.

Problem solved, or was it?

Chapter Four

Coral Stevens was as nice as nice could be. She didn't even mention how unkempt I looked, but then again, she didn't know about my experience with the "Transport of Terror."

Before showing me around, she settled Beau once more in her office where he resumed play with characters from his Early American Frontier box set. He had placed plastic Cowboys around her typewriter. Indians stood in a line atop a stack of colorful pieces of construction paper. He stuffed covered wagons under a beautiful and expensive, cream-colored linen handkerchief held down on one side by a telephone directory. I know an expensive piece of work when I see it.

Watching him arrange his toys, Coral explained the reason her son was there. "The nanny fell ill, and with no alternatives, I had to bring Beau with me."

"It doesn't bother me," I offered, "he's a breath of fresh air."

After leaving Beau alone to start the active performance between the assortment of vinyl pieces, Coral closed the door. Time for my tour of the agency.

Taking in the office layout, I found it extraordinary. Most often in an open concept like this, desks lay in rows with barely enough space to walk between them. Work-related machines covered those desks, leaving no room for the occupant's personal items. However, this floorplan fell completely outside that norm.

Here, an employee's desk, file cabinet, typewriter stand, and large potted plant, outlined a generous square. Having so much surface space on their desks provided plenty of room for personal photos, etc. Privacy came in the way of several tall, individual, mobile screens mounted on metal legs scattered around the floor. Soundproofing, too, perhaps?

"Coral, who thought up such a unique concept as this?"

"I wish I could claim the credit, but I stole the design when living abroad for a few years. I visited several upscale companies and found this configuration to be quite efficient." She swept her hand across the area. "This is a duplication of that strategy where my administrators are among the client assistants. This unites the staff. The longer you work here, Riley, you will discover I have an unconventional thought process. Especially concerning the mental and," she tilted her head and winked, "physical parts of my life."

*What does **that** mean?* I didn't feel comfortable asking for clarification.

After introducing me to the staff of mostly women and only two men, Coral led me back to her office. Once there, we sat at a round table away from Beau's play area.

"Riley," Coral began, "I hope this is not too much for you, but since I had to let our receptionist go, you will assume her responsibilities in addition to your Office Manager duties. I apologize for doing this to you at the last minute, but like my situation with Beau, I had no other choice."

"Not an issue, Coral," I crowed, "I am happy to do both."

"I am so glad you're here, Riley. You will be a tremendous asset to our working family. And," she amusingly stressed, "in the future, I promise to keep Beau on *this* side of the door. Please let me know if you have any questions."

"Uh, not to be a fussbudget Coral, but is there any chance the maintenance crew could repair the garage elevator?"

She raised her brows. "Why would you ask that?"

After recounting my dreadful experience, I received a not-so-amused look from her. "Riley," she stated with a puzzled expression, "that elevator hasn't worked properly for years. That's why everyone parks on the first level. What possessed you to park up there?"

"Because that's the space the receptionist issued when she called me yesterday."

Coral pressed her lips in aggravation. "That, my dear, is a big reason not to hire a family member. I don't care if she *is* my sister-in-law. Gertrude was a menace from the day I hired her as a favor to my brother. She was rude to client and employee alike. And even to you, Riley. I do apologize." Coral opened her lap-drawer and withdrew a notepad. "Here," she wrote a note addressed to the security unit, "give this to the secretary in the main lobby. She'll notify security who will assign you a valid parking space on the *first* floor. I can't imagine the inconvenience you went through because of that woman, Riley. Your first order of business is to submit a reimbursement request for the damage to your belongings."

"Oh, that's not necessary," I urged but didn't put much push behind it. Those items were not cheap.

"Not up for discussion," she insisted. "I will not have my new Office Manager walking around with a crimped briefcase, snagged nylons, and marred shoes."

On the way back to the reception area, I stopped at the supply closet and picked up items to replace those now missing from the desk. Then, I took Coral's note to the secretary in the lobby.

In presenting the note to the pleasant blonde, I glanced at the heading on the piece of paper and received another surprise. My assumption that Coral held the Hiring Manager position was way off base. Coral Stevens was the owner of the company. Pride for the women of the world bubbled up within me.

Returning to my workstation, I decided that nothing would sway me from having anything other than glorious days from now on.

Absolutely nothing.

What a hectic fourth day! People had been coming in and out of the office non-stop since I arrived. To top it off, Coral left for lunch early and had not yet returned. She had a candidate interview in fifteen minutes, so, where was she?

I never ate my lunch, thinking she'd be back by now, and my stomach growled something awful. I glanced at my wristwatch; one o'clock. If I hurried, I could gobble down my peanut butter and jelly sandwich before the next appointment arrived. Before I could, though, the phone rang.

Ugh...damn it!

"Good afternoon, Employment Opportunities for Tomorrow, Riley speaking. How may I assist you today?"

"End this fucking farce of a marriage you have with your husband," the woman demanded in a low, muffled, menacing tone on the other end of the phone. It sounded like she held a cloth over the mouthpiece.

"Excuse me?" My hunger no doubt affected my hearing. "I'm sorry, but I didn't quite get that."

"You heard me loud and clear. Your husband needs someone who can satisfy his needs in the bedroom, and your skills don't come close. Do us all a favor and end it." She hung up.

The receiver remained at my ear when the glass door of the office opened, and an energetic woman bounded in, all toothy in her unusual appearance. Full and thick, chin-length, brown curly hair framed an attractive face with big, bright blue eyes. That was the normal part. The odd part was what she wore: a long-sleeve red and white checkered blouse tucked inside a shin-length, A-lined dark-blue denim skirt. She almost said something, but seeing me "on the phone," she pointed her thumb over her shoulder and sat on the green sofa. In a daze, I cradled the receiver on its base and sat motionless.

Seeing my call end, the perky young woman grasped her red clutch purse with both hands and approached my desk. "Well, good day to you, ma'am!" She spoke loud enough for those in the back of the office to hear her.

Her accent was unquestionably Texan; I know because Sherman had relatives who lived on a ranch outside the Dallas area, and she sounded just like them. With that said, I looked for cowboy boots and a saddled black stallion tied to the light pole outside, neither of which I saw.

"Good afternoon," I replied, "you must be Hazel."

The glowing look on her face would make one think I had just awarded her the blue ribbon for her peach pie at the Texas State Fair. "You are absobloominglutely correct, and I'm here for my interview with Mrs. Stevens. Are you she?"

Her made-up word was peculiar, but at least she used correct grammar. "Uh, no," my mind still reeled with the recent phone call, "she's not back from lunch yet."

"That's all right. Shall I wait right here, or," she pointed to the couch on which she previously sat, "do you want me to wait over there?"

I was not in the mood to have this Howdy-Doody-Ye-Hah so close, but I attempted a smile. "Please make yourself comfortable on the sofa."

A few minutes later, I saw Coral step out of the phone booth in the lobby.

How curious. Why didn't she use her office phone to make a call?

"Oh," I told Hazel, "Mrs. Stevens has arrived."

When Coral stepped into the office, I introduced the two women. Coral whispered to me that she needed a few minutes to freshen up.

"Hazel," I offered, "Mrs. Stevens will be right with you."

"Okee dokee, smokey," Hazel replied with far too much energy.

I bet *she* had lunch and washed it down with a martini to get that over-the-top cheerfulness she exuded.

After showing Hazel to Coral's office, I returned to my open briefcase, but the sandwich didn't seem appealing anymore. What I really needed was a comforting drink like a Pink Squirrel with its almond liqueur, crème de cacao, and heavy cream, but all I had was a thermos of iced coffee. Why didn't I work in a bar, or at least have the forethought to have packed a bottle of Kahlua in my briefcase? Iced coffee and Kahlua would have done the trick.

The workday could not end fast enough. Picking up my purse and searching through it for my car keys, the telephone rang. The wood and metal starburst wall-clock showed ten minutes after five. Not wanting to get involved in another conversation, I ignored the rings and locked the glass door. Perhaps my husband would have a Pink Squirrel waiting for me when I got home.

"I called you at work this afternoon," my other half stated as soon as I set foot in the house, "but there was no answer."

Well, fine; no Pink Squirrel.

After placing my purse and briefcase on the tufted, rose-colored brocade settee, I pulled him into an embrace and squeezed until his body pressed into mine.

"Hey, now," he held me close, "are we competing who can give the strongest hug, because if we are, I'll win."

I increased my hug, as did he until I squealed, "Uncle!" Laughing, I kissed him. "So, what did you want?"

"We need butter, and I was going to ask you to pick up a cube on your way home, but it's okay, we have enough for tonight."

My face lit up. "Are you cooking dinner?"

His eyes twinkled at my humor. "No, Riley, that's your department." He gently tapped me on the nose. "I'm just reporting that we're almost out of butter."

"I'd gladly show you around my 'department,' as you call it. You've been there before and have enjoyed using the features."

He placed his arm lovingly around my shoulders and guided me into the kitchen. Once there, he stopped where the ingredients for the evening meal lay waiting for the "department manager" to make something out of them.

"Will you at least help me?" I asked.

"I always help you, sweetheart." With his strong fingers caressing my shoulders, he nibbled my earlobe. "You cook," he whispered, "and I keep you from burning things." The heat of his breath dancing over my skin as he said *burning things* invoked a different meaning in my groin area.

My expertise in the kitchen was less than stellar, and there was only one explanation for it. Before the stork bundled me up and whisked me away to Earth, God dispersed necessities for me to survive. I received smarts, determination, a half-way decent body, and a strong will to outperform anyone. But I missed the meeting when God passed out skills in the culinary arts. How could I consider myself a perfectionist (which I did) when most of the time my focus was on keeping the house from burning down? Regrettably, there were no do-overs at the check-out line in the Celestial Distribution Center.

Over dinner, I informed my sexy husband of the peculiar phone call I received from a woman who deliberately disguised the sound of her voice when making her vicious demand.

"That's terrible," he offered.

I could have sworn his face paled a little at the onset of the topic, but surely, I imagined such a thing.

"It's obvious she had the wrong number," Sherman firmly stated. He took a deep breath and then comforted me by covering my hand with his. His smile soothed any trepidations I had.

After squeezing my hand, he focused on the piece of obviously overdone round steak on his plate. Though not burned, it had the consistency of leather. I knew this when taking it out of the frying pan. It didn't bend or move at all. It looked fake.

"That's what I thought, too." I dabbed my mouth with a cloth napkin. "I feel sorry for the intended target of that call. Some people have too many screws loose, you know?"

He nodded then focused on his dinner plate. "This looks delicious, sweetheart," he stated, trying to cut through the meat.

"Thank you. I followed the recipe to a tee." No, I didn't. I just threw the meat in a pan and turned up the heat. The quicker I cooked it, the more tender it would be, right?

After finally getting his knife through, he stabbed...twice...with his fork then chewed and chewed. After a while, he discreetly spit the unswallowable chunk into his napkin, folded it, and placed it in his lap. However, covering his next few bites presented a problem. The napkin was not large, and there was an awful lot of meat on his plate. His attempt at keeping his actions hidden failed miserably. Out of the corner of my eagle-eye, I saw every spit and bury.

Poor guy. He went through all that trouble just to keep from hurting my feelings. It happened so often I could recognize compassion when I saw it.

I was the luckiest woman on earth to have such a thoughtful man.

Chapter Five

*E*xcluding the disturbing phone conversation, it took a mere two months, sixteen days, three hours, fifty-seven minutes, and thirty-five seconds for my career bliss to end. Enter Beauregard Fitzgerald Kingston, Jr.—Beau's father and Coral's husband.

The hours before my first encounter with Mr. Kingston and what happened after, were still fresh in my mind. Coral's day had been manic with meetings and work-related fires only she could extinguish. She only took one break, and that was to ask me to cancel the lunch date with her husband when he arrived. The request didn't seem out of the ordinary, so with an air of sympathy, I told her I'd pass along her apologies.

I hated my assigned task at the time—sticking a company flyer in each of a million envelopes and licking them closed. A man had to have invented the wretched envelope sealant that left a putrid taste on one's tongue. A woman would have adhered an agreeable flavor like peppermint or wintergreen to freshen the breath instead of making it reek of glue. The only way to get rid of the bitterness was to scrape my tongue over the bottoms of my top teeth. Then what? Spit or swallow? If I discarded the disgusting film in a tissue every time I licked an envelope, there'd be no more saliva left to do either. That left one choice: swallow followed by a sip of coffee.

Scowling and wrinkling my nose because of the ordeal, I happened to look through our glass office door and into the lobby where a stud—the two-legged kind, not the four-legged kind Hazel would ride—sauntered into the building. What a magnificent specimen of the male species.

In scrutinizing the man, I considered him to be three years older than I. He was tall and smartly dressed from head to toe. His camel-tan suit and white shirt accented by a deep wine-colored tie hung on his frame like a tailor had made the outfit specifically for him. His getup screamed of money as did the obviously pricey, two-toned leather shoes in shades of musk and brown with a detailed cut-out wingtip.

To top off his classy attire, he donned a beige fedora like the style Humphrey Bogart wore in the 1942 production of "Casa Blanca." Secretly in love with Bogart and his ability to almost make me faint dead away when seeing him on the big screen, the same appetite overwhelmed me with this newcomer.

It's okay to swoon; I'm not dead yet.

The way he carried himself oozed of intrigue and mystique like my self-proclaimed Hollywood paramour. My first thought, as I watched this picture of perfection stroll across the floor, was his drop-dead gorgeous appearance.

Nothing wrong with ogling, either.

My second, third, and fourth thoughts were, who was this flutter bum with a sculpted jaw and a hint of dark hair peeking out the side of his hat; which office did he work in; and why didn't I work there, too?

With a glance at his wristwatch, the man came to a complete stop midway across the lobby. Without a care in the world and paying no mind to those around him, he reached inside his suit jacket and withdrew a pack of cigarettes. Two knocks against the side of his hand and the head of a single cylinder popped out. He withdrew it the rest of the way with his lips then replaced the pack to the coat's inner pocket.

Bewitched by this stranger, I forgot all about my tedious task and leaned over the multiple envelopes on my desk to get a better look at him—as if four inches made a difference. Fixated, I saw him feel around in his pants pocket until pulling out a small silver lighter. With the flick of his thumb, he flipped open the hinged lid and twirled the wheel that ignited a spark. Cupping his other hand around the flame, he lit the end of the cigarette.

With his fluid movement, my lungs absorbed every bit of oxygen available around me when imagining myself as that roll of thin paper filled with tobacco pressed between his lips. When he blew out the leftover smoke, my face softened, and I exhaled as he lowered his head to eye-level.

That's when he saw me gawking at him through the wall of clear glass. His mouth curved into a brilliant smile. When he waved at me, I realized my mouth gaped stupidly. There's no telling how many gnats from that ficus tree flew in my open maw.

Without warning, this mesmerizing magician doused his three-quarter-full cigarette in the sand-filled smoking urn and walked, *oh, my God*, my way. In a panic, I took a sip of coffee to moisten my mouth, but that did not stop my heart from racing, or my palms from perspiring. *Holy smokes!* It was twelve o'clock sharp.

Mr. Kingston!

He had arrived to take his wife to lunch. Unnerved, I observed him walk toward me in what I saw as slow motion. One deliberate heel-to-toe step followed in stride by another. My brain waves arrested, and my focus intensified in staring at him. Coral had instructed me to tell him something, but what? Oh, right, she was too busy for lunch and needed a rain check.

The glass door swung open, and the man crossing its threshold in one giant step, made my heart crash into cardiac arrest as he dominated the room. I changed my mind in thinking God had to be male. Only a female God would fashion this man into a sexy as hell creature with whom I would soon engage in conversation.

His hand extended, and with a sensual voice that should not exist on this planet, he greeted me, "You must be Riley."

His demeanor and sultry, deep tone intoxicated me, and before I blurted out something stupid, I attempted to compose myself. "Yes," my pitch was too low and throaty for him not to catch the disquiet in my speech. I stood and placed my hand in his. "I'm named Riley, I…I mean," so much for not saying something stupid, "yes, and you must be Mr. Kingston." My legs were shaking but thank God he saw me from waist up.

"Please, call me Fitz." Keeping the handshake, he covered my hand with his other one. "All my friends do, and I hope I can add you to that category."

I just met the man, and he wanted to be my friend? He didn't even know me. I might be a blood-sucking vampire for all he knew, and if he didn't stop smiling at me like that, he might be my first victim. "Yes, well, thank you, Mr. Kings…um, Fitz."

"It's nice to meet you in person, Riley. Since you started here, Coral has come home every day singing your praises. You have made quite an impression on my wife."

Oh, Fitz, you have no idea what kind of impression you have just made on me.

"I'm sure she was just being kind."

His brow shot up as did the pitch of his tone. "No, no," he stressed, "she truly means it. She doesn't lie. She and I have a relationship based on complete honesty, and when she tells me you're the cat's meow, well, I believe her. You have made a huge difference here, and she appreciates your countless efforts to ensure the office runs efficiently."

My, oh my. That's nice to hear.

"Speaking of Coral," he looked at the closed door as if expecting her to walk through it any minute, "is she ready to go?"

"Actually Fitz, she's been cooped up in her office interviewing clients today and has another coming in later that she needs to prep for. She asked me to tell you she won't be able to do lunch. Perhaps another time?" I asked instead of stated.

"That's too bad," he replied with what I considered sincerity. To my surprise, I caught a twinkle in one of his eyes as an idea seemed to strike him. "Have *you* eaten yet?" he asked. "If not, would you be my lunch date? Through Coral, I feel like I know you, but I'd still like to find out for myself what makes you tick. What do you say?"

Did I want to go? Oh, hell, yes! Should I go? An even bigger, hell, no. Focusing on that stupid envelope again, I placed it on the third of three perfectly stacked piles taking up half my desk space. "Um, well, Fitz," I picked up another without glancing his way, "I have to get these out today or Coral will have my head." This disconnect with my competent self, turned me into a bumbling idiot.

A tender grin crossed his lips and his face grew soft and relaxed. "Oh, Riley, Coral would never do anything to put a frown on your pretty face." He reached over the desk and placed his hand on my arm. "Trust me. I won't keep you more than an hour. Come on. Say you'll have lunch with me."

With his magical fingers burning a hole clear through the material of my dress, it took all I had to urge myself to speak. "Okay," I uttered, "but let me tell Coral."

Free of his grasp, I turned around and walked to the interior door. I sensed his eyes wandering over my backside, which made me self-conscious. Once through the door, I leaned against the wall and recaptured the breath I lost minutes ago.

Since Coral was behind closed doors, I would not interrupt. Instead, I asked Babs, whose desk sat closest to Coral's office, for a piece of paper and a pencil. I wrote a brief note to Coral, then asked Babs for a strip of tape to attach the note to Coral's door. With that done, I gave my fellow employee a forced smile and made my way back to my desk. In silent prayer, I beseeched God (male or female) to have made Fitz change his mind and leave the building. Nope. Still there.

Damn.

"She was busy, so I left her a note," I advised him with that same fragile expression I channeled to Babs.

"Wonderful. Shall we go?" he asked with an outstretched arm toward the exit.

I grasped the handle of my purse for security if nothing else. My hands were shaking so much that if I didn't have something to grab onto, I'd feel awkward and insecure, as if I didn't already fit in that category.

Oh, dear...what have I done?

Chapter Six

*M*y time with Fitz proved interesting. It started as we walked to the client parking lot where a magnificent cherry-apple red, MGA 1500 convertible roadster (top on) waited to take us to lunch. Expecting a gentleman to perform his gentlemanly duty, I paused at the passenger-side door and waited for him to open it for me. I'm glad he did, because I saw no exterior handle anywhere on the side of the car by which to access his vehicle on my own.

I sank into the tan bucket seat where the rich, soothing scent of leather enveloped my senses. The durable material caressed my palms as I ran them over the animal hide. Drinking in the details of the grand interior, I imagined myself zooming down the highway toward a secret rendezvous with my lover; my hair becoming one with the wind as he and I threw care away while breaking all the rules—*all* the rules. Because of my detachment from reality, I didn't hear Fitz slip into the bucket seat beside me.

Poised, he eased back with his gaze directed at me. "I take it by the look on your face you approve of my transportation."

"Oh, Fitz," I sighed, "this car is dreamy, and having you behind the wheel adds to the vision." I transferred my attention to the glossy exterior.

"You think *I'm* dreamy?" he asked in a deep voice to stress the word.

"Hmm?"

"You just told me I was dreamy."

His statement touched a brain nerve.

He said I said what? I never told him that, did I? Oh, my God, did I?

My body went ridged. My eyes widened, and my head jerked in his direction.

Recognizing my embarrassment, he threw his head back and exploded in laughter. I needed to defend myself, but the words stuck somewhere between my brain and my mouth. To top it off, he planted his hand on my thigh, which brought an instant contraction to my leg and a rising heat to my face. Using my purse, I indiscreetly pushed against his hand as if trying to brush a bug away. It was a stubborn bug.

My action kept his ear-to-ear grin as if he enjoyed his little cat and mouse play. "It's all right, Riley, I get that a lot." He squeezed and released my leg.

I clasped the handle of my purse in my lap and focused forward as he put the motorcar in gear. Without another word from either of us, Fitz left the parking lot and waited to find an opening to enter the heavy traffic.

Cars, carrying impatient passengers to their destinations, zipped around each other. I couldn't help but think *those people* weren't expecting Lucifer to be waiting for them that night like I was because of my sinful thoughts of a man who was *not* Sherman.

What drew me to this man whom I just met? His masculine physique? The fact he was wealthy? His sensual voice? *Uh, yes, yes, and yes.* I behaved no better than a teenage schoolgirl who had a crush on the quarterback of the football team. Jesus Christ! This was not me.

See...Lucifer is making me act this way.

I always knew my mouth would get me into a lot of trouble someday. However, I thought it would be a slip of the tongue of unladylike vocabulary, not this kind of stupidity.

Pulling into the lot of the local diner, Fitz parked his car. Getting out of the roadster, he came around to open my door and offered me his hand to help me out. No way would I touch any part of him. If I did, I'd evaporate in a puff of smoke and go straight to hell; would not pass go; would not collect two hundred dollars.

"Riley?" His pearly whites sparkled.

What choice did I have? None. Therefore, I placed just my fingers in his cool, dry palm. He waited while I swiveled and planted my high heels on the asphalt, then in one fluid movement, he lifted my hand as I raised myself from the seat. As he reached around me to swing the door shut, I caught a whiff of the salty and refreshing notes of his subtle cologne.

Why does he have to smell so good, too? Get behind me, Lucifer! Stop tempting me!

Entering the eatery, I found the volume of noise almost too loud to hear myself think. Dishes clattered behind the counter; women laughed two octaves too high; men roared and slapped each other on the back after saying something funny.

It was glorious!

Fitz and I grabbed an empty booth the moment a couple vacated it, and after sliding onto the red, vinyl seat, we perused the menu.

Once the waitress cleaned the table and took our order, Fitz began a barrage of questions. "From what Coral has told me, I already know about the efficient Office Manager Riley. Now I'd like to learn about who Riley is outside the office. Tell me about yourself." He reached into his jacket pocket and withdrew his pack of Pall Malls. "Smoke?" he offered.

The man was such a cool cookie how could I refuse? After I slid one out of the pack, he retrieved his lighter and lit my cigarette before lighting his own. Inhaling my first puff, I turned my head to exhale the smoke. "There's not much to tell," I said. "I'm a simple woman with simple needs and wants."

Staring, accompanied by a smirk, he studied me for a moment as he allowed his cigarette to burn down untouched. "Somehow, I don't think you are as uncomplicated as you say."

He needed to stop looking at me in a way that penetrated my clothes. Where was our food? I needed it to keep from slobbering all over my lunch partner.

"Were you born here in Detroit?" he asked, after taking a deep drag from the filtered end of the cigarette.

"No, Muskegon." I tapped the cigarette ashes into the ashtray. "My family thought about moving after my adoption, but they nixed the idea."

"You're adopted?"

"Yes."

"Do you mind me asking how that happened?"

I shrugged. There was no shame on my part. "When I was old enough to understand, my adopted parents told me my biological father had perished in a car accident a few months before I was born. My biological mother had died in childbirth—mine."

His expression turned compassionate. "I'm sorry, Riley. So, when and how did your adoption take place?"

"After I lost my birth mother, her best friend became my foster parent. Right after that, she and her husband started the adoption process. Our DNA doesn't match, but they are my parents just the same, and I refer to them as such. That's pretty much it."

"Anyone younger or older in your household who could have taken the blame for breaking a window other than you?" he joked.

My eyes flashed with amusement. "No, I'm an only child, which makes me my mother and father's favorite."

A grin crossed his lips as he kept the questions coming. "Do your parents still live in Muskegon?"

"They certainly do. I can't think of anything that would entice them to move; not even my leaving town."

The waitress brought our meal, and we doused our cigarettes in the ashtray at the end of the table. "Coral tells me you're married," he continued as the woman set our plates down. "Enlighten me. What kind of man can snag a catch like you?"

I nearly spit out my chocolate milkshake at such boldness. After swallowing in a hurry so the patrons didn't see me spew like an erupting volcano, my face flushed with the intensity of heat from that non-existent lava. "Uh, thank you?" I asked instead of stated. "My man, I mean, my husband's name is Sherman, and we've been married for just over two years."

"What does *your man* do for a living? I hope it's something lucrative that keeps you in furs and diamonds," he glanced at the off-brand purse sitting beside me, "and not somewhere that earns him merely enough to keep you dressed and fed."

Well, that's rude!

My admiration for Fitz fell several notches at his unsubstantiated insinuation. I squared my shoulders. "As a matter of fact, Fitz, Sherman's company just promoted him to Vice President, which pays quite well, thank you very much."

Fitz smirked. "Good to know. What company does your husband work for?"

"Unified Automobile Company," I bragged with confidence.

Now *he* practically choked on his food. My narrowed brows and cocked head prompted Fitz to explain his shock. "Really? You are aware that UAC has been struggling to survive as a company since two car manufacturers merged to form it. The new company has not even reported a profit yet. Worse than that, the firm's largest loss occurred this year. I hope your husband still has a job in a couple of months, and you don't end up on skid-row."

I wanted to show him how unladylike I could be and give him a knuckle sandwich right in the kisser. I mean really, who in their right mind had the audacity to insinuate someone they never met would soon lose their job?

It took all I had not to reach across the table and throttle him. Instead, I lowered my head and counted to ten to control my temper. "You must be mistaken, Fitz," I cockily addressed this insolent bastard. "UAC would not have promoted my husband, offered him a raise, and paid for our move here if that were the case, all of which they did."

Fitz retracted the inference. "I'm sure you are correct, Riley," he agreed. "No enterprise in that dire situation would be foolish enough to do something so extravagant for a new employee."

I loved winning against an insensitive pig like Beauregard Fitzgerald Kingston. The win, though sweet, did not lessen my bitterness.

Most of the remaining time at the diner ticked by in tempered silence. When Fitz raised a topic he thought might interest me, I had little if anything to say about it. As a result, he stopped trying and ate his food without engaging me further.

Returning to his motorcar after leaving the restaurant, I waited for him to open the door for me, which frosted me to Heaven's Gate.

Jesus Christ! Where is the handle to this cracker box?

As soon as the poor excuse of a gentleman opened the door, I plopped myself on the seat, crossed my arms, and stared straight ahead.

"Riley, I'm sorry for upsetting you," Fitz apologized, entering his side of the car. "Let's not let this mishap end our first meeting on a sour note. I refuse to move this vehicle until you tell me I'm forgiven." He draped his arm around the back of my seat and made tiny circles on my upper arm.

I bristled at his touch.

His lofty attitude annoyed me as much as the antics of trying to smooth over being a king-sized jerk. Then he put the cherry on top by getting a little too familiar.

Hacked off to the gills, I clenched my teeth and gave him a scathing glare.

Not a chance, buddy boy. If you're going to just sit there, I'll find my own way back.

Satisfied with my mental decision, I reached for the inside door handle, but couldn't find it!

How is a body supposed to get out of this tin can?!

Watching my frantic search for a way to escape, he grabbed my arm to get my attention and keep me from pulling the wrong thing. "Oh, come on, Riley," he pleaded, "don't be so stubborn. I told you I was sorry. What more can I say?"

I didn't want to walk the two miles to the office, and I didn't bring any cash for the bus. I couldn't call Sherman to come get me. Yeah, that would be awkward. My choice was obvious. "Fine," I spouted, "just get this Mickey Mouse excuse for a car fired up and get me back." One insult deserved another.

Shaking his head, he started the engine, backed the car up, and entered the flow of traffic. To keep him from saying anything else, I focused out the passenger side window until reaching the complex.

Once free of the vehicle, I pushed my way past him and never glanced back. At my desk, curiosity got the best of me. I looked through the large outside window and saw Fitz standing by the side of his roadster. He lit a cigarette and nonchalantly smoked it until throwing the butt on the ground and grinding it out with the ball of his shoe. He threw one more glance in my direction, then slid into his car and drove away.

Instead of working on the letter Coral had given me to type, I rehashed what happened at lunch with her husband. Why would a man I just met taunt me so? What happened to making a good first impression? Whatever his reason, he did not put his best foot forward with me.

A drawn-out breath left my lungs. I typed what Coral had written and placed it in an envelope. I licked the disgusting sealant, closed the flap, placed a three-cent stamp in the corner and put it where the postman would pick it up tomorrow.

Time dragged on, but five o'clock finally arrived.

The drive home was still too slow for my taste. I pulled Bluebell up our driveway to the covered carport at the top and stopped over the old layer of oil. Depressed by the day's event, but glad to be home, I gathered my belongings from the passenger seat and walked into the house.

To my surprise, Sherman stood in the foyer wearing my red and white-checked apron and holding a dry martini in his hand. Speechless at his gift—not to mention the heavenly aroma of roasting chicken—my eyes misted as I dropped my briefcase and purse on the floor. Relieving my husband of his offering, I wrapped my arms around his shoulders, trying not to spill one drop of the rehabilitating liquid. How could my melancholy continue with such a warm welcome?

There was no doubt my Adonis with the potbelly, trumped the Adonis with the spitfire red chariot any day.

Chapter Seven

I **went to work a much happier woman.** Last night, my husband and I talked after the scrumptious chicken dinner he prepared. "Talk" in this sense, however, wasn't with words, but using one's mouth in a different manner.

I could never accuse my husband of being sexually unproven at pleasing me. Regardless, there was a disconnect with reciprocation. Sherman expected me to return the favor in the oral gratification department, but the act itself made me feel uncomfortable. It had nothing to do with a physical inability, but a mental one. That kind of activity repulsed me, and I refused to do it.

My negative attitude about performing oral sex, stemmed from my childhood. My parents never discussed the subject of sex with me as a youngster unless it was on a need to know basis. Obviously, they didn't think I needed to know much.

To cite an example, one of the seven boys I played kick-the-can with as a pre-teen tomboy accused me of being a cockteaser. His statement confused me. I didn't own any roosters, and if I did, I wouldn't tease them—cocks are mean animals.

Thinking it funny, I laughed in recounting the story over dinner. My parents saw no humor in my remark *at all*. They sternly told me *that* term was offensive, and I should never say it again. Seeing their shocked faces gave me the impression I would not get an explanation. It flabbergasted me when the older girl down the street later explained the expression had a sexual connotation.

Holy crap!

Since I had to learn on my own concerning sex, my education came from the rumor mill. My girlfriends who knew about the topic, made it sound disgusting and nasty. Guess some of it stuck with me as I got older.

I may have been a novice at sexual activities in my early twenties, but the man I married was excellent at *everything*, especially how he claimed my virginity on our wedding night two-and-a-half years ago.

Oh, my God. Talk about a sexual revolution rising; it not only rose but crested the horizon in full regalia! The sensations I'd been missing all these years bloomed into action. The techniques he used on my exposed flesh rattled my bones.

Consummating our marriage that night in the hotel room had made me as nervous as a cat on a hot tin roof, but the patience Sherman displayed put my mind at ease. Being ten years my senior, meant he had more experience in mastering sex. By teaching me about my body first, he gave me permission to feel the unfamiliar sensations. *A lot* of unfamiliar *everything*!

Our bodies lay side by side with nothing covering us but the night's breeze as it drifted through an open window. The cooling effect nipped our skin, providing an added sensual atmosphere.

Sherman recognized his new robotic wife. How could he not? I lay flat on my back with my head pressed into the soft pillow, and arms stiff alongside my torso. Trying to focus on level breaths became difficult because my heart raced as if I were about to meet a peril of unknown proportions. I don't know why I felt that way. Sherman was my husband and protector. He would never hurt me. Therefore, I trusted him.

In contrast, Sherman lay next to me, relaxed with his head propped up in his hand. He lightly glided one finger across the worry lines on my forehead. "Sweetheart shut your eyes." His calming tone melted the anxiety consuming me, and his smile reassured me I had nothing to fear. He leaned over and kissed each lid closed.

Darkness. Nothing good ever came out of darkness.

What was he doing?

My chest heavily rose and fell out of anticipation.

"Breathe, my love, slowly in, slowly out," he whispered so close to my ear that I felt the warmth of his breath.

He moved away from me, then repositioned himself by straddling over my hips. I may not have been able to see it, but I sure as hell knew what part of his body took up residence on my belly.

Starting at my shoulders, he barely touched my skin as he drew two fingers down each arm, prompting goosebumps to form over my entire body.

When reaching my wrists, he captured each one and raised them over my head. This simple action made my breath hitch.

"Now," his voice sounded more demanding, "lie still." He lightly kissed my forehead. "No matter what you think is happening, don't look." He duplicated the action on the tip of my nose, followed by a velvet kiss.

What if I open my eyes just enough to see what is coming? No. Where's the fun in that?

Apprehensive, but curious, I did as he instructed.

In the silence and self-imposed darkness, something light and delicate brushed the right side of my collarbone, then slowly tickled its way across to the other side. It made me smile as chills puckered and enveloped my body, but then I frowned in thinking more about it. "Sherman, are you using a feather duster on me?"

"Shh," he sounded, "quiet your mind and concentrate on the sense of touch."

This fluffy implement trailed between the valley of my breasts, then traveled underneath one and lightly circled the now taut point.

My skin heated and my heartrate shot up. The more he played, tentacles of liquid fire licked my most intimate place. Trying not to cave into the eroticism, I did my duty and kept my eyes tightly shut.

Moving on, Sherman tabled the downy article and introduced something else. By paying attention to the material and the fragrance of the thing he drew lightly over my breasts, I recognized it as a flower. He must have removed one of the two roses from the bouquet the thoughtful hotel manager placed in the room earlier that day to celebrate Sherman's and my nuptials.

How romantic on both men's part.

Sweeping underneath my bosom, Sherman traveled the same route, completing the journey at each rosy tip. There, he provoked them repeatedly—tip to tip—by swooshing the top of the flower across my hard nipples, then batting each with the flower head. Swoosh, bat…swoosh, bat. He moved the bloom to my temple. At a snail's pace, the tightly grouped petals drifted down the side of my face, across my lips, and under my chin. Then silence.

What is he doing now? Oh, God, this is driving me insane!

I found out when his tongue, slick and warm, glided over my lips and skimmed down my neck. The air hit the lines of moisture, creating more goosebumps. My back arched as I released a guttural moan. With these few elements of seduction, blood flooded my lady parts like a party erupting *down in the valley.*

Continuing his path lower, he hesitated at my belly where he cavorted within the confines of my "innie" navel and manipulated the skin until I thought he'd redesign it into an "outie." His movements were erotic, and I squirmed at his expertise. Involuntarily, I anchored my head to the pillow; my jaw tightened, and I panted in submission.

With tension building, I fought the need to curl into a tight ball to ward off his caresses as he continued nearer to the source of the fiery pulses. I opened my eyes to meet his. By the softness of his look and his lips slightly turned up at the corner, I knew my arousal pleased him. With that said, my head nearly exploded from the hammer driving out a message for him to move on. He got the mental clue. Our inhales and exhales matched in a rhythmical union.

He interlocked his fingers with mine as he masterfully drew lower. I released the grip and grabbed handfuls of the sheet. Audible groans bubbled out of me and intensified with every passing second. The pulses within my private "V" grew stronger and more vigorous as did the rapid, violent beat of my heart. My mouth gaped. My neck tensed. My torso visually rippled like an earthquake. The engulfing blaze tormented my outer flesh and left me glowing with a ravenous appetite in wanting the bounty of his offering.

He did not disappoint.

I couldn't think rationally when his voyage rested on the oversensitive nub driving this titillating desire. A primal instinct I didn't realize existed within me, assumed control. "Sherman! Sherman! Oh, Sherman!" I cried out as I drew my legs up and placed the balls of my feet on the bed. Arching my back and lifting my butt in an overwhelming sense of euphoria, I gave him easier access to what he captured.

Excitement consumed me at his expert stimulation of the tiny pearl. Spontaneous groans became out-and-out cries from deep within my gut. A multitude of spasms sent waves of shimmering warmth throughout my body. This electrifying experience resulted in the climactic frenzy at reaching my first exploding orgasm.

God, thank you for this man and his sexual prowess!

After allowing me time to recover, Sherman started the lesson on *manual* reciprocation to gratify him. Taking self-pleasure was one thing; providing it for your partner was different. I didn't want to fail as a student at "Sherman's Academy for Sexual Satisfaction."

He poured baby-oil in my hand. "Riley," he murmured, "rub your hands together then take hold of my cock, but not too tight."

There's that horrible word again. Overcome it, Riley.

Nervously looking at his hard and upward-curved shaft, my mind drifted to elephants and the luck they brought with their trunks turned skyward. Was Sherman's "trunk" a sign of good luck?

In performing the act, I wondered if I held him tight enough; rubbed long enough; went fast enough at the proper angle.

Assuredly, if I strayed from the objective, or my arm got tired, he coaxed me back by covering my hand with his and bringing me about. Though focusing on my own task at hand, I couldn't help noticing the way his body moved at my actions. The muscles of his inner thighs flexed and relaxed; his chest surged upward and fell; his eyes closed, and the back of his head buried itself into the pillow.

"Yes, Riley, like that…" He sucked air through his closed teeth and hummed a groan. Though not as boisterous as I had been, the sounds he made rung out, but in a more strained and gravelly way. Blood flowed into his member, deepening the pale color to a darker shade of red that made the baby oil glisten with every stroke of my hand.

I held it tighter in fear it would shatter from how inflated it became. Then his thigh stiffened. An audible moan escaped his lips, then a low, "Ahh" that grew into what sounded like a painful, "Ahh!" His tight facial expression scared me. Did I hurt him? Should I stop? My answer came—as did he—when he erupted like Mt. Vesuvius. Holy hell, what a sight. My orgasm was internal, but not his. The creamy stream shot straight up and fell on my hand.

Ewww. Note to self: next time, angle his penis toward his chest.

After a respite for both of us, my next lesson in the fervent exchange continued, and that's where the whole kit and caboodle collapsed.

"You did great, sweetheart. Now I'll teach you the art of *orally* making me come." He positioned himself, and then me. "Pick up my cock and place it in your mouth. It's softer now so you shouldn't have any problem."

Wait, do what? Put it where?

"Uh, Sherman, I, I can't do that."

He stroked my hair and looked directly into my eyes. "Of course, you can, sweetheart. It's not hard." He smiled. "Did you get that? It's not *hard*."

Yeah, I got it, but he would not get it from me. I didn't care how much he tried to convince me it was a natural act, rumors of what I heard as a young teenager came back to haunt me. In my mind, I could not place my lips on what looked like a tiny, bald head with a slit of an eye staring at me. He peed out of that thing, for Christ's sake, and he wanted me to put it in my mouth? Not in a million years. I would do anything he asked, except that.

I rose from the bed and backed away as if his *cock*—I mentally frowned—would pounce up and devour me. If Sherman wanted more sex from me, it would have to be by normal means; no *cockamamie* penis dinner for me.

I won that battle, thank God.

The coitus that followed our mutual interaction in the matrimonial bed was engaging, passionate, and loving. However, for me, foreplay took the cake as the overall victor of the two methods by which both of us achieved orgasms.

The lessons Sherman taught me on our wedding night thrust me into another realm where my mind expanded and *mostly* accepted a satisfying world I never wanted to leave. Especially when it involved a feather duster. Yes, the next morning, I discovered the thing on the floor next to the bedside table.

My man was so creative.

Chapter Eight

A month passed without seeing Fitz again. That didn't mean out of sight, out of mind. I mentally rehashed our lunch meeting and wanted to ask Sherman about the car manufacturer company's financial trouble Fitz had mentioned that day. After dinner, over wine and dessert on the back porch, I'd do it.

"Darling," my voice strained while cutting into the slice of decadent chocolate cake that slanted like a ski slope, "I have something to ask you."

Noticing the obvious concern in my tone, he rubbed my back. "You can ask me anything, sweetheart."

On second thought, maybe I shouldn't say anything. He'd tell me if he's about to lose his job, right? He never did, so that means...

"Riley," he softly urged, "what do you want to know?" With his thumb, he tenderly brushed my cheek. "Whatever it is, I can see it's bothering you, so out with it."

"A while back, Fitz Kingston...you know, Coral's husband."

Sherman nodded his acknowledgment.

"Well," I continued, "we were talking one day, and he happened to ask me who you worked for. When I told him, he informed me of something that sent my hackles rising."

He narrowed his eyes. "What did he say?"

I took a sip of wine. "He said UAC was in financial trouble and you would probably lose your job. I told him he was mistaken and got all bent out of shape over his assumption. There's no truth to his statement, is there?"

He bit his inner lip; a sure sign of his deliberating how to say something uncomfortable. "It's true that UAC is not where they expected to be after the merger, but that's why they promoted me. I am the 'financial fixer,'" he stated with air quotes. "It's my job to develop an initiative for promoting the company's performance."

"See, I had nothing to worry about. I knew in my gut that Fitz was out-and-out lying to me. He's such a jerk."

He gathered me in his arms and rubbed my back. "I have no idea what gave him that impression that I had a short time left with UAC." He kissed my forehead. "Don't worry your pretty little head about my position with the company, sweetheart. My job is secure."

I hugged him tight. "Good to know, darling." I squeezed harder.

But then, while still in a warm embrace, he asked a question in return. "I don't remember you telling me you and Kingston had, what sounds like, an in-depth conversation." He released me, looking me in the eyes. "When was this?"

"About a month ago. He and Coral were to have lunch together, but she couldn't go, and he asked me to take her place."

I took his nod as accepting my answer without reservation. *Wrong.*

"How did he know about UAC's situation? Does he work for the company in some capacity?"

"I have no idea what kind of job Fitz has. As far as I know, he could be living off Coral who gives him an allowance to spend on expensive clothes and cars. But if he worked for UAC, I think he'd tell me."

"I see." He narrowed his eyes. "What else did you two talk about?"

I took another sip of wine and shrugged. "Nothing much after I blew up at him."

His attention remained on his glass. "Why didn't you tell me about this earlier?"

"What, about my conversation with Fitz, or about our having lunch together?"

"Both."

"I didn't think it important to rehash having lunch with someone. And as far as the other, well…as I told you, I convinced myself that Fitz lied. Just out of curiosity I had to make sure."

Vertical furrows creased between Sherman's brows as he glared at me. "You keep referring to him as Fitz. You call your boss's husband by a nickname?"

"He asked me to, so I do."

"Have you and Fitz engaged in any more revealing conversations?"

"No," I stated with my own pinched brow. "In fact, I haven't seen him since." I hoped that would put an end to any concern Sherman had.

He picked up his dishes, and walked to the back door.

"Are we done with dessert?" I called after him.

He did not turn around. "*I* am," and disappeared into the house. Alone now, I realized my perfect life had somehow taken an imperfect turn.

Suddenly, a previous conversation with my mother came back to haunt me. "Riley, dear," she had told me, "if you work outside the home, nothing good will come of it. You need to be a dutiful wife who stays home to cook, clean, and raise children without questioning why like I have done and still do for your father. A woman working outside the home is nothing but trouble; be it she who disturbs the order of affairs, or the affairs discombobulate her. You don't want to be that woman, Riley. Mind my words."

"Yes, mother," is all I had said.

My how things changed.

As time went on, and I thought about what I wanted to accomplish in life, my total acceptance of what my mother pounded in my brain turned to a partial one. The difference between my mother and me was that I wanted it all—marriage, *job*, and children—and come hell or high water, I would achieve my goal.

The first of the trifecta had taken a hit, and because of that, the next few days were unusually quiet at my house. That all changed when we received an invitation to a New Year's Eve dinner party the following month at the Kingston's house.

"I don't really feel like going to this party, Sherman. Don't you think it would be nice if we stayed home and celebrated the New Year, just the two of us?"

He took on a dubious expression. "You always look for an excuse to go into the house of the well-to-do, so why not this time? It's unlike you."

I didn't want to go because I'd have to see Fitz again, but how did I explain that to my husband? It looked as if I had no choice. Besides, I had always enjoyed getting a glimpse of how green it was on the other side of the fence.

I smirked slyly. "You're right, as usual, darling. I *have* wondered what Coral's house looks like inside and this is the perfect opportunity to see how gorgeous it is. But why do you want to go?"

He took on a smug look. "Because I want to meet the man who raised the hair on the back of my wife's neck." He pointed at the invitation. "Mark the RSVP as a 'yes,' Riley. We're going. End of story." He ended his demand with a tender smooch.

Men.

The New Year's Eve party was the event of the season. Coral invited a ton of people including the office staff and their spouses along with neighbors and friends. Her beautiful two-story mansion had more than enough room to accommodate everyone.

Just entering the dramatic entryway with warm woods, stunning leaded glass windows, and gleaming wide-plank wood floors sent shivers down my spine. Silver balloons clung to winding stairway balustrades. A five-piece live band played popular songs on a raised dais at the end of the longest ballroom I'd ever seen—the *only* ballroom I'd ever seen. On one side of the room, gold glitter sparkled on black tablecloths covering buffet tables filled with foods I couldn't even pronounce. Pewter punch bowls—with and without alcohol—laid atop credenzas. Dessert tables covered with mouth-watering delicacies lay alongside the opposite side of the room. The Kingston's spared no expense in assuring their guests had a grand time.

When our plates held a pile of food, Sherman and I entered the adjoining dining room where several large, round tables bore name cards at each table setting. We found our names placed at the office staff table that included three couples—Sherman and I, Brendon and his wife, and one other pair I didn't know very well. Hazel and Babs made up the only two singles at our table of eight.

While we women reminisced and swooned over previous television shows we'd seen featuring Elvis Presley and his gyrations, *oolala,* I overheard the men speak about some boxer named Rocky Marciano who retired the previous year as the only undefeated Heavyweight Champion, or some such drivel.

Liquor flowed constantly, making my head feel like a hot air balloon—light and airy. The way Babs smiled and giggled suggested she felt the spirits, too.

Fifteen minutes before the celebrated hour of midnight, Coral turned on the television set to CBS then asked the band to stop playing. Moving to the microphone, she made an announcement. "Okay, everyone," she clanked a spoon on the side of her glass, "it's time to gather around to watch Guy Lombardo and his Royal Canadians perform from New York."

To bring in the new year, the professional wait staff Coral hired for the evening, distributed party hats and noisemakers to all those present. As the clock's secondhand converged on the stroke of midnight, the promise of bringing in 1958 soared. With seconds to go, everyone started the final countdown—ten, nine, eight, seven, six, five, four, three, two, one!

"Happy New Year!" we shouted simultaneously followed by blowing the loud and obnoxious horns.

The masses embraced their significant others and planted huge kisses. Even Hazel and Babs found themselves in the arms of single men wanting to celebrate. Sherman did the same by dipping me back and kissing me. Coming up for air, I became even more lightheaded. Could it be the excitement, the kiss, the liquor?

In the entanglement of people bumping into each other and grabbing onto someone—anyone—to wish them a fruitful 1958, I lost grip on my New Year's Eve partner. A few minutes later, I spotted him with Coral on the floor space designated for dancing. She had one hand lying comfortably atop his shoulder and the other relaxed within his open palm. His hand rested on the middle of her back in proper hold as they glided effortlessly around the hardwood parquet floor to the band's rendition of "Only You" by the Platters. It seemed odd to see my husband dancing to this song with a woman other than me. Then I lost sight of them. People blocked my viewpoint when passing in front of me, but tilting my head from side to side, I found them again.

Before I ventured out on the floor to cut in on my boss, I couldn't help but watch the graceful movements she and Sherman exhibited as they turned and weaved among other couples attempting to perform the same magical steps. They were so good together; Fred Astaire and Ginger Rogers would have been jealous. I was.

I smiled, unexpectedly, when Coral threw her head back in laughter at something Sherman whispered in her ear. What did he tell her that was so funny? I would ask when the song ended, which it did a few seconds later. I waited for my husband to rejoin me. Waited and waited. He had still not arrived when the band began playing another song.

Once again, I searched the crowd only to find Coral and Sherman standing close to one another outside the dance circle. Telling myself not to jump to conclusions, I assumed a strong posture. Displaying a playful grin, I approached them with as much ease as they had shown on the dance floor.

Getting close to them, I about tripped over my feet when coming to an abrupt halt. My eyes practically popped out of my head when Coral wrapped her arms around Sherman's neck, and his hand caressed the small of her back. A split second later, she moved in for a kiss lasting way too long for two people not in an intimate relationship.

I wasn't *that* drunk to be seeing things, but maybe Coral was *that* drunk to be doing things—inappropriate things. What surprised me even more, was the man who declared undying love for me didn't try to break free of her grasp. It looked as if he enjoyed another woman's lips on his. My face burned at the scene, but when I glanced lower, my face flamed. Sherman seemed very much at home with Coral's hand plastered to his crotch! What the hell!

Does Coral being my boss give her the right to sexually assault my husband? And how can Sherman allow such an act to begin with?

Booze or no booze, this was my husband and my boss attached in unacceptable behavior. It had to stop, but before I could put the kibosh on it, someone from behind grabbed me and pushed me against a table. Before I knew what hit me, Fitz's lips were on mine; his tongue down my throat and celebrating in a different way.

The mission of rescuing my spouse from his New Year's Eve sparkler disguised as a man-eating lioness evaporated, replaced by a new awareness. My head whirled. The beat of my heart created a drum cadence within my chest as I pushed back from my presumptuous friend with eyes of cobalt blue.

The trance broke when he looked over my head and took on a look of, what…satisfaction, concern, dread? I turned around to find Sherman scowling in our direction.

To hide my—and his, I suppose—embarrassment, Fitz took hold of my arm and led me to my husband who stood very much alone now. With an unpretentious smile, he gently shoved me in Sherman's direction.

"Your wife wandered away from familiar territory," Fitz shouted over the celebratory noise. "As a gentleman, I thought it best if I delivered her safely back to you."

My husband was no fool, and only a fool would think he was one. Sherman captured me around my waist to keep me steady.

"Thank you, Fitz," Sherman cuttingly replied in an indignant tone. "In a crowd like this, you never know who is lurking in the shadows to take advantage of a situation."

Sherman's statement didn't seem to faze our host. Fitz nodded at both of us, turned and strode away, I assumed in search of someone else with whom to play tonsil hockey.

Neither of us spoke on the ride home. My husband fumed. My head spun from the liquor I had imbibed, and my teeth clenched at remembering what Coral had done to Sherman, and that Sherman accepted her actions. Jesus Christ! What a turn of events this turned out to be.

Happy New Year, 1958; hope you're a good one. However, it may not start out very well in the morning.

"I didn't kiss him on purpose, Sherman!" I yelled. "Why are you insinuating there is more to this than meets the eye? Fitz kissed me. I did not kiss him!"

"I saw how you looked at him when he broke the kiss." He glared at me with his brows drawn close and lips pressed tight over his teeth.

With that statement, I took long strides to stand in front of my husband who sat with his legs crossed and arms in combat mode at the breakfast room table. If he wanted a fight, by God, I was bound and determined to give him a good one.

"How in the *hell* could you see how I looked at him when Coral was playing handball with *your* balls?"

"She was drunk, Riley, like the rest of us," he blocked my punch. "It's obvious by this accusation you didn't see me remove her hand a few seconds later, now did you?"

Point, counterpoint.

I hadn't seen that because Fitz distracted me. Sherman barely escaped that one by the hair of his chinny-chin-chin. "All right, that explains that." My glare turned even darker like my tone, but not to the point of losing control. "What about you and her getting intimate over an eternal kiss? And I don't want to hear the same reasoning she was drunk."

When he couldn't come up with a response, I crossed my arms and leaned into his personal space. "You can't answer that, can you? That's because **there *is* no answer**! You crossed the line last night, Sherman. I hope you realize that." I marched to the kitchen where I blankly stared out the window over the sink.

Sherman rose, walked over, and stopped behind me. Slowly and quietly he placed his hands on my upper arms. I shrugged off his touch. But then he tried again and turned me to face him. "I'm sorry, Riley," he apologized, looking straight at me with a soft glint of remorse in his eyes. "I don't know what came over me to return the kiss with Coral. It was completely stupid of me. You are also correct about my not seeing your face after your kiss with Fitz, but the expression on *his* face afterwards, made my blood boil."

I tempered my rage at his atonement for starting this idiotic fight. "What expression did he display that got you all hot under the collar?"

Noticing my calmed demeanor, he tucked a strand of unruly hair behind my ear. "It was one of challenge."

That caught me off-guard. "Challenge? What kind of challenge?"

As if regretting he had pressed the subject, he sighed when putting his arms around my waist, tightly embracing me. "Never mind. It's over now and there's no reason to carry on about it. We both...uh, I behaved badly last night." He broke the hug and slid the back of his fingers down the side of my face.

I was about to say something in return, but before I could, he tenderly pressed his lips against mine. He took a breather but remained close enough that his breath caressed my mouth. "I love you, sweetheart," he murmured, "and I get jealous when another man touches you like he did." He kissed the tip of my nose and cupped my face with both hands. "Can you forgive me for thinking you had something to do with it?" he expressed with an impassioned plea.

Again, he did not let me answer. Instead, his lips zeroed in on mine, allowing his talented tongue to play its way between my lips, performing a symphony within the silky hollows. When Sherman helped himself to a handful of my fanny cheeks and drew me tighter against his body, I literally felt how much this amorous exchange affected him. The roar of the sleeping giant awakened and came to life beneath his zipper.

Lip-locked, we fumbled our way to the adjoining breakfast room as we freed ourselves of angry thoughts and every stitch of each other's clothing. Sherman sat me on top of the glass table and kissed my mouth and breasts before moving his lips down my belly to his destination. My head fell back, my eyes closed, my heart pounded violently as I leaned on my hands behind me to keep some sort of balance. Once again, he promoted my eagerness to have sex by elevating me into that distant land of fanciful abandon. Never had he put me in such a position, but God Almighty! I climaxed thirty seconds after he *had breakfast at the table*!

We stumbled back to the kitchen and fell to the floor. While Sherman lay on his back, I straddled him. Getting down to business, I kissed a path down his chest.

"Ah, I love your lips on me," Sherman cooed. "Don't stop."

I did stop, just because he didn't want me to. I lightly dragged my nails down and alongside his torso, creating delicate ribbons of pink on his skin. "How does this feel, darling?"

He moaned. I stopped again.

He lifted his head. "Why do you keep doing that?"

"Doing what?" I asked all doe-eyed and innocent.

"You start arousing me then stop."

I took his enlarged member in my hand and began stroking it. "You mean like this?" Then stopped once again.

"Yes, like that," he groaned.

I replaced his penis on his stomach and leaned forward to kiss him. "I'm just yanking your chain, darling."

"Yeah, well, could you yank my cock instead of my chain?"

I laughed and began massaging the subject of conversation. I had no baby oil, so the act did not last long. Instead, he massaged my bottom and flexed the muscles in his own to forge a dry rhythm. His action allowed me to adopt the same cadence and drive my hips forward and back, causing friction on my privates.

No sooner did I get into a comfortable pattern, Sherman grabbed my shoulders and flipped me, exchanging places. Not hesitating, he positioned himself and thrust his pelvis forward, penetrating my primed sheath with his ultimate sex tool. The curvature of his fleshy unit and the multiple propulsion thrusts he used, stimulated the hell out of my vagina's roof to where I wanted to scream. So, I did.

The flesh on my shoulders dimpled with the strength of his grasp. With each frenzied drive, he achieved extra power in plunging deeper. Over and over. Faster and harder. My God, he was about to rip a hole through my stomach wall with that jackhammer of his, but then relief came when he emerged and ejaculated all over my torso almost up to my neck. His manhood rested on my stomach as he bellowed out an animalistic groan.

What started out as a spiteful repartee, ended up in an ardent exchange with our appetites fully quenched.

Lying quietly on the cold linoleum, we embraced each other. I don't know what he was thinking, but I knew I needed to wipe the kitchen table down with Clorox. And wash the floor.

Anyway, check that off the list. We had christened our breakfast room *and* our kitchen.

Most gratifying.

Chapter Nine

Friday night meant getting together with Mayzelle and Gene. Shortly after we moved into our home, Sherman and I hit it off with our neighbors across the street and had become instant friends. We loved this couple because they dragged us into a world of making the most mundane activity into something extraordinary.

We had planned to go to the racetrack and place bets on a couple of horses, but Mother Nature was of a different mind. To prevent us from winning our way to retirement, the Goddess of Weather decided we needed to stay home. To ensure that, She opened the skies and released a deluge that flooded the track, causing cancellation of all the scheduled races for the next three days. So, here we were, stuck at our house, playing Yahtzee.

"This game is getting boring," I lamented to the three people sitting at the game table. "No one has even come close to making a Yahtzee yet." I cocked my head, contorted my lips, and tried to speak in that position. "Are we not holding our mouths right, or are the dice stacked against us tonight?" I released the pose and looked at my scorecard with every square filled with a numerical value except for that elusive five-of-a-kind.

Gene agreed that our evening lacked luster. "Let's spice up our game, shall we?" he began, getting his creative juices flowing to ditch the current doldrums. "Here's my line of thought; would you all be up to playing Shotzee instead of Yahtzee?"

"What does that entail?" Sherman squinted his eyes and crossed his arms in interest.

"Well," Gene continued, "when someone throws a five-of-a-kind, everyone but the one who threw it has to take a shot of whiskey."

My brows shot up. "Even us women?"

Gene sneered and cocked his head with a raised brow. "Yes, Riley, even you and Mayzelle. Don't you think you can handle it?"

The gauntlet fell at my feet and I snatched it up. An inner brilliance flashed through my eyes displaying my scrappy side. "Without a doubt in my mind," I addressed his ridiculous question. "Anything men can do, women can do better." Was I kidding myself? Absolutely, but I'd never back down from such a challenge.

To begin this new round of play, I brought in a bottle of Jack Daniels and four shot glasses. Ten minutes in, Gene threw the first Shotzee.

Really? Did it take whiskey for the Yahtzee gods to take notice?

Having the honor, he filled everyone's jigger and applauded as we drank. Fifteen minutes later, Mayzelle earned fifty points with a Shotzee and watched the rest of us swig whiskey. After Mayzelle threw the third five-of-a-kind, things around me got blurry. I could still make out the dice, scorecard, and dice cup, albeit with difficulty.

When having to drink whiskey a fourth time—*damn it, Mayzelle, cut it out*—I slammed my jigger on the tabletop. The jolt made the shot glass fly out of my fingers and bounce onto the floor beneath us. Leaning my weight against the edge of the table with one hand, I reached down and blindly waved my other around our feet to retrieve the shot glass but didn't find it and gave up looking.

When Sherman rolled Shotzee number five, I wasn't about to get on hands and knees to retrieve the jigger. If I so much as got out of my chair, I doubted I'd get back in it. As a replacement, I grabbed the dice cup we used to shake the dice and attempted to pour the liquor in it myself. Inebriated to the point of dizziness, I spilled liquor on the table but managed to wave the bottle over the cup enough to get some in.

"Cheerrrs!" I slurred, waving the cup in the air. Down the hatch, and I followed suit by falling right off the chair, shoulder first onto the floor, and into a nebulous darkness.

"Good morning, sweetheart," my husband hummed in my ear, "it's time to rise and shine."

Refusing to comply, I snagged his pillow and pulled it over my head. That was his signal to leave me alone so I could nurse the worst hangover known to mankind, but Sherman would have none of that. He knelt on the mattress and cuddled up beside me. "Forget it, buster," I said through the satin-covered, goose feather pillow, "there will be no sex from me." I lay still, hoping he'd get the message.

He lightly stroked my bare arm. "Riley," he whispered, "I have something to help take that nasty headache away, but I need you to sit up."

"No," I muttered, "go away and let me sleep."

He pushed the pillow aside and pulled my shoulder to roll me on my back. "Come on now," he reached his arm under my back and raised me to a sitting position, "you'll feel better."

He hopped off the bed, fully clothed, and walked to my side where a glass of water and a packet of Alka-Seltzer were waiting on the bedside table. Tearing open the little envelope, he poured the two tablets containing ingredients that would relieve my hangover, which Lucifer bestowed upon me, into the glass of water. He waited until the fizzing settled down before giving me the glass.

"There," he kissed my forehead after I drank it, "that wasn't so bad, was it? Now, get some rest. I'll come get you when it's time to eat."

At one o'clock in the afternoon, I rolled out of bed and blindly reached into my closet for something to wear. It didn't matter that the color of my Capris clashed with the color of blouse I chose. Who says a woman can't wear red and orange together? I did and it looked, well, atrocious, but so what. I had no intention of going anywhere, and Sherman couldn't care less about the coordination of my clothes.

Wrong, again.

Once I put on makeup to hide my senseless folly from the night before, I followed a heavenly aroma down the stairs, through the foyer, and into the kitchen. Sherman stood at the stove, leaning over the deep well and stirring a steaming pot of chicken soup. He smiled when seeing me up and around. He laughed when noticing the color combination of my outfit.

He raised a brow while checking me out. "Is the circus in town?"

In my state of post-inebriation, I still had the energy to come back with a sarcastic remark. I projected a scathing scowl minus the glimmer of appreciation for his humor. "Aren't you a barrel of laughs? If it were, then you'd be my companion on the tiny tricycles. Is the soup ready?" I opened the cabinet and withdrew two soup bowls.

Amused, he sampled it one more time. "It is. Here," he reached for my bowl, "I'll dish it out; you go sit down."

Whoever invented chicken soup had my utmost respect. It was a comfort food that made all the difference in the world when re-energizing a body, and Sherman had the best recipe. He should take up cooking, and I should sit back with a cigarette in one hand and a beer in the other. Uh, uh, forget that. Beer tasted like dirty feet. Not that I've ever tasted dirty feet, but I assume beer would taste like that.

Since we had a late lunch, our dinner at the normal hour of six o'clock was light, a de-light in fact. I convinced my adventurous partner we should eat dessert first to be different. Without reservation, he agreed.

After consuming our banana splits, we never imagined eating anything of nutritional value. Once I cleaned the bowls and placed them in the cabinet, we plopped ourselves in our respective chairs for a leisurely night of watching TV. We had no sooner turned it on and got comfortable when the phone rang. It was my mother.

"Riley…" her voice cracked and audibly shook.

Instantly, my heart flip-flopped in my chest. "Mom, what's wrong?" I asked.

"It's your father, dear…" she hesitated.

"What about him?" She scared me.

"He had a heart attack this morning, and…"

I waited for her to complete the sentence, but she sniffled in the silence. "And what, Mom!" Why did she stop?

"The doctor's tried everything they could to get the beat regulated, but…"

"But what!" I shouted through the receiver. By this time, Sherman had turned off the television and came to me, putting his arm around my waist.

"Riley…" my mother began again.

"For God's sake mother, tell me what happened!"

She broke down in tears. "He didn't survive, Riley." More sobs rolled over her. "Your father died thirty minutes ago."

All I heard from her were wails pouring out in heaping waves. On my end of the phone, I couldn't move. I couldn't speak. I stood there, grasping the receiver so tight, my knuckles turned white. Sherman pried the receiver out of my hand and took over the conversation with my mother.

Tears should have spilled their sadness down my face, but they didn't. Not one teardrop fell, and it baffled me why. My parents and I had always been close, so news like this should have reduced me to a bowl of melted wax. Could past experiences have caused a callous interior to adhere itself within the recesses of my heart that kept me from crying? To illustrate, when my mother found a lump in her breast several years back and the doctors discovered it was malignant, I held my father's hand at the hospital during her operation for a radical mastectomy. After she came home, I stayed at their house an additional two weeks to help them both.

And when my father had a severe case of influenza three years ago, I helped her nurse him back to health. Last year when they came back from traveling out of the country and my father developed some strange lung disease, I again lent my comfort and support. Those were instances where my parents lived and continued to do so. Now, one of them had passed over Life's threshold, so why in the hell was I not a blubbering mess?

When Sherman hung up the phone with my mother, he saw I hadn't moved an inch. Wrapping his arms around me in a warm embrace, he tried to console the stone statue I had become. My arms dangled at my side and my breathing barely existed. Releasing me, he walked me to the couch and urged me to sit down. "Riley," he looked me square in the eyes that looked void of consciousness, "Riley," he repeated, gently shaking my arm to snap me out of this stupor.

With hands in my lap and shoulders drooped, my gaze went blank. "My father is dead," I muttered in a state of shock. "He died while we were eating banana splits." A pool of liquid collected in my lower lids, waiting for permission to pour over the edge.

"We enjoyed ourselves while my father drew his last breath," I continued in a flat, monotone voice. He handed me a tissue, but I didn't take it. Cocking my head, I focused on his face. "I wasn't there when he died." I gazed then at the floor with an empty stare. "Why didn't my mother call me sooner? I could have made the trip to be with him, but she didn't call me. Why didn't she call me, Sherman?" I beseeched him with a slack expression and dull, wet eyes. Only then did I allow the avalanche of tears to yield.

He knelt in front of me and caressed my face with his hands, wiping the continuous stream of moisture away with his thumbs. "I don't know, sweetheart. Maybe she thought he'd get better. Maybe she didn't have enough time before..." He stopped, which brought my attention to order.

My emotion spun on a dime. A sudden rise of anger coursed through my veins. Not able to take in enough air from the weight bearing down upon me, my nostrils flared, my lungs filled, and my eyes practically bulged out of my head. "Before what?!" I demanded. "Before they rushed him to the emergency room? Before the doctors went through the motions to try and keep him alive? Before they told my mother that my father didn't have a chance in hell to survive?" I sat straight up. "Before she called the priest to administer last rites? When didn't she have enough time to pick up a goddamned phone and call me to inform me my father was dying!"

I flew off the couch, nearly knocking Sherman over. With my hands balled into fists, I stood erect in the middle of the room like a proud bull waiting for the matador to finish it off. Pain washed over me—*me!* I didn't even consider what my mother experienced. It was all about me and how I suffered from hearing this devastating news.

I needed to escape; to go somewhere where the subject of death did not exist. I grabbed the keys to Bluebell from the basket on the kitchen counter. I snatched my purse off the settee in the foyer and fled to my car parked on the lower half of the driveway.

Sherman ran after me. "Riley, wait!" he yelled, but I didn't stop. Once in my car, I smashed into the bumper of his that sat at the curb as I backed out of the driveway. Squealing the tires, I sped toward the intersection. In my rearview mirror, I saw him run back into the house. I could tell he intended to follow me, but with the sun about to go down, he would be hard-pressed to do it. I drove fast on any given day, but tonight my speed would increase to the point no one could catch me.

Chapter Ten

I never saw my husband's car after I drove onto the main thoroughfare. If he looked for me, I doubt he'd find me at The Midnight Lounge on the far eastside of town. I had been on my way to Hazel's house but slowed down when seeing a ton of cars in the club's parking lot.

Lots of people meant they did lots of talking, which meant I did lots of listening, which meant very little thinking on my part.

The instant I walked through the door, I stopped cold. Thick cigarette smoke penetrated my nose and burned my eyes. Laughter and voices rose above the clanking of martini and whiskey glasses. Waitresses barked drink orders to the bartender, which he mostly ignored. "Oh, Lonesome Me," blared from the jukebox. What a fitting song.

Do I dare stay? sounded my little angel voice on my right shoulder. *I have never been in a place like this on my own. Ladies like me don't go to bars without a chaperone.* But then the devil voice on my left shoulder chimed in. *What the hell. I need to grow up and show some gumption. I'm here and I'll stay here.*

The devil won.

I clung to my purse with both hands, almost embedding the handle into the skin of my palms. The only place available to sit was at the bar, so I slid onto the square black leather stool and inched this way and that to get centered. After planting my purse squarely in my lap, I perused those around me.

To my right sat a nicely dressed man in a full three-piece suit. When accidently meeting his eyes, I lowered my head and stared at my purse. Suffering from nerves, I smoothed a wayward strand of hair behind my ear and fingered the collar of my blouse.

My limbs refused to relax. If I sat any straighter, my back would snap in two, turning me into a contortionist in that make-believe circus Sherman insinuated was in town.

Decked out in casual wear, the man to my left didn't tarry in speaking to me. "Well, hellooo there, doll. Cannn I buy youadrink?" he offered with an obvious slur from imbibing too much liquor.

Barely giving him the time of day, I timidly turned my head to look at him, but not in the eye.

Never in the eye.

Eye contact meant interest, and I most definitely had no interest in carrying on a conversation with this man. "No, but thank you," I replied with trembling lips.

He leaned into my space. "Whaaad you say? You're gonna have ta speak up ta hear ov'r…the mussic."

I cleared my throat and looked directly at the long straight hair protruding from the tip of his nose like the horn of a unicorn. "I said, no thank you," then quickly put my focus on watching for the bartender. Though facing forward, I could feel the drunk's beady little eyes roaming over me.

"If you're not here…ta driiink," he lightly drew a finger down my arm, "you must be here…in 'nother c'pacity."

His flirtatious behavior repulsed me and made my stomach turn as I flinched out from under his contact. "Look, I'd appreciate it if you refrain from touching me." By this time, the man on my right had vacated his seat.

The drunk leaned back. "Well, ex-cuuuse me. Aren't you…the hoity-toity one?"

Not wanting to make a scene, I slipped off my stool and occupied the open one. Another woman took my previous seat. Good. Let her deal with that jerk. Back to the business of getting a drink.

Every time the bartender came within reach of me, I peeled my fingers from the purse handle and raised my hand to put in my order, but he kept passing by without so much as an acknowledgement. Men, who came up to the bar and yelled their drink order received service almost immediately. Was that the method by which a person got a drink here?

"Whiskey," I shouted when the bartender passed by again, "neat," I added, whatever that meant. I heard someone shout it over the counter and decided if that guy liked it, it was good enough for me.

When the bartender sloshed a glass of amber liquid in front of me, I nearly fainted. It had no ice or ginger ale in it. Thoughts of "Shotzee" night resurfaced, making me want to gag.

"Charley," a deep, booming voice called over my shoulder. The bartender stopped moving and paid close attention to the voice. "I think the lady would much prefer a glass of champagne."

"Right away, Mr. Kingston," the bartender replied with all due respect.

Before I could turn around, Fitz tapped the shoulder of a different man sitting to my right. The seated man nodded back at the gesture and vacated his stool whereby Fitz sat down.

Fitz placed his half-empty drink on the counter and turned to face me. With my mouth agape and the dazed look on my face, he saw how shocked I was at seeing him.

"What brings a girl like you to a place like this?" he asked with a tone filled with sarcastic humor.

Now, *this* kind of man engaging in *this* kind of wordplay was what the doctor ordered. Wit and fortitude distracted me from the painful burden of my father's death. "I could ask the same of you."

The bartender slapped a paper napkin on the counter, placed a coupe glass of the sparkling wine on top of it and pushed both toward me.

Fitz took possession of my unwanted whiskey and twirled the contents, focusing on the liquor as it coated the interior of the glass. "I've been coming here for years. What about you? I've never seen you in here before tonight." He glanced around the room. "I don't see Sherman. Please tell me you're not here alone."

At the statement, I bit my lip in thoughtful contemplation of the champagne bubbles racing up from the bottom to celebrate their journey when making it to the top.

I threw my shoulders back and raised my chin. Before answering, I took a deep sip of the sparkling wine. "I see a lot of women here alone," I boosted the strength of my tone. "That tells me it's not unusual for a woman to come to a bar by herself."

Fitz lowered his head and grinned. "Most of these ladies you see here are, uh," he cleared his throat, "working women."

"See, you just made my point, Fitz," I announced. "Be they secretaries or housewives, they work hard at the office or in their home and need a place to let their hair down. A drink can be a relaxing activity to take the edge off their day." I raised my glass and nodded my head. "I'm no different."

Justified in my reason about being there without a man on my arm, I took a validating sip. Fitz's grin grew larger; I didn't know why, and I didn't care. Drinking mattered, and I got after it.

Lightly holding the glass of whiskey between his index finger and thumb, he proposed a toast. "You never got to drink your glass of champagne before Sherman whisked you away at our New Year's Eve party. So," he raised his glass and waited for me to pick mine up. "Here's to 1958," he announced so I could hear over the crowd, "may it be a year to remember," then he winked at me, "and maybe parts of it to forget."

I did not understand what he meant…again. I clinked his glass and emptied the contents of mine. He ordered me another. Three glasses of champagne at the bar with Fitz eased my mind. Having him by my side to protect me from assholes like the lascivious letch who hit on me earlier, made me fearless.

With my hand now in his, Fitz helped me off the stool and maneuvered me around the crowded floor to a table filled with people. He pulled out an empty chair and waited until I sat down to scoot it in. He knew these men and women and made the introductions. Not a single name stuck in my memory.

Everyone sitting at the table had something funny to say, and I almost peed myself when laughing at their jokes and stories. No one ever saw the bottom of their glass, either. Fitz made sure of that. Martinis and champagne were aplenty for the women, and the men drank whiskey of the neat order.

All too soon, the bartender yelled *last call*. Downing one more champagne ensured my inability to drive home. *Shit*. I lived on the other side of town. I'd end up in the pokey even before getting out of the parking lot. A taxicab was the only option left in getting back home.

As I reached into my purse, Fitz put his hand over mine. "Forget your car keys, my dear Riley. You can't drive in your condition."

"III'm not go-ing to," I slurred as I removed his hand from mine with two fingers as if picking a rotten peach from the fruit bowl.

I pulled out everything in my purse to locate my wallet where I kept the number of a taxi company in case Bluebell broke down. "III'm drivin' a taxi home."

His grin grew larger. "You're not driving anywhere."

My head snapped up, and I wagged my finger at him. "You're not the boss-a-me, missr Fitz." In my drunken state, my bravado rose. "But," I giggled, "you *are* a goof-ball. Look," I poked him in the arm, "this-s how it works—the driver's drivin' the cab. I'm just drivin' innit. See?"

Before putting my attention back on my purse to find the wallet I had already removed and placed other items on top of, I witnessed Fitz's enjoyment. Was he mocking me? If so, he'd better be ready for a slug upside the head. Fitz was no match for me. As a woman, I knew how to fight and win.

He placed both hands over mine. "Riley," he tried to gain my attention, "I'll take you home."

I may have been three sheets to the wind, but I knew *that* was not a good idea. "Oh, no you won't," I protested, lifting my finger that waved around in front of my face due to impaired faculties. When doing so, I frowned with perplexity and focused on this digit as if it belonged to someone else. To stop its movement, I grabbed it with my other hand then passed a hefty burp from deep within my stomach. I giggled at how loud it came out. "'Scuuse me." The fact I didn't even try to suppress the manly-sounding belch made it funnier still.

I put on a serious face and placed my hand on my hip to show determination. My fingers kept slipping down as if I had spilled oil on my capris pants. Instead, I shook my head, and triggered my index finger.

My hand flew across my body from one shoulder to the other and back again. "Sherman woudant like me in 'ur car…" I warned, taking a deep breath. About to finish the sentence, my thought process crossed wires. With the tip of my finger poking on my temple, I narrowed my eyes. "Uh, what waz-ur-queshion?" I dislodged my finger and cocked my head. "Wait. Waz-ere a queshion?"

I looked up as if the answer hovered in the thickness of horizontal, vaporous smoke hugging the ceiling. "Oh, yeah," I came out of my fog, "no, no, no, no. You can't take me…to…that place I live in. My Sherman willll knock your block *off*, and that would be baaad. No," I shook my head. "That would be very, very baaad. I'm drivin' me… a taxi home but," I turned my now empty purse upside down, "I canna find my…" I tried to focus on Fitz's face, "…that thingie I put my license in?"

"Your wallet?" His grin stretched from ear to ear.

Everyone at the table roared at the comedic entertainment. I joined in having no clue to what was so funny.

Fitz relieved me of my purse and placed the items back in it, including the elusive wallet. "If you won't let me take you to your house, I'm taking you to mine. I'll have Coral call your husband and tell him you're spending the night with us. Then I'll take you back tomorrow morning. How does that sound?"

As I weaved and bobbed in my chair, I decided he had the right idea. "Yeah, okay," I furrowed my brows, "why didint you say that before?"

Helping me rise, he then scooped me up in his arms and carried me to his car. When arriving at the MGA roadster, I scowled. "Fitz, you putz 'round in that sstupid, li'l beasty thing with no door handles. You need tooo return it. Iss defective."

He folded me into the passenger seat and went around to slip into his. He watched as I arched my back to find a comfortable position. The show got better when thrusting my bust forward and moving my hips back and forth. Once my butt found its place, I heaved a deep sigh and closed my eyes. *Oooo...bad idea.*

In my intoxicated state, it startled me when Fitz leaned over and lightly kissed me. I moved to resist, which meant raising my chest in protest, but then he quelled my fear. "Riley," he spoke low and slow as he considered my movement an offering and took advantage of the situation by wrapping his hand over the presented gift, "relax. You are in good hands. Very good hands."

He placed feather kisses on my ear and followed the contour of my jawline before landing once again on my lips. All the while, he did wonders in awakening what was under my bra.

I knocked his hand off my breast and pushed him back. "Hey, you canna kiss me or touch me like that," I sputtered in the best angry tone I could muster. "My lips and boobies belong to Sherman, and only *he* can touch 'em. You take that kiss back!"

"You are so right, Riley." A sly grin crossed his face. "I overstepped. Let me take it back."

My head bobbled at his apology. "And dooot now," I garbled.

In taking the kiss back, he kissed me again, deeper and more exploratory. It left me spinning like a tornado and caused an unexpected excitement in the way he manipulated my tongue. The way he tickled my lips made me coo with pleasure. I felt my heart pick up its speed and the skin on my body prickle with bumps as the blood heated in its flow to my down under.

"There," he whispered in my ear and over the staccato breaths I heaved from the heady kiss, "I took it back. Are we all square now?"

With my eyes partially closed, my head nodded in agreement. "Mmm, hmm, all square now," I mumbled.

After arriving at Fitz's house, he carried me through his front door and took me straight to the guest bedroom where he lay me on the bed, shoes, and all. I had my wits about me, but barely. He must have thought I was out cold because his fingertip glided down my cheek and stopped at the tip of my chin. I felt the warmth of his breath as he neared my mouth.

Was he gonna kiss me? Oh, goody, goody. Come on Fitzy boy. Lay one on me. I'm ready for 'ya. I won't tell Sherman if you won't.

"Son of a bitch," he growled. "I want you so bad, but not like this." He kissed my forehead and disappeared from the room to let me sleep it off.

In my state of impairment, I would have let him do anything he wanted to me because this was a dream, right? And dreams don't count for shit, now do they?

Ahhh, Fitz…don't leave.

Chapter Eleven

Morning's announcement came as most did; with a blinding stream of sunlight beaming its way into the **room.** Feeling the brightness on my eyelids, I opened them no more than a slit.

Shielding my eyes, I slowly surveyed the surroundings of the room I did not recognize—the furniture style I did. A mahogany Queen Anne highboy sitting atop its spindly cabriole legs looked as though it walked straight out of 18th century England. On the wall to my right sat a matching dressing table with companion stool and attached mirror. To finish off the ensemble, I lay in a four-poster bed in the same style.

I had no idea where I was or what mischief happened last night to get me to my present location. It hurt my head when reality came crashing in.

Oh, God. What have I done?

In an instant, I glanced down at my clothing. Same bright combination as the night before. Shoes still on. I fingered the buttons on my blouse. All intact. I sighed in relief.

Forgetting about the height of the bed, I rolled out of it and nearly twisted my ankle when finally reaching the wall-to-wall carpeted floor. Before I ended up in a broken heap, I entwined my fingers securely within the quilted bedspread, grabbing a handful to anchor myself.

In a world of hurt from head to toe, I took baby steps in shuffling out the doorway, holding onto whatever I could wrap my hands around. Keeping my shoulder pressed against the hallway wall, I came to a library where a comfortable leather chair invited me to pause a moment. Plopping down on the broken-in softness of the discolored brown cushion, I bent over. Cradling my head in my hands and closing my eyes, the bold and nutty aroma of freshly brewed coffee reached my nose and triggered my senses.

Hearing voices coming out of the next room I assumed to be the kitchen, I listened in on the conversation. Immediately, I identified the individuals.

"What was she doing there alone in the first place?" I heard Coral ask.

"I never got that out of her," Fitz replied.

Making my way to the kitchen, I leaned against the doorframe with one hand on my aching head and the other over an irritable stomach. As a moan escaped me, both occupants heard it and turned; Coral holding a coffeepot mid-air and Fitz mid-chew.

Coral immediately rushed to my side and helped me to a chair at the kitchen table. "Riley," she stated with a tad of irritation, "I don't mean to be abrupt, but what in Heaven's name got into you last night? Why did you get drunk, and more importantly, why were you in a bar without your husband?"

"May I please have a drink of water?" I asked quietly so as not to increase the constant sway of the pendulum swinging back and forth careening against the walls of my brain with each energetic motion.

"Yes, of course, dear," Coral's tone changed from exasperation to one of sincere compassion. "I'm so sorry. What was I thinking?"

It took only seconds for her to fill a glass with ice water. "Are you hungry?" She placed it in front of me. "There are croissants, but I can make eggs if you'd prefer."

Food sounded disgusting and even the water had trouble going down. Not even Alka-Seltzer could fix this magnitude of stupidity.

"No, thank you, Coral," I mumbled, "I'm fine, a little hung over is all."

Fitz raised a brow. "A *little* hungover? Looks to me like you're a *lot* hung over."

The sarcastic tone of his voice brought my attention to him. "Yeah, I suppose I am. Thank you for seeing after me last night, Fitz. I don't know what went on at the bar but," I breathed deeply, "the fact I woke up in your house makes me think it was not pretty."

"You were out of your element, that's for sure." He then reiterated his wife's question. "So, tell us, Riley, what took you to The Midnight Lounge, and without an escort no less?"

I lowered my head in complete humiliation. Here I sat, at my boss's house in a disgraceful condition of my own making. How mortifying. Sherman would be very angry.

SHERMAN!

He must be out of his mind wondering where I was. "May I please use your telephone to call my husband?" I asked.

"I called him last night, dear," Coral stated, her eyes reflecting a spark of kindness. "He'll be here soon to pick you up. We offered to take you home this morning, but he wouldn't hear of it."

I gulped and deep lines creased my forehead at her statement. Yes, I deserved a good tongue-lashing from Sherman. A heavy sigh left my lips as I placed one hand over the other on top of the table. No sooner had I done that the doorbell chimed a three-toned tune. Coral rose from the table, squeezed my shoulder in passing and headed for the front door.

That left me with Fitz. Reaching across the table, he covered both my hands with his one in a comforting gesture. "If you need to talk about anything, Riley," he locked eyes with me, "anything at all, I've been told I have broad shoulders to bear the burden."

Sensing a sexual uneasiness in my gut as it braided itself into a knot, I disengaged my hands from under his before Sherman walked into the kitchen with Coral. Seeing my husband, I rose, and like a child with her hand caught in the cookie jar, I bent my head in shame. I could not bear to witness his disappointment.

"Thank you again, Coral," Sherman hesitated. I felt the intensity of his eyes on me, and not in a good way. "I hope she wasn't any trouble." His statement could not have been any sharper, and its cut any deeper.

"None at all," Coral sincerely offered. "I'm glad she's all right. All I can say is thank goodness Fitz was there. Otherwise, there's no telling what could have happened to her." She shot her husband a scowl. "That establishment is littered with drunks and prostitutes."

The remark Fitz made at the bar last night suddenly became clear to me. The working women he referred to were prostitutes.

Jeez-Louise.

And that drunk bastard who sat next to me and violated my arm with his disgusting touch must have thought I was one.

Double Jeez-Louise.

Sherman glared at Fitz who appeared mockingly smug. "I suppose I owe you my gratitude, Fitz." I knew my husband hated saying that, but my actions made him do it.

"No problem, my man." Fitz remained seated while quietly tapping the end of his coffee spoon on the tablecloth. "I did what any gentleman would do." Again, the two men engaged in eye-to-eye combat. "Bars can be a wretched place, Sherman," Fitz continued, "especially for a naïve woman like your wife."

I saw Sherman clench his fists at Fitz's snide remark.

With drooped shoulders, I moved to my husband's side. "Thank you both again," I addressed my hosts. To make this pill a little easier to swallow, I engaged in a bit of humor. "But it's time I get the spanking I deserve for being a bad little girl."

I received a frosty stare and grim silence from my husband.

Coral gave me a big hug, "Stay strong, Riley," she whispered. "This, too, shall pass. I'll see you tomorrow morning, dear." She broke the embrace and presented a gentle smile to alleviate my frazzled nerves.

In that same humor I started, Coral turned to Sherman and embraced him. "Don't go too hard on her. She's a good little lamb who went a bit astray. I'm sure she won't do something so dangerous in the future." She then bestowed a different kind of smile to him than what she gave me. I couldn't discern what it meant.

Coral escorted us to the door and waved goodbye as Sherman took his lost little sheep home for a good shearing.

"Aren't you going to say anything?" I asked my husband who sat motionless at the wrought iron kitchen table with his hands folded on its glass top. I, on the other hand, kept my still weak knees from collapsing by wearing a path in the linoleum. "You should be yelling instead of sitting there with your mouth shut." I rose my voice, but not enough to irritate the headache raging within.

Sherman was livid with me, and I didn't blame him one iota. My actions last night were inexcusable, and the fact I never considered what he must have gone through not knowing if I was dead…He had every right to be angry.

He kept his focus on the tabletop. "What do you want me to say, Riley?" His tone was low and exuded control. "That I'm shocked you would do such an idiotic thing as walk into a bar without me?"

His pitch got louder. He turned and looked at me full on with a glow of hostility in his narrowed eyes. "That you lost your ever-loving mind getting drunk in a place where perverts hang out waiting for someone like you to take advantage of?" He jabbed himself in his temple to accentuate the point.

He then leaned forward in his chair to present a ferocity he wanted to get across to me. "That you didn't even have the decency to call me yourself to let me know you were still alive? Is that what you want me to say," he bellowed, "because if it is," he vehemently thrust his finger toward me in a swinging motion, "then you got it!"

His eyes revealed an inferno raging within each pupil and it scared me to death.

Putting aside the fact my breathing grew more rapid, I rushed to kneel beside his chair. Drawing his demonstrative hand off his thigh, I clutched it to my breast for dear life. "Yes, darling," my breath broke, "that's exactly what I want you to say because it's true. I did all those things without thinking about anyone but myself. I was so upset over my mother's news about my father, I just needed to go someplace where I could disappear. I am very, very sorry. You've got to forgive me. If you don't, I'll just—"

"What?" Sherman yanked his hand out from under mine. "Run away again? Get drunk and have another man drag you to his house again?" He rose from his chair and crossed the room in a fiery rage.

I fell back on my heels and lowered my chin to my chest. I profoundly bruised our relationship and severed a vein of respect he once had for me.

Drawing both hands through the stubby hair follicles on his head, he turned to face me. "By the way, not that you're interested or anything," he remarked with malice, "but your mother has called three times asking for you. She wants to tell you about the arrangements for your father." With that, he stomped out of the room and left the house.

Oh, God. My father.

My throat tightened as the conversation with my mother flooded back. Recreating the ire that previously held a darkened spot in my heart, I considered this all her fault. No, it was *both* their faults. My father's fault for dying, and my mother's fault for not allowing me to be there when it happened.

Picturing that image, I fully collapsed to the floor and brought my knees up to my chest. Wrapping my arms around my legs in a fetal position, I allowed the flow of tears to spill freely until they pooled around my cheeks on the hard surface.

When I finally got hold of myself, and my breathing became settled, I slowly sat up using my hands for support. Noticing the liquid on the floor, I rose on rubbery legs and made my way into the kitchen where I found a dish towel to wipe up the salty moisture before someone slipped on it.

The next morning, Coral stood by my desk when I arrived at work. Her stance said it all. Because of my late night stupidity, she was about to say those two career-ending words. I wouldn't blame her for giving me the boot, so I prepared myself for the worst.

"Riley," Coral's tone was smooth as it rolled off her tongue, "would you please follow me to my office?"

Yep, fire away, Coral. I hope your aim is perfect and you get me with one shot.

After closing her door, Coral motioned me to sit in the chair across from her desk. She sighed and took a seat. "About last night." She hesitated briefly. "I asked Fitz why you put yourself in such a precarious position, but he couldn't answer me. We never did get around to hearing it from you, either." She interlaced her fingers and laid her hands on the desktop. "Just because I'm your employer, does not take me out of the friendship circle. In this company, I want my employees to see me as an ally they can approach when faced with a situation, be it work or personally related.

"As an outsider, Riley, I see you are going through a rough patch in your life. As your friend, I would like to think you could confide in me. But before you say anything, please feel confident the conversations in this room never reach outside ears."

Coral didn't fire me; she wanted me to open up to her about my life. It seemed a small price to pay for keeping a job I loved, so I'd give her what she asked.

I drew a barely moist tongue over my dry lips before beginning. "I received news that my father had passed away and didn't know how to process it." I kept my hands clenched in my lap to tell the skeletal version of the story. "The news came as a shock, and instead of accepting the truth of it, I escaped to a place where I didn't have to think. It was stupid, and I have disappointed a few people," I raised my eyes to her, "including you, Coral."

Coral's expression softened, and her tone turned sympathetic. It almost looked as if she were about to cry. "I am truly sorry for your loss, Riley. A father plays an important role in his daughter's life and discovering this kind of news about yours must be devastating for you."

I let out a ragged breath. "Thank you, Coral, it is."

She then took on a questioning look. "Dear, why are you even here? Why aren't you on your way to your mother's house? Don't you think she needs your support right now, not to mention her support for you?"

I didn't want to talk any more about the subject, but I certainly couldn't tell my boss to leave me the hell alone. I made the decision to stay here, but how could I help Coral understand without my looking like a coldhearted beast?

"I still need time to wrestle with my emotions, Coral." I made the purely ridiculous excuse sound convincing. "I can't comfort my mother if I'm a blubbering mess. I'll know when it's time to go."

"Well, alright dear," she rose from her chair as did I, "but, you don't need to be here at the office. Go home and find something constructive to do that will help console your grief." Her lips curved into a soft and sympathetic smile. "Bars aren't your answer."

With my embarrassment at its peak, I mumbled, "You can say that again."

Hearing my own words, I thrust out my chest and stood at attention. "If I need to act out my grief again, I'll make sure I do it at home. But if it's all the same to you, Coral, I'd like to stay and get some work done. Right now, I need to keep my mind pointed in the opposite direction of where it's been lately."

She raised her brows at my statement. "Oh. If that's what you want to do, Riley. Feel free to go home if it gets to be too much." She walked to my side of the desk and embraced me with a soul-bolstering hug. "I can't stress enough that I am here to listen if you need to vent."

I returned the gesture. "Thank you, Coral." *And Jesus.* "I'd best get to work now."

Chapter Twelve

"*E*xcuse me?"

"I didn't stutter, Sherman."

He shook his head as if clearing cobwebs from it. "Riley, why in God's name would you not go to your father's funeral?"

Separating myself from the crux of the situation, I nonchalantly picked off two small lint balls from one wrist of my peach-colored cardigan. "I don't *want* to go, so I'm not going to." I extracted a cigarette from my gold case, lit it, then drew in deeply to inflame the end with a fiery glow. Blowing out the smoke, I watched the wisps dance gracefully as they scattered through the air before disappearing like how I wished I could.

I did not look my husband in the eye. Instead, I gazed out the living room window. "My mother can handle this without me," I stated with more ease than I should have. "She has a ton of friends who will be hovering over like mother hens." I inhaled another puff of tobacco, raised my chin to accentuate its exhalation, then tapped the burned cylinder of ashes over the green, metal ashtray.

"My father is no longer on this Earth, Sherman, and I am not going to put myself through the agony of watching his remains be placed into the darkness of it." Only then did I turn to see Sherman's reaction of pure shock.

His mouth hung open and his eyes bulged as he glared at me. "Have you lost your ever-lovin' mind?"

I looked passed him while biting my lip. "No, last I checked, it was in its proper place."

He stepped toward me, removed the cigarette from my fingers and placed it in the ashtray. He then took both my hands in his and brought them to his chest where he caressed them. "Riley," his tone softened, "you can't mean that. Your mother needs you at a time like this."

He searched my eyes for understanding. It was there; just hidden behind a bleak case of sadness and an undeniable state of stubbornness. "You two may not share the same blood," he went on to say, "but you are the sole remaining member of her family." He tried hard to get through the towering barrier I placed around my heart. "How could you even consider the thought of not being at her side to comfort her when she has lost her husband and you have lost the only father you have ever known?"

I did not wince at his words but remained steadfast and heart-locked.

"Look," after kissing my knuckles, he lowered my hands and let go, stroking my arms instead, "I understand how upset you are, but this is not up for discussion." In a fluid movement, he smoothed my hair then cupped my face with both hands. "You're going…we are going and that's all there is to it. You will regret it for the rest of your life if you don't."

With no other motion, I furrowed my brows, unleashing the depth of anger radiating from my steel-blue gray eyes directly into his brown ones. "The only thing I regret is what my mother did to me concerning my father when he fought for his life. She stole the last moments of my father's life from me, and I will never forgive her for that. Ever."

Sherman exhaled a long, low breath when releasing my face, taking on a sternness I had not expected. "If you won't go for your mother, or for yourself, then go for me, because," he lowered his head and licked his lips again before looking back at me, "I would think less of you if you turned your back on your mother in a time when family means everything."

I stood still in contemplation of the choices placed before me. One, I could go through the motions of attending the funeral with resentment aimed directly at my mother. Two, I could stand my ground and refuse to go with the possibility of Sherman holding the decision over my head which would result in taking another notch out of our marriage.

It was a no-win for me either way. However, I loved my husband more than my mother right then, which wasn't saying much. "Fine, Sherman." I straightened my spine, determined to make the best of this pitiful situation. "I don't want to be the wedge that splinters the love you and I have, so I'll go. Now, I don't want to hear another word about it." I abruptly turned, snatched my cigarette case and lighter off the end table and went to the bedroom.

Sherman and I attended my father's funeral. At the church service, my rocklike resolve waned, and my spirit collapsed in on itself, creating a gaping hole in my soul.

I could not escape the overwhelming anguish that shattered my world in creating this new reality: the death of the man who raised me as his own. My father was the man who, having no son, taught his daughter-tomboy how to build and use a rubber band gun out of old wood and strips of tire innertubes. He was the man who, in my teenage years, tried to teach me how to play golf, unsuccessfully I might add. He showed me the correct way to repair cracked plaster and how to play chess; I mastered the repair but not game.

I remember a nightly ritual he and I participated in when I was little. He'd be sitting in his armchair smoking a pipe and reading the newspaper when I came into the room carrying my favorite storybook. He doused the pipe, folded and placed the newspaper aside, then lifted me onto his lap. The first thing he did was give me snuggle kisses under my chin, which created a roomful of giggles. Then he opened the book—the same book every time—and read it to me, never giving the impression of boredom.

My father was patient, kind, considerate, helpful, and a hundred more positive adjectives one could think of. But now…now…the man whom I cherished was no longer with me. Now, only a representation of who he used to be lay within the confines of a wooden casket. Shards of grief embedded themselves deep within my broken heart.

And the burial.

My mother pressed me into standing directly next to her at the gravesite so she could cry on my shoulder. I had intended to avoid having to watch the proceedings by standing in the far back where sympathetic mourners obstructed my view. But no. She clasped a bible to her chest with one hand, and with the other she dragged me with her to where the casket lay supported over the open grave.

My stomach churned, and my nostrils flared in trying to gather enough air to keep standing. If I gnashed my teeth any harder, I'd crack them all. Normally, mourners did not stay for the lowering of the casket, but my mother insisted she and I watch.

Morbid woman.

It ripped me apart to witness the attendants lower the hardwood vessel of death shrouding my father's remnants into the cold, dark earth. My sight clouded with moisture, but no tear did I allow to fall.

To vanquish the somber vision playing out before me, I allowed my mind to enter an equally despondent place. The fact I would never again hear my father's voice over the telephone or throw my arms around him when we all got together to celebrate birthdays or holidays, sent me further into a fit of despair.

Breathe, Riley, I repeated over and over to myself. *You can get through this. Take one breath at a time. You're a fighter, and you will not allow this war within your heart to annihilate you. Get with the program. You can rise above and conquer.*

And by God, I did.

From the very first day of returning from my father's funeral, I tried to erase the misery of that scene and rekindle a more current one—Sherman's and my happy life before that fateful phone call regarding a tragic passing. My efforts were failing. I did what he demanded of me for Christ's sake, and that was to stand by my mother's side as my father's lifeless body found its place six-feet underground, so why did Sherman insist on giving me the silent treatment? I finally sought council about what to do—Hazel.

I never expected to befriend such an unusual person as Hazel, but she was just the one I needed in my life to bitch to about Sherman among other topics. She reciprocated to me about her dating life. Yikes! What a rodeo. She had men on a revolving door. No sooner had one man swooped in and courted her, Hazel gave him the cowboy boot and entertained another, giving him the same treatment. One day I asked her about it.

"Hazel, why can't you hold on to a man for very long?"

"Oh, darlin', it's not that I can't hold a man because I most certainly can. It's that I enjoy catching all the different kinds of fish in the sea."

"Aren't you ever going to settle down with one of those fish?"

"One day, maybe, but until then, I'll take the good, the fun, and the entertainment my fish have to offer. When one has served its purpose, I'll throw him back into the sea and catch another."

"When do you stop fishing?"

"When my appetite turns to steak."

Hazel had a different way of thinking about relationships and that's why I sought her advice this time about Sherman's and my un-fairytale path.

At the end of the two weeks of trying to improve things between Sherman and me on my own, I tried the Hazel method.

I snuggled up against my husband's back and draped my leg over his in a spooning position, but what did I get in return? "Riley," he gruffly stated, "your body is too hot to have you hanging all over me."

I tried my attempt at humor. "Is that your way of saying you find my body a sexual inferno?"

To ensure I understood his real message, he pushed my leg away and rose to begin preparing for the day. The sun had not even risen yet, for crying out loud!

Every morning since then, I stayed on my own side of the bed leaving an empty void between us. Not just a physical space, but a mental one as well.

Strike one.

Sherman's timetable changed, too. In my opinion—the useless one, per my husband's recent neglect in asking for it—he was over-zealous in his new arrival time at work. He now rose at five o'clock a.m. to leave thirty minutes later, allowing him to be behind his desk by six o'clock. That's even before God opened Her eyes!

I surmised that my two "life crises" in relation to my father—my drunken state at The Midnight Lounge where I ended up at the Kingston's home, and the one before and during the funeral itself—had to be the cause for this radical change in Sherman's behavior.

To rectify the situation, per Hazel's suggestion, I tried making amends by writing silly notes to him and leaving them in different places around the house for his discovery. Getting creative and knowing the one room he went to every morning without fail, I carefully scripted my undying love on six contiguous squares of toilet paper then rewound them on the existing roll located in the main bathroom.

The anticipated positive reaction I expected from him, turned sour when he neglected to mention anything about it one way or the other. After he left for work, I found the squares folded neatly on the bathroom sink. I had no idea if he had even read the heartfelt affections I poured out.

Strike two.

At Hazel's behest, I booked a romantic weekend for my husband and me in a fancy hotel that included a fruit and champagne basket. The hotel room was elegant, and we enjoyed the fruit that proved ripe and delicious.

Finally, success.

Wrong again!

After relishing the succulent treats, it all went downhill. Opening the bubbly, Sherman poured me a quarter glass and decided the rest belonged to him. I would have enjoyed more but got no opportunity since he downed the champagne one glass after the other.

His body language told me what he wanted next. Sex. The corner of his lips curled up into a sneer, and his eyelids lowered a bit like that of a lion sizing up its prey. The words he used were not kind, soft, or romantic. His quest for sex frightened me. His actions were primal in that he practically ripped my clothes off. If I hadn't intervened, my new blouse would have been in tatters as would my lace panties. I'd never seen him like that before.

After I stood naked before him, he shoved me down on the bed, followed by him swiveling my legs up on the comforter. I barely batted an eye when he straddled me, his clothes still on but zipper open and penis exposed and fully aroused. He fell upon one elbow beside me and hung over me while he positioned his shaft with his other hand then forcefully entered me.

What the hell! I wasn't even ready. It hurt when he made his first thrust. Where was the gentle preparation that made me quiver and get my juices flowing so I could enjoy the act as well? He did not engage in tickling my neck with light, feather kisses. Not once did his magic touch leave a trail of goosebumps over my naked flesh while venturing toward the tender erogenous zone between my legs. His normal, gentle entry fell away to that of a wanton man determined to get what he needed and to hell with my needs.

I kept my eyes tightly closed and held onto the comforter for dear life as he pounded his dick in and out of me like a whore he picked up in some back alley to fuck then get rid of when he completed the job.

"Sherman!" I finally screamed out when my vagina became raw and irritated, "why are you being so rough! You're hurting me! Stop it, please!" The only reason he pulled out was to come on my stomach, not because it had anything to do with the pain he inflicted. When sated and exhausted, he collapsed on his side of the bed without a word to me.

I lay still except for the heaving breaths that left my lungs, as tears streamed down my face in complete disbelief of what just happened. Where did all this violent and pent-up emotion come from? My adoring husband who used to take pleasure in watching my reactions to his slow and sensually doting ways, fell by the wayside.

It broke my heart to see this side of my husband. Could his drinking all that champagne so quickly turn him into a wild animal who I never want to see again?

When he fell asleep, I quietly got dressed, took the door key, tiptoed across the floor and left the room. I needed clean, crisp air to obliterate the vile stench that hung back in the hotel room. Thirty minutes later, I walked back in and slipped between the sheets, clothes and all. If he wanted an encore sex performance, he'd have to work for it. This would not happen to me again.

The weekend may have started out well enough but ended up a total bust. It relieved me to see it end.

The next morning, we packed up our bags in silence and left the hotel. Neither of us spoke about that night's experience. I buried it deep inside and tried to forget.

Strike three.

Hazel had no more ideas after hearing about this last debacle. "I am so sorry you went through such a horrific experience, darlin'. Sometimes men are cruel. Don't know what drives them to be that way, they just are. Eventually, you will put that night behind you. I wish there was something else I could offer up to you, but I am fresh out of ideas. Who knows? You might think of a way to mend things with Sherman all by your lonesome. Don't let it get you down, though." She gave me a strong hug.

There was one more person who could help me—Mayzelle. I engaged her and Gene to come up with a special game night of charades that included wacky people, places, and things.

They did, and it worked.

The fact we were with other people and doing something we enjoyed created that icebreaker. I couldn't do it by myself or with Hazel's help. I hoped Sherman's and my path advanced in a positive direction. Thank God for good friends and great neighbors.

Chapter Thirteen

I flopped my head back and closed my eyes at my mother's monotonous instruction for making the perfect meatloaf. "Okay, thanks mother, I've got to hang up now, Sherman's calling me. Bye." Did I write the recipe down? No. Did I even listen? Tried not to. Did I lie about having to go? Yes. Sherman wasn't even home to call me away from the conversation. My husband, once again his adoring and caring self, went across the street to help Mayzelle move a dresser. Gene had run an errand for her, and as impatient as she was, she couldn't wait for him to return to help her. Like all women, she wanted what she wanted when she wanted it.

Sherman returned to that knight in shining armor who always came to the aid of a damsel in distress. Today, Mayzelle took on that role of a helpless lass.

Ever since my father died a month and a half ago, my mother deemed me his replacement, as far as talking went. She and I had always been friends, so it should not have surprised me this would happen. It's just that now she called me on a daily basis to complain and whine.

"Riley," she sniffed, "this house is so lonely without your father here, and so am I."

"I know it's hard Mother, but you have wonderful friends to occupy your time."

"Yes, I do have the most adoring people around me. But that's not the only thing I'm worried about."

"What else is there?"

"I'm not sure I have enough money to survive very long when I get old."

I shook my head and grinned. "Oh, mother, you know that's poppycock. You inherited a boatload of money when your parents passed away, and I know you squirreled it away for a rainy day. Not only that, but dad earned a ton on his own. Also, when he died, he had a lucrative life insurance policy, so you can't convince me you have financial woes going into the future."

She sighed, and from her tone of voice, I heard a smile. "Your father did take excellent care of me, didn't he?"

"Very. So, is there anything else concerning you today?"

"Should I get a puppy?"

Where did *that* come from? "Do you want a puppy, mother?"

"It would be a good companion for me, especially at night. That's when I get the loneliest and scared."

"True. Think about it before you do anything rash, though, mother."

"I will, dear. Should I take sleeping pills? Some nights are unbearable without someone else in the house. I stay up late, even until ten or eleven at night thinking about this and that. I can't seem to turn off my brain."

Ten or eleven is late?

"Mother, that is something you have to take up with your doctor. Last I checked, my name didn't have an MD after it."

"You are right again, dear. You are so smart. You get that from your father, you know."

"I get that from *both* my parents, mother."

"Thank you dear. Now, on another note, how are you and Sherman doing? Last I heard from you, there was trouble in paradise."

"It's good, mother. We are back to being us again...the happy us, not the sour-pickle us."

"That pleases me to no end, dear. When are you coming upstate to visit your old mother?"

"As soon as I can."

Countless times she asked me that question, but I kept putting her off. Why? Hearing her complain over the phone, I could tune her out; hearing her clamor on in person was completely different. I'd avoid it if possible. Don't get me wrong, I loved my mother dearly, but her plaintive cries bugged the hell out of me.

"You know what will take my mind off your father instead of getting a dog?"

Uh oh. Did I dare ask? "What mother?"

She got all excited. "You and Sherman having a baby!"

Really? Did she expect me to have a child to keep *her* occupied? But then I thought more about it. Was I even ready to venture out of my comfort zone and enter the joyful realm of motherhood? Was Sherman ready to take the throne beside me and take on the role of father? Was now the right time to increase our family? We just overturned a bad situation in our relationship.

Mentally debating the subject, I concluded that my husband and I were in a good enough place to begin thinking about starting a family. Not only that, he and I had been married going on three years now, and perhaps we should take that step. After dinner, I'd bring up the life-changing topic and get his reaction. First, though, I went to the flower shop and bought one red rose to brighten the mood.

⁓

"Thank you, sweetheart, not only for the rose you laid across my plate, but for this meal. This is one of the most delicious dinners you have ever prepared." Sherman purred his approval as he wiped his mouth with his napkin. "Did you get this meatloaf recipe from your mother?"

"As a matter of fact, I did." No, I didn't; I got it out of the latest edition of the Better Homes and Gardens Cookbook.

"I'm glad you two are getting along better these days. I thought for a minute there you'd never forgive her for insisting you go to your father's funeral."

I picked up our plates and took them to the sink. "She's my mother, so of course I've forgiven her for that."

When the meal ended, Sherman and I cleaned the kitchen. I washed the dishes, rinsed, and put them away while he watched and commented on what a good job I did.

Teamwork at its best.

Ending that chore, but before starting my subtle spiel on having a child, I reached into the cupboard for a bottle of port and placed it on the kitchen counter. Withdrawing the brass corkscrew from a drawer, I positioned it on top of the cork and pried it out. An entrepreneur should invent a device that makes this job easier, like an electric wine opener.

Only in my dreams.

"Darling?" I took the wine-filled glasses into the living room.

"Yes." Sherman lit a cigarette and settled in his favorite armchair.

"Let's have a baby." So much for subtlety.

It took a lot to shock my husband, but that did. "Really?" He nearly missed the round, sterling silver and glass starburst ashtray when placing his cigarette down before he dropped it. "Are, we ready for that kind of responsibility?"

I handed my husband his glass of wine and placed mine on the coffee table before sitting in the companion chair. He lit a cigarette and handed it to me.

He's such a gem.

"Is anyone ever ready for a baby, darling? Sometimes you just have to do it." I cocked my head and practiced my bewitching skills. Looking sideways at him, I raised my shoulder and rested my chin on top of it. "Don't you want to," I rotated my shoulder, "do it?" I asked with a sensual tone.

My attempt at being sexy brought a smile to my husband's lips. "With you? Always, but I thought we were talking about having a baby."

I took a long drag off my cigarette followed by a deep sip of port. "We are."

"So, when would you like to, as you say, do it?"

With excitement building, I folded my legs under me and sat on them. "The sooner the better," I suggested.

"What about starting tonight?"

I raised one brow and exhibited a come-hither look. "What about starting, now?"

Sherman inhaled one last take on his cigarette, smashed it out in the ashtray, downed the half-full glass of wine, and shot out of his chair. Standing in front of me, he took my hand and helped me up. Leading me up the stairs into the main bathroom, he butted me up against the double sink and closed the door. There, he stood completely still while his eyes roamed over every part of me.

Suddenly, that awful night at the hotel blasted into my memory.

Now? You're going to think about that now? Stop it! That was a one-time occurrence that happened because Sherman had too much champagne. This is totally different.

I took a deep breath and noticed him staring at me. "Sherman, what are you doing and why are we in the bathroom with the door closed? You and I are the only ones in this house. Besides, I thought we were going to make a baby."

He scanned me up and down. "We will, but first, I want to remember you as slim and trim," he drew his palm over my stomach, "and not with a bun in the oven."

He pulled me into a strong embrace and pressed my body into his until I felt his testament to full arousal. He showered kisses over my ears, nose, and jaw, then stopped, but only briefly to observe my reaction. Seeing my eyes closed and a light smile on my face, he tenderly nipped my lips before putting his plan in motion.

Placing the amorous escapade on pause, Sherman turned on the water in the peach-colored tile shower. Resuming where he left off, he proceeded to unfasten each of my shirt buttons one by one. Taking his time, he slid my blouse off my shoulders, inflaming the smoldering embers pulsing under my skin and especially under my brazier.

In my surrender, I swayed as his fingers incited a riot of shivers up my spine while he loitered over the individual swells of my bosom trapped in their encasement. His hands slipped around my back to liberate the multiple hooks in the taut material of the bra. Slowly dragging the straps down my arms, he followed the path with his lips until coming parallel with the ample suppleness of my now unencumbered breasts. Cupping one in his hand, he circled the area around the widest part of the areola with his tongue, then on every pass, the circle got tighter and tighter until he captured the nipple itself between his teeth, lightly bearing down until he heard me gasp. The other breast got the same treatment, thank God. You can't do one without doing it to the other. Fair is fair.

"Our baby is going to be well fed by you, Riley," Sherman whispered. "I'm going to be jealous when he or she suckles you and I can't."

Taking a knee, he licked down to the top of my capris, leaving a trail of glistening moisture on the miniscule hairs. I watched as he adeptly unfastened the zipper then lowered the pants to the floor.

Only my black satin panties with pink embroidered butterflies remained. Consciously, he massaged my pubic bone with his thumbs. Placing enough pressure in the right places, he watched as I began to writhe in place. With eyes closed, I melted into the pleasure and thrust my pelvis toward him while throwing my head back almost hitting the medicine cabinet behind me.

He then reached around and grabbed my fanny. Keeping me still, he lowered his mouth near the under edge of my pubic bone still wrapped in satin and blew several breaths that penetrated the material. The air he expelled felt warm. Erotically warm, and the more he did it the warmer it got, and so did I.

Next, the panties had to go.

When I couldn't stand the torture any longer, I started removing them myself, but Sherman put an end to that lickety-split. Taking hold of both my wrists, he placed my hands back on the sink. "Settle," he cooed, "let your mind and body drift as if you are floating in the ocean current that is carrying you to a deserted island where you and I are the only occupants."

Closing my eyes once more, I nodded, inhaled deeply, and pressed my lips together. Mentally, I cast myself into that sea of sexuality.

Yes, the panties had to go, and he shimmied them down around my ankles. He then nuzzled the exposed blanket of hair surrounding my sex, making the follicles on my arms stand on end.

My face flushed with fever. My nipples became so hard they could no doubt cut glass. Electric pulses rippled between my legs indicating my readiness for him, but he was not willing to move beyond foreplay yet. Rising, he quickly undressed.

Pulling me into the shower with the warm water splashing over our bodies, his own fever engulfed him as he pushed me up against the hardness of the four-inch square tiles covering the walls. Our shower stall was small and coupling up in it created an added intimacy.

Falling to his knees with the water spray pelting his back, he spread my legs farther apart. With his eyes closed to avoid water trickling in, he blindly kissed and bit his way up my inner thigh to the upper region. The anticipated plunder of my privates caused me to jerk when reacting to his manipulating the tender skin at the highest point before reaching my nubbin.

OH, GOD...OH, GOD!

As my pelvic muscles started to spasm and the nerves launched a million pleasure signals to my brain, I pressed my head, arms, and shoulder blades against the shower wall so hard, the porcelain squares would surely crack.

To amplify this communion between physical and mental plains, I reached down to separate the swollen outer lips that concealed my pink diamond that melted back into its protective hood. Grateful for the assistance, Sherman delved in by ever so lightly bearing down with his teeth so as not to inflict pain but to send acute flashes of fire into my genitals.

Surging eruptions rattled my inner core. I gasped for air and got water in my mouth. I had to spit it out, but at this point, portraying the epitome of a lady was the furthest thing from my mind. I wanted my husband to dispel all my angelic qualities and turn me into something savagely primitive that could ravage and take ravaging in return.

He seized and pulled my backside flesh forward, fusing his facial lips to my genital ones. Imprisoning my jewel, he nearly dislodged me from this earth as the blood came crashing into my head causing a sudden rush of adrenalin. Nearly lacerating his flesh by clawing his shoulders with my fingernails, I could no longer hold anything back. Seconds later, he brought me to completion as I loudly roared a barbaric acclamation of unadulterated abandon.

He stood with bent knees and quickly entered me, gliding in and out at a slow, even pace. As he gripped my hips to steady himself in his acceleration, I buried my face between his pecs and bound myself to him with a constrictive hold around his neck.

The water pulsating over him did not seem to distract him in moving faster and thrusting deeper. Keeping a firm hold, he leaned on me and groaned his satisfaction when making his final thrust.

With his own ass muscles still fixed and flexed, he remained inside me until every bit of his seed had found its way into my womb.

I feel pregnant already.

Chapter Fourteen

My mother squealed enthusiasm over the news of becoming a grandmother. At least it kept her from droning on about how miserable she felt. It did not, however, keep her from frequently lamenting over how nice it would have been for my father to have witnessed the birth of his grandchild.

I agreed with her on that point. I just wished she agreed to talk about certain topics with me. Sex to be specific and those topics related to it. But no.

I tested that Pandora's box not too long ago to see if she continued to keep it tightly locked. Sherman and I had a big fight over my not wanting to perform oral sex on him, and I considered approaching her about it.

But then my thinking veered in another direction. *She's never been open to talking about this kind of thing, so maybe I should forget it. I'm not even sure I can spit out the words I need to convey to her. Why do I feel so guilty about starting up this conversation? God, please give me the strength to do this.*

"Mother, you and I can talk about anything, right?"

"Of course, dear, what's on your mind?"

I cleared my throat. "Sex."

She immediately choked on her own spit. "Riley that is not a subject we normally discuss," she croaked out.

"Yes, I know. But if I can't speak to you about sex, who can I talk to?"

"Your husband, dear. You talk about..." she couldn't even say the word, "that kind of thing, with Sherman. He's more experienced than you and probably more than I."

"But it's something he wants from me that I can't bring myself to do. I just can't. He wants me to put his, his...in my—"

"Riley, stop! I don't want to hear about what he wants you to do. I'm sorry, dear, but I don't know what I can say that will help you in any way. A wife does what a wife must do to keep her husband happy. Only you can determine what's best for your marriage in that department. Now, that's all I'm going to say about the subject."

After that, I never ventured down that road again with my mother. That's when Hazel became my confidant about such things.

I did, however, get the broken record advice from my mother about my role as Sherman's wife. "Riley dear," she stressed, "God put a woman on this Earth to accomplish four things—marry, keep an orderly house, bear children, and stay home to raise them to become honest and productive individuals. That's what I did when I married your father, and that's what Sherman expects of you."

At least I was in the process of carrying out requirement number three of my mother's list of womanly duties—that of being with child. She had never approved of my choice to work outside the home, so there went number four on her list.

In addition to the preliminary announcement to her that I had a bun in the oven, as Sherman referred to my pregnancy, I went as far as asking her to come down and stay a week or two after the baby's birth to help me. She could not have been happier but added she would not come until the first day of the child's third month. She didn't want unnecessary germs floating around that could harm her grandchild, and insisted I do the same by keeping the baby indoors and not go outside with him or her. I agreed. Finally, we were on the same page and once again had something in which we shared excitement.

Cloud nine had room for one more smiling soul—Sherman. I burned dinner; he laughed it off by saying charcoal was good for his teeth. I over-starched his shirts; he said it made him stand up straighter. I used his good screwdriver to dig up weeds; he agreed it was the only thing long enough to get to the roots.

And pampering? Oh, my. He wouldn't let me lift a finger around the house except for cooking, and he did all the cleanup. Not wanting me to overexert myself with the housekeeping, he hired a maid service to clean the house. Was he being over-zealous? Perhaps, but with all this attention, I should have gotten pregnant a long time ago.

At work as a new mama-to-be, my co-workers advised me what to do and what to steer clear from. "Don't raise your arms over your head Riley, because that will cause the umbilical cord to wrap around the baby's neck," one woman advised. "If you sit on cold cement, you'll get hemorrhoids," stated another. Even Brendon gave me advice. "I had to drive my wife up and down the bumpiest road I could find when she was past her due date," he offered.

I readily listened, but being only one-month in, I had plenty of time to take their added suggestions of going on a strict diet and refraining from reading "exciting books." I already smoked and drank alcohol, which doctors promoted for relaxation. God blessed me in many ways.

Ah, the weekend. I loved sleeping in with my husband and reveling in our spooning position. Not ready to rise yet on this beautiful Saturday morning, we both rested on our sides, perfectly joined like two tight-fitting jigsaw puzzle pieces. With his one arm slipped under my pillow and the other draped possessively over me, the heat of his bare flesh pressed into my flimsily clothed body. His grasp around my torso drew me closer into him as if preventing me from leaving this cozy cocoon. I loved how we fit together like peanut butter and jelly; bread and butter; Bogart and Bacall.

Hearing the morning song of a warbler, nudged the rest of my senses to life as did the single ray of sunlight spilling through the non-closing curtains and blinding me. Note to self—never be stupid enough to purchase curtains during a spontaneous sale without having the precise window measurements in your purse; the panels won't fit, ever.

With a low, husky moan, I alerted Sherman of my needing to shift. Giving me ample space, he removed his arm and inched back to his side of the bed as I uncoiled myself like a housecat awakening from a long, winter's nap. I hated putting an end to the tender moment, but my legs would remain crooked if I didn't unfold them.

In keeping with the drowsy laziness of the morning, I kept my eyes sealed to their lids when slowly stretching my legs to relieve them of the tightness. When rotating my shoulders, I garnered a peak at my husband who offered a whimsical smile; his head propped up in his hand and watching my flexibility in the way I shifted.

"Good morning, beautiful," he cooed with droopy eyes from sleeping heavily.

Reaching my hands up and back over my head, I began to complete the lengthening of my body. Interlocking my fingers together, I sank my shoulders into the mattress. By arching my back, it not only fully awakened my husband who admired the slow exercise, but also the healthy peaks of my fleshy breasts revealing themselves through the cream-colored, sheer negligée I wore.

Recognizing his intent by watching him lick his lips, I magnified his appetite by turning a simple activity into a sensual performance. I rotated my shoulders and elongated my neck, sinking it further into the pillow. Keeping my eyes shut, I raised one knee and slightly lifted my lower body. Twisting toward him by stretching one elbow to the ceiling, he received a full-on frontal view of my chest. Coming back to a resting position, I released a subdued moan of pure satisfaction.

Lowering my arms, I rested my hands on my bent knees. Adding to the allure, with a delicate and sensual touch, I drew my hands down my thighs then upward, following the contour of my body until lighting on the sides of my breasts. Once there, I fondled them with a circular motion over the garment's thin material, enticing the peaks to keep their perky position. Firmly taking each aroused nipple between two fingers, I repeatedly twisted and pulled them until my mouth fell open and my breath became ragged.

In unison with my own excitement, Sherman's breath grew louder and more rapid. Wanting my actions to rip the very wind from his lungs, I traveled down my abdomen where my skin turned into tiny tents of raised flesh when brushing smooth fingernails across it. He came alive with a spontaneous, guttural groan when I proceeded to pull my nightgown up and over my bent knees.

Sherman touched my arm, but I flipped it off. He was the spectator, not a participant.

"Come on, Riley," he moaned, "let me play, too."

"Shut up, Sherman," I hushed him with staccato breaths. "Lie there and enjoy the show." He protested but complied.

My panties were the only thing veiling my next destination. Prolonging the sexual display, I rubbed on top of the fabric before venturing on.

After shimmying off my panties, I turned to the soft powder puff of curls guarding my nether region. Caressing the follicles to further develop the fiery sensation, I moved lower. Finding the cavity wet and demanding possession, I inserted my middle finger. Easing it from pillar to post across the fleshy roof, I arched my back when simulating penile penetration. One finger did not do the trick.

In my euphoric state, I added my index finger to the mix bringing about an intensification of rapture so powerful, I fell into a trancelike detachment of all things around me. With my free hand, I spread the dewy folds of the hood protecting my tiny organ and used my body's natural lubrication to coat it. I massaged and pinched the swollen bead. I whimpered. The orgasm escalated, fulfilling the promise of delivering me to a groundswell of blissful release. Quenched, I collapsed my legs to recapture my breath and unplug the highly charged electric current flowing throughout my entire body.

Oddly enough, the bed continued to move. When I opened my eyes, I turned to see Sherman with his eyes tightly shut, a grimace on his face, and his shaft in hand. He took himself off to his own never-never land. I smiled at thinking I turned him on that much. He couldn't play with me, so he did the next best thing and played with himself.

That's my man.

My intent in starting this erotic exhibition was to brew a slow burn in my husband. Somewhere along the way it backfired on me. Though surprised, I didn't mind going off-script and creating my own climax in the performance that benefited me in the most *masturbateable* way.

"Want me to butter your toast for you?" Sherman asked when scraping the pieces of overly browned bread after removing them from the broiler. While at the kitchen table, I had kept his attention on me instead of the oven by engaging him in a tickle fight. We could have thrown the burned pieces out and started over, but jelly covered up a multitude of sin.

"Would you be so kind?" I replied, loving every minute of having my husband be so attentive. He'd most always been considerate, but even more so now.

Taking a sip of coffee, I sat up straight to relieve the pain in my lower back. I must have pinched a nerve when bedazzling Sherman with my horizontal dance of seduction. A sharp stab like a knife pierced my lower abdomen. Focusing on extinguishing the pain, I grimaced then relaxed as mind overcame matter.

Sherman noticed. "Riley, are you all right?" he asked with concern.

"Yes, it's just a little cramp. The women at work told me it might happen and not to fret." But then a stronger assault in the same place cratered me.

He rushed to my side. "Let's get you over to the couch. You obviously pulled a muscle or something this morning. Here," he reached under my elbow and helped me out of the chair.

When I rose, his eyes flew wide at blood on the vinyl seat cushion. "Jesus," he mumbled.

Holding onto the table for support, I glanced over my shoulder to where he stared. "Sherman," I loudly groaned, "something's wrong. This can't," I severely cramped again, "be normal." This time, my knees nearly buckled.

"I need to get you to the hospital. Can you stand here while I get the keys?"

"Hurry," I urged with tears streaming; my fingers practically denting the table's wrought iron edge that kept the glass in, I gripped it so hard.

It only took minutes to get me in the car and for him to screech out of the lower driveway. Once he got to the main drag, he bobbed and weaved around cars at break-neck speed. Not even the police car blaring its sirens and flashing lights behind us slowed him down.

Pulling in the emergency drive of the hospital, both Sherman and the policeman exited their vehicles—Sherman to help me out of the car, and the policeman to arrest him for speeding and failure to pull over. With one glimpse, the officer understood why his male offender did what he did. My clothes were bloody, and I writhed in pain.

While my panic-stricken husband took one of my arms, the policeman took the other and helped me into the emergency room. Everyone moved out of our way when seeing my condition.

"My wife is pregnant and is in pain! Can somebody help her!" my husband cried out. No one moved fast enough for him.

"Goddamn it! Can't you see she's bleeding?!" Almost immediately after that, a nurse yelled for two orderlies to get a gurney. Once they did, they whisked me away before I said anything to my husband.

Later that day, I lay listless at home, underneath the Martha Washington bedspread as if a hundred-pound weight pressed down on my chest. My limbs were heavy as if made of iron. I internally shivered as though my insides had turned to ice, and they might as well have. Nothing in there worked anymore, especially my heart that resembled nothing more than a frosty muscle. My warm tears hastened their disappearance into the threads of the satin pillowcase.

My loving husband sat next to me in a chair, holding my pallid, limp hand and smoothing my hair. "You're going to be all right," he soothed, "it will take time, but you'll get through this. We both will." He kissed my knuckles, "We'll try again, and we will, I promise." He brought my hand to his cheek and caressed it. "I love you Riley. Remember that, okay?" His lips trembled on my skin as he kissed me on the forehead.

He tried to inject his strength into me by using assurances that rationalized the situation. It wasn't working. Not for me...not for him. Through my own misery, I could easily sense his bereavement and heavy heart. With wet, dull eyes, he lowered his head on the edge of the bed and released the tears he tried to hide from me. I didn't have to see them to know they were there.

Sherman tried hard to console my grief, but I fixated on the source of my suffering—my baby's death. My numb brain prevented me from talking. I didn't even have the strength or desire to comfort my husband. And he kept speaking, and soothing, and touching me. Finally, I couldn't stand him in the same room anymore.

"Sherman," I barely spoke above a whisper, "could you please leave me alone for a while. I want to sleep."

Sleep.

My bereaved heart would never allow my body to experience that revitalizing balm of sweet restorative surrender again. My baby died due to my self-absorbed actions and dereliction of faith. In my religion, God frowned on masturbation, but I hadn't cared. My disregard of religious teachings was a sin, and as punishment, God reclaimed the precious fruit of Sherman's and my union.

Sniffing back waiting tears, I rolled over and slowly drew another pillow to my chest. Wrapping my arms around it, I buried my face into the top of it as I clung to the down-filled softness as if it were my only lifeline.

It was no one else's fault I miscarried. That burden was mine alone to carry until the day I died. In the meantime, I would never forgive myself for being selfish and immoral.

Damn me to Hell.

Chapter Fifteen

"They"—whoever *they* are—say "time heals a broken heart." That may be, but the restorative process is not swift. Losing my child was difficult to overcome. I could not turn my mental state on and off like a light switch. I saw it taking months and years for the profound sadness of Sherman's and my loss to lessen, but it would never fade completely.

Getting back into a routine at work helped take my mind off the "should-a, could-a, would-a" scenarios plaguing my mind. It was a blessing to have people around me like Hazel who deepened our friendship with the over-and-above care and gingerbread consideration she showered on me. She had become my go-to-gal in all things sexual (things I could bring myself to bear to her, that is) and otherwise. I considered her one of my best friends.

Arriving at the office, I received two treats. One was a bouquet of roses mixed with daisies sitting on my desk from Sherman, and the other a visit from a little angel—Coral's son, Beau whose speech had greatly improved from just a year ago. He sat at my desk drawing on a piece of construction paper with the colored pencils I kept in a cylindrical container. The mere sight of him always brightened my day.

"Beau," I cheerfully greeted the now five-year-old, "what brings you here today? No nanny?"

Putting the pencil down, he pushed off the desk with his hand and twirled around two rotations in the swivel chair before coming to a stop. "My nanny quit."

I placed my purse in the bottom desk drawer. "Why?" I jokingly nudged him on the arm. "Were you a bad boy?"

He cast himself off again. "No, she had a baby in her tummy and needed to stay home instead of watching me." He shrugged when coming to a stop. "That's okay. I didn't like her anyway."

His statement about the woman being pregnant pierced my heart, but I forced the cresting sadness to wash over me like water off a duck's back. I leaned against the desk's edge and crossed my arms. "Why not? Did she do or say something mean to you?"

"No, she was," he hesitated to find the right word, "*angry* all the time. Mommy said my nanny didn't want to be fat."

"Oh," I wistfully sighed, "that's too bad. Having a baby should be a happy time."

He went back to the piece of construction paper. "Do you like my picture?" He showed it to me. I had no earthly clue what he had drawn, but I ooed and ahhed anyway.

"So, is your mommy going to get you another nanny?"

He shook his head and his soft curls bounced around like jubilant coils filled with springy enthusiasm. "No. I get to come here every day." He twirled one more time. "I like this chair. Can I have it?"

I plucked him out of it and plopped him on the floor, then took his place. "No, you *may* not have it. It's my chair."

"Mommy says I have to share. Why don't you have to?"

"Because I'm an adult and don't have to share my things if I don't want to, and I don't want to share my chair," I tapped his nose, "with you, little *boy*." At that, I grabbed him and began tickling his ribs. Trying to fight off the onslaught of my fingers, he squirmed this way and that, but could not escape the Tickle-Spider.

The joyous laughter exploding in the reception area caught the ear of my boss. When Coral walked through the connecting door to see what caused all the hubbub, she stopped dead in her tracks.

"There you are you little escape artist." She shook her finger at her son, but the invented frown she portrayed displayed utter failure in showing anger. "I could hear you two all the way in the back." She attempted to keep a straight face.

"Mommy," Beau yelled, running to give her a big hug, "can I stay out here with Riley? I won't be any trouble, I promise."

Before she answered, I gave her a nod that allowed her to give Beau an affirmative answer.

"Alright, young one, but," she wagged her finger at him, again, "don't you dare give Riley any cause to spank you, because she has my permission to do that if you misbehave."

"Yippie yi yo kayah!" he screamed at his mother's green-light response.

Glancing at me and seeing an imaginary spider inch down, Beau lost his smile and took on a cautious stance before me. His already rosy cheeks turned a tad darker when exchanging a knowing look at what loomed ahead.

I squinted my eyes with mischief, behaving like the child with whom I played. Trying to escape, my target burst out in laughter and started running around the desk to avoid the Tickle-Spider's impending strike. Coral stayed for a bit to absorb the entertainment then left her son and Office Manager-slash-Receptionist to play childish games.

Having Beau around brought cheer to my soul, but it made me blue at the same time. His drawing pictures on colored sheets of construction paper, or sorting colored pencils I had mixed up, made me envision doing these activities with my own child had he or she lived. At least I could do them with Beau for now. My time would come when I interacted with my own child—Sherman promised.

Beau became a permanent fixture at the agency for quite some time. In watching and playing with this little handful of rascality and exuberance, I considered myself with a new position: Office Manager-slash-Receptionist-slash-Nanny.

I looked forward to seeing this adorable cherub, until one day, my chair had no one in it. "Where's our little bundle of fun and frolic this morning?" I asked Coral when walking into her office and glancing under her desk to see if he hid there.

"I found this wonderful, new privately-owned daycare where I've enrolled him during the week. It comes highly recommended, and it's on my way to the office."

"So, no more playing Tickle-Spider with Mr. Beau?"

"No," she laughed at my shenanigans, "no more Tickle-Spider, which means you can get work done without having to do double-duty. Speaking of which," she opened her lap drawer and presented me a check, "this is a little something to express how grateful I am for the time you spent babysitting my son."

My eyes lit up at the amount. "Coral, this is not necessary. Being with Beau was a salvation for me. I could never accept compensation for the pleasure of his company, but I appreciate the thought." I immediately handed it back in exchange for a strong hug.

This gesture on Coral's part and mine in return went a long way in strengthening a friendship bond.

The next few months flew by with activity. On a personal level, Sherman and I dabbled again in the baby department, and again, "the rabbit died" as they say when a woman conceives. I'm three months along. Now, if I could carry this baby to term, it would be marvelous.

On a mother level, mine came for a week's visit when learning about my pregnancy.

On a husband level, Sherman was a trooper. If he saw a pleasant conversation between my mother and me heading in a nasty direction, he'd voice a different viewpoint that ended up turning the discussion around. He saved me from myself on many occasions.

On a friend level, Mayzelle, Gene, Sherman and I won three hundred dollars total between the four of us at the horse races. The share of the money Sherman and I won at the track went for a nice dinner-for-two at a swanky restaurant.

On the work side of things, Coral added an employment agency in Lansing, Michigan, making it number six in her respectable business repertoire.

Once again, Coral's unconventional sense of thinking at work surprised me. Most often, a woman announcing she was expecting a child resulted in her ensuing dismissal, but not here. Coral told me I could work as long as I felt up to it, and if I had the need to leave early because of not feeling well, to do it; no questions asked. That gave me peace of mind. At six months along now, I suffered no morning sickness, no cramps, no nothing, just joy at getting this far without difficulties.

Sitting at my desk and listening to my transistor radio playing the number one song at the time, "At the Hop," I couldn't help but start quietly singing along as my foot tapped out its beat. Be-bopping in my chair, I glanced at the wall clock that revealed the time as two o'clock.

I loved two o'clock because Sherman called every day at that time to say hello and check on my health. When I shared this with Coral in passing one day, she called it endearing. She also expressed her jealousy because Fitz never did anything so considerate when she was pregnant with Beau.

The main reason I received this kind of attention was that Sherman wanted me to put my notice in to stop working. We fought tooth and nail over the topic and finally, I emphatically told him that if I deemed myself healthy, I'd keep my job, thank you very much. He didn't like it. Too bad. I oversaw the health of my baby as long as he or she kept their end of the bargain and stayed put until time to leave the protection of my belly.

Right on schedule, my telephone rang. Answering the phone in the manner expected of an excellent receptionist, I greeted the caller with a pleasant tone. "Good afternoon. Employment Opportunities for Tomorrow, Riley speaking. How may I assist you today?"

It was not Sherman, but a voice from the past.

"Hello, again, bitch," the despicable woman enunciated in a low tone, "I bet you thought you were rid of me, didn't you, Riley?"

When hearing the foul-mouthed caller I'd heard months ago, and who now used my name, I swore my baby turned a somersault in protest. In a state of disbelief, I couldn't think fast enough to respond to the woman's question.

"I'm back," the woman sneered; I could hear it over the phone. "And I have something to say, so listen up buttercup. I bet you don't know where your cheating husband went for lunch today, and who he fucked afterward, do you, bitch?"

My rage rose ten-fold at this absurdity. "Listen here, whoever you are," I raised my voice, taking care not to speak too loudly so others could hear, "I don't know what your game is, but you've got the wrong player, so do *not* call here again!" I slammed the receiver on its cradle. "There!" I glared at the inanimate source of my rage and nodded with a jerk. "Take that, *bitch*!"

Having to type a letter, I snatched a piece of letterhead from the tray on my desk. "Sherman is *not* a cheater," I mumbled. Perturbed by the caller's question, I inadvertently placed the paper upside down in the typewriter and began typing. "Of course, I know where my husband went for lunch today." I ripped the paper out, crumpled it up, and threw it in the trash. "He went to the office lounge with the other department heads to talk about work-related topics." I jerkily rolled another piece of letterhead into the machine. "And the only woman my husband fucks," I angrily mumbled, "is me, you sadistic, whoring slut."

A minute later, the phone rang again. It could have been a client, but in my mind, it was that same woman. "I swear," I stated, "if you call here one more time, *you fucking whore*," I emphasized the words, "I'll report you to the cops, and they'll be down your back so fast, you'll see skid marks down your ass. Got it, *bitch*?" I snarled.

My declaration and, quite frankly, my use of terminology, shocked Sherman. As a result, he stumbled over his answer. "Uh, wow, Riley. Can you tell me what I've done to deserve being called a fucking whore and a bitch, and having you sic the cops on me?"

I nearly dropped the receiver. "Sherman!"

"Of course, it's me. Who did you think it was?"

"That woman I told you about a while back, you know, the one who called and told me to divorce you? I just hung up the phone with her."

"She called back after all this time?"

"Yes, and if she calls again…well, you heard what I'm going to do."

"Loud and clear," he replied. "She's got you pretty upset, doesn't she?"

"She *did*," I huffed aloud, "but I don't want to talk about such a vile person. I want to hear you tell me how much you love me and our baby."

"Of course I do, and that's exactly why I'm calling. Are you sure you're okay?"

"Hearing your voice, I'm as fine as frog's hair split two ways. I'll see you tonight. I love you."

"Love you, too."

Chapter Sixteen

Three Months Later —

Our spanking new baby girl had ten perfect little fingers, ten pudgy toes, a round face with a few rosy splotches here and there, and barely visible blonde peach fuzz on her head. This described Kathleen Marie O'Keefe to a tee; our gift from God.

My mother offered to fly down and help me, but, as she reminded me, it wouldn't be for a couple of months. Fine with me. I figured, Sherman and I could manage until then. We could do fine without her coming at all, but I didn't want to disappoint my child's grandmother.

The morning of Kathleen's third month birthday, my mother knocked on our door.

Thank you, God, for giving me someone who loved me enough to take away some of my frustration.

It seemed I had misjudged the expectations of my husband when Kat came into the world. I thought he and I were equal partners in caring for our bundle of joy.

Surprise!

He had little to do with Kat when it came to feeding, changing the cloth diapers, and rocking her to sleep before and during the night. In his way of thinking, only mothers did that. He took the role of tickling and trying to make her smile…period. In fact, one night, when Kat let out her highest pitch of crying, he went so far as to tell me to keep the baby quiet because he had to go to work in the morning.

What a son of a bitch.

It was a blessing having my mother relieve me of my daughter who repeatedly tried to fully develop her lungs. Heavens to Betsy! How could such a tiny human emit a volume of sound like that of a wailing banshee? And sleep? No, no, Kathleen didn't know what that meant. She either took a bottle, cried, or messed her diaper, and sometimes, all three at one time. Hell, the child never closed her eyes, which meant neither did I. Again, my mother stepped in to take over. I had a new appreciation for her patience and tenacity in all things infant, but especially when rocking her grandchild to a tranquil state of slumber. When I tried it, the only one who fell asleep was me. Thankfully, I awoke before my baby's head slipped down between my knees.

I couldn't believe six months had passed since our tiny angel joined our little family. My how time flew.

Placing Kat (her new nickname) in the playpen to interact with her toys, I went into the kitchen to lay out the ingredients for dinner. Placing the roast on the counter to defrost, the telephone rang. It was Coral.

"I'm checking in to see how things are going today," she stated with a smile I could hear over the phone.

"Splendidly, actually," I told her because they were.

"Well, remember Riley, if and *when*," she stressed the word, "you want to come back to work when Kat gets older, say the word.

It's not the same here since you left, and we all want you back as soon as you can get here."

Since leaving the agency on what I considered maternity leave, I periodically received a phone call from Coral. Her show of concern in how life with a baby affected me and the stresses on a marriage that went along with it, made me feel comforted. The laughter we shared about things happening at work reinforced my belief about what a caring boss she was. Obviously, she cared about the baby and me but also wanted to remind me to come back as her Office Manager. No one knew this, but I seriously considered it.

When Sherman came home from work, he was happier than I'd seen him in a long time. The countless nights of not sleeping when Kat had colic, or diaper rash, or countless other reasons why babies cried, had taken a toll on my husband, too.

Waltzing into the kitchen—literally, waltzing—and humming the tune of "Blue Danube," he held one hand over his stomach and the other up as if holding an imaginary partner. Imitating Fred Astaire, he danced over to me, took me into that position and without warning, we moved around the kitchen, through the door and into the living room.

"Darling," I squealed, enjoying his spontaneity, "what's this all about?"

"We're dancing, sweetheart."

"Yes, I know," I laughed, "but why are we dancing?"

"Because I have an announcement to make."

"Are we going to keep dancing while you tell me, or shall we sit down and, whoa," Sherman twirled me under his arm, "that was fun. Now, where was I?"

"You are here, you are there, you are ubiquitous," he twirled me again, then dipped me in a low backbend and kissed me deeply.

Coming up for air, but remaining in his arms, I couldn't get over the sudden change in him. "Hey handsome, what has gotten into you?" I held onto him so I wouldn't fall.

Bringing me to a full standing position, he smoothed my mussed hair then drew his hands easily down the length of my arms until grasping my hands tightly in his. "I've been promoted, Riley."

I took on a cocky stance with a surprised expression. "To what? You're already the Vice President of the Finance Department, what else is there?"

"Chief Financial Officer of the entire company. I've been promoted to CFO, Riley, CFO. Isn't that stupendous?" He grabbed my waist, and when I threw my hands around his neck, he spun me, bringing my feet completely off the floor.

"Oh, darling!" I exhaled my enthusiasm, "that's wonderful news!" He put me down. "But then," I removed his tie that had come loose in all the hoopla, "I knew you would make it big someday. UAC has finally come to their senses and given you the position you deserve for getting them out of hot water. Congratulations, darling." I planted a heartfelt kiss on him. No sooner had we broken the embrace Kat cried for her dinner.

With a well-fed Kat back in her playpen, Sherman and I sat down to a beautifully presented dinner of our own. The perfectly browned roast with crispy edges laid on a serving platter surrounded by cooked carrots and tender green beans. A bowl of mashed potatoes—including lumps—seasoned brown gravy with a thin layer of oil floating on top (and a few lumps there, too), and a covered basket of hot rolls finished the menu. It pleasantly surprised us that I hadn't burned anything. Not one thing.

Handing the carving knife to my husband, I sat tall and steadied my gaze on how adept he was at slicing a piece of meat. My heart swelled at knowing I succeeded in cooking the perfect meal. If I had feathers, they'd be spread like a peacock.

His first slice was just the right shade of pink.

Carving a piece for himself, he loved the couple of shades darker. On drawing the knife through again, it stopped when crossing a bone.

This confused me because I specifically asked the butcher at the grocery store to give me a boneless beef roast. Digging the white paper packaging out of the garbage, I read the type of meat I had purchased; it was the correct kind. I followed the Betty Crocker Cookbook instructions when setting the correct temperature and roasting it for the right amount of time. What the hell?

It didn't take a sleuth like Sherlock Holmes to discover the problem. The knife came across, not a bone, but ice. I did everything precisely as prescribed except for allowing the meat to thaw completely before placing it in the oven. The words of Doris Day's recent release came to mind—"Que Sera, Sera"—and in our exuberance over Sherman's promotion, we merely laughed and cut around the frozen section if we wanted more.

The next day, I decided to bring up the subject of my rejoining the workforce. I considered the timing of Sherman's new position as a sign of destiny in our favor. Making more money would allow us to place Kat in an affluent daycare facility like the one Coral had Beau in where the child/assistant ratio was two to one. Only one caveat kept me from signing my daughter up; she had to be nine months old. I could wait three months. Now to convince Sherman.

"Absolutely not!" Sherman voiced in a strong and almost vicious way. "I will *not* allow my baby girl to step one foot in a daycare facility, which means you will *not* go back to work!"

"*You're* baby girl?" I yelled in return. "When did Kat become yours alone?" I walked over and stood in front of his brand new, leather recliner where he sat inhaling cigarette smoke.

He doused the butt in the ashtray. "You know very well what I mean, Riley."

"That's beside the point," I told him with my arms stretched out to my side. "I *want* to go back to work, and besides that, Coral is holding my job for me."

When hearing my declaration, he leaned forward in the chair and narrowed his eyes. "What do you mean she's holding your job? Have you and she been conspiring behind my back?"

At the accusation, I placed my hands on my hips. "She and I have not been *conspiring* about anything. She simply told me if I *wanted* it," I stressed, "I could have it, and...*I...want...it*," I poked myself in the chest after every word as I leaned into his space.

Sherman rose from his chair, brushing me aside as he did, and walked into the kitchen to pour himself a drink. He strode across the kitchen floor, put one cube of ice in a rocks glass then poured in two fingers of bourbon and took a deep sip. Afterwards, he placed his hands on either side of the glass, and in deep concentration, stared at the amber liquid. He remained that way for a good minute. Standing in the doorway, I silently watched and waited for his next explosion.

When he spoke again, it was softer and more controlled. "Why is going back to work so important to you? I'll be making enough money so you will never have to work again." He raised his eyes to mine. "But more than that, Riley, I can't understand how you could let someone else raise *our*," he accentuated the word, "daughter." He stood up straight. "I tell you what, you give me a *good* reason, and maybe I'll reconsider, but so far, I haven't heard it."

He was being so obstinate. It's not like I would be handing our daughter over to people I didn't know. Well, okay, I would be, but Coral spoke very highly of the assistants at Beau's daycare.

I stepped into the kitchen and took a deep breath in getting ready to defend my position. To match my husband's tone, I softened mine. "Listen to me, I love working at the agency. I'm good at my job and am making a difference in a positive way there. Coral and I have developed a strong boss/employee relationship, but not only that, she and I have become friends.

"At work, she has no qualms about relying on me to get things done. She shares work-related issues with me and asks my opinion about how to handle certain situations. Coral depends on me, and in many ways, I depend on her. Her calls to me these last several months have been an escape from the constant routine of my day."

I quickly made my way toward him. Placing my hand on his arm, I locked eyes with him. "I need this. "I really do." I searched his eyes for understanding but didn't find it.

Allowing my touch, his stare penetrated my eyes. "What you have just described, Riley, is how you should feel about raising our child who, by the way, depends on you more than your boss. You make a difference *here*," he jabbed his index finger on the counter, "in this house, by caring for and nurturing Kat. Your bond should be with your daughter, not Coral. And speaking of your *ex*-boss, it's too bad you feel the need to escape the routine of your day. I didn't think Kat was such a burden on you."

His words burned like a hot poker. He turned everything around to make me feel guilty, and it worked. I couldn't defend myself against his argument. No doubt, he won this battle, but the war was far from over. I needed a new strategy, and I had three months to come up with one that would change his mind.

A week later, the morning crept through the window sheers of our bedroom. The soft rays cast a warm glow over the man sleeping soundly beside me as if he were about to fade away and become one with the dust particles floating in the muted stream of light. Moving an inch at a time, I lifted the bedsheet and slinked toward my side of the bed.

Stepping out, I tiptoed to the closet where I donned my clothes and quietly made my way down the hallway and into Kat's room to check on her. Peacefully asleep, she lay spread-eagle on her back in a pink romper with her arms comfortably alongside her head, and hands loosely folded. By the way her lips were moving, she dreamed about sucking the living daylights out of a bottle.

My heart stirred with love for this babe whose features favored her father more than mine. How could I not want to spend every waking hour with her?

For days on end, guilt had taken up residence within my soul and riddled my mind. But then God granted me a happy ending, or at least I hoped it would be happy.

My solution hit me like a bolt of lightning. If I wanted to work outside the home and at the same time foster the mother/daughter bond with Kat, I had to take her to work with me.

When I spoke to my free-thinking boss about the possibility, she readily agreed to allow it. She knew from my time with Beau that I could juggle work and babysit with little difficulty. Sure, the ages were a mile apart. When I watched Beau, he was a toddler; able to walk, talk and get into trouble. Kat, on the other hand, was in the crawling stage, couldn't tell me what she wanted, and yes, got into trouble, too. However, with her in a playpen beside my desk, I could keep an eye on her and provide those motherly moments daycare would eliminate.

Now I could go to my husband with the ammunition I needed to get my point across that I could do it all—hold down a job, a marriage, and nurture Kat as well. This spiritual intercession reaffirmed my belief that God was definitely a woman.

Chapter Seventeen

"We're not starting this again, Riley." Sherman's drawn face and plunging brows showed a crestfallen disposition. "I've had a hard day, and I refuse to fight with you."

"What happened?" I was not without compassion for his feelings.

The muscles in his neck tensed. "Simply put, the CEO wants to expand our office space, and I advised against it to save money. I lost the argument."

"Oh, I'm sorry, Sherman." To hit him with my idea of taking Kat to work with me would not improve his mental state, but then again, I had to speak my mind before I chickened out. "I'm not starting anything, Sherman," I assured him without raising my voice or putting on battle armor, "but I want to tell you how I plan to keep working and nurture Kat as well. I'm taking her with me."

He looked at me as though I'd hit him square between the eyes with a Louisville Slugger baseball bat. His nostrils flared, and his muscles strained against his shirt. His lips got so tight it looked as if he didn't have any. He raked his fingers through his short hair, trying to appear calm though there was nothing in his posture that showed a relaxed state. To keep from blowing a gasket, he closed his eyes. "Why do you insist on making life so difficult, Riley?" he stressed, his tone low and gravelly.

"You're the one who's being unreasonable," I argued. "This is a perfect solution, so why can't you accept it and let's move on?"

"Move on?" That got his attention. He took several slow and deliberate steps in my direction until he loomed over me. "Move on where, Riley?" His stare meant to frighten me, and it did a little, but I held my ground. "I can tell you right now it's not down a smooth path," he warned.

The jitters took hold as the memory of that fateful night reemerged when he got drunk and had rough sex with me. I shuddered at the route this conversation took. Still, I would not allow this man to upend my mission. The blood pulsed harder and faster through my veins, providing the adrenaline I needed to bring an end to this utterly stupid dialogue.

Ready to put my ultimate plan into action, I took a step in, putting me nose-to-nose with my adversary. My facial expression relaxed. My chin strengthened and jutted toward him as I visually probed his eyes. "You don't have to confront me with idle threats, Sherman. I am your wife and the mother of our child. You are inferring that if I take Kat to work with me, I fall into the category of being a bad mother. That's ridiculous. You are simply being stubborn."

He did not step back.

Neither did I.

"You are *not*...taking...Kat...to work, Riley," he enunciated. "She needs looking after *here*, not in an office where your job will take your attention away from her. End of story." His tone was flat and severe at the same time.

My brows arched as I looked up at him with soft eyes. A smirk crossed my lips when delivering my sharpest blow. "You are perfectly correct, darling," my words dripped with honey accompanied by a vinegar chaser. "Kat needs tender loving care on a daily basis in this house." I turned away from Sherman, picked up the pack of cigarettes from the end table and pulled one out. After lighting it, I took a deep draw and blew out the smoke. I briefly turned to face Sherman who had relaxed in thinking he won the debate.

Not so fast, dear husband.

"Tomorrow morning," I placed the lighter next to the ashtray, "I shall call my mother who will jump at the chance to fly down and babysit until you come to your senses and change your mind."

Sherman's head flinched at my statement, and his eyebrows squished together. "How is that solving anything?" he questioned. "If you're here taking care of Kat, we don't need your mother."

"Oh, but we do." I sauntered across the hardwood floor with a poised gait, my heels tapping out their subtle warning. Even the cigarette between my fingers cast a trail of ominous smoke in my wake. "I'm going back to work, regardless. If you don't want me taking Kat that's perfectly fine. My mother proved herself a treasure when Kat was a couple of months old. She'll do it again. There should be little doubt that our daughter will be in the best hands and get that daily maternal nurturing you so rightly declared she deserves."

The calm state Sherman momentarily captured, vanished in the blink of an eye. His face glowed crimson as if a fire simmered under his skin. The intensity of his stare made it clear that my husband could explode at not only my statement but also my logic. "That's the most ridiculous thing you've ever said, Riley," he sneered with a scathing tone.

I cocked my head and thought about his remark. "I don't think so, which means you have a choice to make Sherman. And it is *your* choice. Allow me to take Kat when I return to work, or have my mother move in." I licked my lips. Eye to eye, I pressed, "Which do you prefer?"

"*Neither.*"

"Choose, Sherman."

His posture stiffened. His mouth turned down over obvious clenched teeth as he visibly ground them. He sat between a rock and a hard place. "You've pushed this to the limits, *sweetheart*," he stressed the word, "you do realize that."

I merely shrugged. "That's your opinion. What's it going to be?"

He unleashed a loud exhale. "I'm giving you this one only because I don't want your mother under foot." His demeanor darkened. "But hear me loud and clear, Riley, don't make this kind of demand a habit. Do you understand?"

Victory was mine.

"Perfectly, darling. Now let's seal the deal with a kiss, shall we?" I would not allow Sherman to take any glory here whatsoever. *I* was the winner here, and *I* made the rules. Rule number one and the only rule: make up and move on like I had recommended. If he had listened, none of this would be happening.

I snuffed out my cigarette in the ashtray. With the ease of a cat, I strolled to my husband and put my arms around his waist while resting my head on his chest. "No more quarreling, my love," I purred, then lovingly looked up at him. "Now kiss me and tell me you love me."

"I may love you, but I don't like you right now."

I smiled. "That's okay. I'll take it. So, what about that kiss?"

When placing my hands on the back of his head and pulling it to mine, he hesitated, but finally gave in.

It was wonderful having Kat with me at work, but it didn't last. Coral told me about a friend of hers named Meredith who babysat Beau after school. With me in mind, she asked Meredith if watching an additional child was too much. Meredith saw nothing wrong with that, and Coral gave her my contact information.

Even Sherman loved this angel sent from Heaven who exuded a friendly disposition with an easy-going manner. And talk about efficient. If you looked up the word in the dictionary, you'd see her picture plastered next to it. The best part, she offered to pick Kat up at our house every weekday morning before I left for work. She would take her to her own home and entertain my daughter with age-appropriate educational activities. When Beau got out of school, she and Kat would pick him up and stay at Coral's house until Coral came home. After that, Meredith would bring Kat to our house. It was the perfect arrangement.

Instantly, married life got better.

"Come on, Bluebell," I encouraged my car. How dare it overheat while running an errand for Coral. "Don't do this to me. If you're gonna die, do it in my driveway, not here on the highway."

A steady fog of steam plumed from under the hood, prohibiting safe visibility. Pulling off onto a wider part of the road as far as I could, I killed the engine and watched the windshield mist with moisture.

The inconvenience of the event sent my teeth gnashing. I peeled my hands off the steering wheel and slapped the hell out of Bluebell. I hit the dashboard, wheel, and everything else I could abuse within reach. "Goddamn you son of a bitch car!" I screamed, the sound reverberating around the interior of the vehicle. "What am I supposed to do now!? There's no phone anywhere around here! How in the *hell* am I supposed to call somebody?!" I threw open the driver-side door and dashed to safety on the other side of my beloved Rambler.

Cars sped past me, and my only hope was one of them would stop and help. I bit my bottom lip that became the object of concentration as I corrected my posture to ensure oncoming traffic saw me.

Shit! Where were all the humanitarians? Did I have to revert to raising my skirt and showing a little leg to entice a car to pull over? *I think not.*

Unfortunately, I had but one option: put shoe to asphalt. My rising blood pressure would help propel me; the extensive pounding in my ears from the massive headache building would drown out the sound of traffic; my rapid heartbeat would pump enough oxygen to the muscles of my body to get me to Lansing in no time.

With a new mindset, I opened the passenger-side door, grabbed my purse, and slammed the panel in hopes the window would shatter to pieces. "Well, isn't that peachy-keen!" I yelled. "Your body is as strong as an ox, but your guts are made of Jell-O! Fine, be that way! See if I care!" I looked at the stretch of road. "Something told me this was *not* going to be my day," I grumbled. "I should have taken Mayzelle up on her earlier invitation to join her for lunch. But no. Instead, I am about to traipse down a fucking road."

Two minutes into my heated walk, a vehicle pulled over and stopped in front of me. It was a rusted pickup truck vacated by an equally old, scraggy geezer who walked in my direction.

"Hey there, honey," the old-timer called out then pointed his finger over my shoulder, "that yer car pollutin' the air over there?"

The Good Samaritan's appearance was not appealing. His denim overalls were filthy as if he worked on an oil rig; his hair separated in sections from lack of washing; and he was missing several teeth. I got the heebie-jeebies looking at him.

"Yes, it is," I yelled, keeping a commanding tone as well as some distance between us.

"Where you be walkin' to, sweet pea?" He kept advancing toward me. "If'n you hadn' noticed, you be out in the middle o' nowheres. I be happy to give you a lift."

"No, no, I..." I had to think fast, "I'm doing a little exercise while waiting for my ride who should be here any minute, but thank you anyway," I lied.

He saw right through me. Thumbing his ear, he smirked. "Izzat right. There's no phones out here, darlin', so how did you call someone to come get you?"

Shit, oh, shit. Then it came to me. "A car stopped by and the driver told me he'd call my husband when getting to a phone." That sounded reasonable.

"Uh, huh," nodded the man who spat a brown liquid on the ground several feet away from me. "If'n a driver stopped to help, he would not a left you out here by yerself, so yer gonna have to do better'nat."

"You don't have to believe me, and that's fine, but it's the truth." Though losing a bit of moxie, I remained firm. "Another thing you should believe is my husband is a very jealous man, and if he sees you trying to pick me up, well, it won't be pleasant for you."

"You don' say." He stood within a few feet of me. "I be thinkin' I can take care o' myself." He spread his arms out to his side. "Why not let me help you?"

He reached for my arm, but I jerked back to avoid his touch.

His grin grew wider. "Come on now, honey," he cajoled. "Be a good li'l girl and come on now with me so I can drive you to town." He shook his head. "There's nothin' to be afraid of. I won't bite."

"I'm not afraid of you," I again lied with a failing bravado. His mannerism disturbed me, and my stomach clenched at the sight of him. My body trembled and sweat drizzled down the edge of my hairline. "I would like you to leave before my husband gets here," my voice hardened, but noticeably quivered. "It's for your own protection." From fear, beads of sweat drifted down my spine and soaked into the fabric of my dress.

He lunged for me and grasped my upper arm with one hand. With all my might, I slugged him with my purse, hitting his shoulder. Instead of letting go, he yanked the purse out of my clutches with his free hand and threw it into the prairie grass.

"Why, you li'l vixen," he snarled. He seized a handful of my hair on the back of my head and twisted the tresses into a ball then pulled hard to keep me from fighting against him. I tried not to gag at the wretched stench of his breath that stunk like chaw mixed with rotted teeth when he came closer. "So, you wanna play rough?" he growled in my ear. "Alrighty then." He tightened his grip. "Let's you'n me go a round or two. It'll be fun."

With my head tilted back, he stood behind me and pushed me toward his pickup. I screamed, which made him tighten his grasp even further and throw his other nasty hand over my mouth, pulling me close into his body. With all my might, I clawed at his hand, while at the same time, tried to bite his palm. Finally, I dug my fingernails into his bony knuckles, and my teeth connected with the calloused flesh. He let go, but that bit of freedom did not last. Before I had a chance to take two running steps, he threw his arm around my neck, nearly choking me. Then, I felt a hard object press against the small of my back.

A gun? Does he have it inside his overalls pocket? Jesus Christ!

"You feel that bitch?" he snarled. "Don't make me use zis on you. Jus' settle down and do what I say, and you won' get hurt."

In my position facing away from the road, I heard a car's tires screech to a stop close by. I also heard a door open and slam as someone got out of their vehicle, but I couldn't see them.

"Hey, you there!" a man's voice yelled. "What's going on here?"

Thank you, God, for sending someone to help me!

"You say nothin' girl, you hear me?" the creep growled in my ear. "If'n you make one sound to tip off yer si-tia-shun, yer gonna make me have to shoot him and then you." He shoved the barrel of the gun harder into my spine. "Do I make myself clear, sweetpea?"

Tears formed in my eyes as I hummed my acquiescence.

"Das a good girl," he said. He left the gun barrel where it was and tightly held me around my waist to prevent the protrusion of the concealed weapon digging into my back. He then loudly addressed my potential liberator. "There's nothin' goin' on here, mister, that a bit a displin' won' fix," he sneered with a smirk on his lips that came across loud and clear to my ears. "The wife here thinks buy'n a fancy dress and spikey heels at Goodwill gives her the right to up and leave me without discussin' the *par-ti-cu-lars*." "She don't know I know she's headed off to see 'nother man, and that just ain't gonna happen as long as I draw breath. So, don't you worry 'bout nothin' mister," he mocked. "She be in no danger. She just requires a li'l attitude adjustment."

"You don't need to be so rough with her."

"Das a matter o'pinion. She's one hell-of-a fighter this one is," the villain stated. "Once she's in the truck, though, she'll settle right down. I have a bottle of her fav'rite whiskey in there. After a few swigs, she'll be a pussycat," he smiled at me, revealing stained teeth, "won't you, sweetpea? Then we can get back home to our five kids who've been callin' out fer you." He turned his attention back to the observer. "You can unnerstand kids need'n there ma, now cain't you, mister?" He never loosened his grip on my hair.

"Yeah, well, I suppose. Just don't hurt her or get her drunk…for your children's sake."

"I hear you. Now," he returned his attention to me, "let's get in the truck, sweetpea. The kids is waitin'." He looked over his shoulder and nodded at the onlooker.

Words speak louder than actions because the witness got in his car and drove away. There went my lifeline. I closed my eyes and willed myself not to cry.

"Dat was close, wazzant it sweetpea?" he smirked.

God, give me the strength and wisdom to free myself without getting shot.

She answered my prayer.

I realized my arms remained unrestrained. With my right hand over my left fist, I thrust my left elbow straight into the disgusting man's gut.

Bullseye!

The blackguard released me, allowing me to make a mad dash back to Bluebell. High heels were not the best form of footwear when running from a bullet. I thought about kicking them off, but that would take too much time I didn't have. I'd die anyway at the brute's hand, so I might as well die with my heels on. Maybe he'd be a lousy shot and miss me.

I was close to grabbing the passenger-side door handle of my car when a set of fingers dug into my arm and twisted me around. Realizing the barbarian was about to back-hand me, I drew my hands up to shield my face. With closed eyes, I gritted my teeth and waited for the impending blow, but it didn't come. Instead, he released me.

With no support, I fell against Bluebell. In a daze, I slowly brought my head around to see what happened. To my grateful surprise, he grappled with another man—Fitz!

Fitz had ripped the brute off me, and with his fisted hand, savagely introduced his *five brothers* to the opponent's chops. A right punch followed by a left found the attacker's jaw. Brown chaw juice shot out of the barbarian's mouth from Fitz's forceful blows. It happened so fast, all I could do was watch in awe at the agility Fitz presented, and his perfect aim when rearranging the bastard's face.

When the scoundrel fell to the ground and didn't get up fast enough, Fitz reached under the man's overall straps, grasped a handful of shirt material, and lifted him to a standing position. Loosey-goosey, the man—with additional chewing tobacco spattered over his cheeks and missing one more tooth—wobbled in place.

"I take it you never learned it's not nice to strike a lady," Fitz loudly growled. "How about some of your own medicine?" Fitz backhanded the man. "How does *that* feel, you cock-sucking son of a bitch?"

Fitz must have felt the guy was no longer a threat and rushed to my side.

Before reaching me, I yelled, "Fitz! He's got a gun in his left pocket!"

Fitz stopped mid-stride and turned around to see the man struggling to stand. The geezer never made it. Fitz ran back and kicked him in the side, flattening him once more. With his foot on the back of the guy's neck to keep him down, Fitz reached into the man's left pocket and withdrew a socket wrench, not a gun. Fitz threw the tool as far as he could into the grass before running back to the roadster.

He cupped my face in his hands. "Riley, did he hurt you!?" He kept staring back and forth into my eyes.

Before I toppled over from relief, Fitz encircled my waist to keep me upright. "Here Riley, lean on me." I nodded but kept silent. He led me to his car, opened the door for me and guided me into the passenger seat.

"My purse," I mumbled. "He threw it over there." I pointed to the place I remembered the man taking it from me,

After situating me in the car, he searched in the grass and found my purse concealed within its tall, honey-colored blades. He dusted off the handbag and returned it. With one last glance over his shoulder, Fitz watched the pervert clasping his ribs as he rose and stumbled back to the dilapidated pickup.

Now in the driver's seat, the vile man peeled out onto the road, the smell of burning rubber crinkling my nose. As he sped away, he stuck his arm through the open window and flipped us the bird.

Before rejoining the masses on the highway, Fitz took my hand and squeezed. "Riley are you hurt?" he repeated in a stronger tone.

The inside of my nose prickled as if tiny warriors pierced it with itty-bitty spears announcing the onset of tears. The single, salty drop that slid from my eye, ventured to my chin where I quickly wiped it away. "Where he pulled my hair, but that's all. If you hadn't come along when you did…" Staccato gasps caught in my throat as surging emotion consumed me.

Fitz reached into his jacket pocket and offered me a cotton handkerchief. The dike that held back my waterworks cracked, and

I couldn't stop the flow. With the soft cloth, I wiped away tears and streaked mascara.

I felt safe now with Fitz beside me. As we drove down the highway, he found a level place in the weeded median and carefully maneuvered his roadster across to the opposite side of the road.

"For God sake, Riley," his tone drifted over the noise from his open car, "what were you doing out here by yourself?"

I sniffed back more tears and blew my nose in the hanky. "Coral asked me to run an errand for her." I took a deep breath. "After my car broke down, I started walking to find a phone and that's when that man…"

Fitz patted my thigh.

At once, the situation sunk in. "What about my car, Fitz?!" I frantically asked.

"Don't worry about that. I'll call my mechanic when we get to my bar and ask him to tow it to his service garage and give it a good going over. Then I'm going to buy you a drink."

His statement caught my ear. "Your…your bar." I wiped my nose. "You own a bar?"

"Do you recall the night you got drunk and wound up at The Midnight Lounge?"

My shock-factor shot up a notch. "You own The Midnight Lounge?"

"I do indeed," is all he replied.

The memory came back, in part. "That makes sense now," I nodded in understanding, "as to why the bartender turned on the formalities when seeing you."

He turned smug, "I'm the boss, and what the boss wants, the boss gets."

"I suppose."

In our current direction, I saw Bluebell on the opposite side of the highway. She looked forlorn as she sat abandoned.

Oh, my God! My mission!

"Fitz!" I raised my voice to a critical level. "You have to go back to Bluebell!"

"Who's Bluebell?" He had no idea what I was talking about.

Right, I'd never mentioned to anyone that my vehicle had a name. "My car!"

He looked at me as if I had two heads. "You named your car, Bluebell? Why, because it's...blue?"

I didn't care if he thought I was a loose nut. "Yes, because it's blue, okay? I need to deliver the envelope to the Lansing office, and it's in the front seat. Coral is depending on me, so *please* take me back, and then will you drive me there?"

Some depraved maniac just ambushed me and all I could think of was completing a task for Coral. After another median crossing, we were on our way toward my precious, broken-down Bluebell.

Chapter Eighteen

When getting to the Lansing office, Fitz telephoned his mechanic on my behalf while I called my husband. Sherman was away from his office, so I left a message that my car had broken down, and I'd get a lift home. That's all I said. I handed my special delivery package to the person whose name was on the envelope, then Fitz and I bid the folks there goodbye and returned to the roadster.

"Feel better now?" Fitz asked. He took my hand once again and repeated that comforting gesture of squeezing the anxiety out of me.

I tried to hide how his touch liberated tingles down my spine, but the heat rising to my face revealed the instant emotion. I should have drawn my hand back but didn't. In fact, I returned the act with a tight clasp of my own. The man saved my life, for Christ's sake. This was not the time to rebuff him.

His thumb stroked the back of my hand. "Riley," he practically whispered, causing an undercurrent of seismic waves to surge through my veins.

It petrified me to gaze into those circular bands of deep blue surrounded by pitch-black centers, but I couldn't resist. Gingerly, I raised my eyes to his. What I saw reflected in them frightened me as much as having that creep-o-potomus nearly kidnap me.

"Yes...Fitz," I murmured.

"I don't know what I'd..." he stopped mid-sentence, "I mean, what we all would have done if something happened to you."

His mistake caught my attention.

Why does he care about me, and why do I want him to care?

My brain began a tumultuous tango with my heart. Neither would come out on the victorious side of that dance.

He stared me down, then leaned in as if to kiss me. I withdrew my hand from under his and leaned back toward the door. "What about that drink you promised me?" I asked. Decorum needed to rule here.

I bested him, and he understood that fact. Graciously, he started the motor—the car's; his was already in full gear—and we made our way to The Midnight Lounge.

At the bar's entrance, I looked skyward and witnessed dark clouds assembling for an impending storm. When we exited the bar an hour later, the merged clouds engaged in a turbulent ruckus of breaking the sky apart with thunder, lightning, and driving rain. Fitz left me standing under the building's awning as he ran to his convertible and attached the rag top. Soaked to the skin upon his return, he put his arm around my shoulders to keep me from slipping on the wet asphalt when ushering me into the car's water-logged seat. No matter how I squirmed, I couldn't avoid the liquid soaking into the fabric of my dress, causing it to cling to my body.

Fitz was much worse off than I. His wavy hair lay flat on his head like a helmet, and his smart-fitting blazer clung to his body as if painted on. I giggled.

"What are you grinning at?" he grumbled.

"You look like a drowned rat in a rain barrel," I boldly laughed.

"Yeah, well, Mrs. O'Keefe, in your present condition, Marilyn Monroe would not want to be seen with you." Somewhere along the way, I must have mentioned about my crush on the Hollywood starlet.

His statement threw me into a fit of hilarity in agreeing wholeheartedly with him. The attitudes in the car while Fitz drove to my house were much lighter than before. Gone were the moments of rising sentiment that might have led to a dangerous place.

By the time Fitz pulled into my driveway, the rain stopped pelting the windshield of the MGA. He put the car in gear but left the idle running.

"Fitz," I focused on my hands clasped in my lap when beginning a speech I neglected to deliver hours ago, "I never thanked you for rescuing me from that horrible man." Only then did I glance in his direction. As I suspected, he stared at me.

"You're welcome, Riley. I happened to be in the right place at the right time. The fact you're safe is all that matters. When I hear from my mechanic about your, 'Bluebell'," he grinned at the reference, "I'll call you with the details."

"I appreciate that, too, Fitz. There's one more thing I need to ask."

"Anything."

"You and I need to keep the facts about my being assaulted and you interceding and bringing me home, between us, okay? I'm not telling Sherman."

"Okaaay, but don't you think, he deserves to know about a major occurrence that happened to his wife?"

"Let's say it's better if I keep certain parts of the ordeal a secret. I'll think of a way to explain about Bluebell and how I got home. I don't want you to tell Coral, either. She'll think it was her fault since she sent me on the errand." I looked him square in the eye. "Promise me, Fitz, that you won't say a word about it, please."

"No can do, Riley," he said, to my chagrin. "Coral and I have a pact about secrets; we don't keep them from each other."

"Really? Never?"

"Never. We have a tell-all relationship. It strengthens us as a couple."

Wow. Fitz is as out-of-the-box as his wife.

"Okay, you can tell Coral, but you can't breathe a word to Sherman. Promise?"

"With your husband, mums the word." He brought two fingers to his lips and turned as if locking his mouth and throwing the imaginary key over his shoulder.

With a nod, I grasped the handle of my purse. Before I pulled the inside cable, which I found out opened the car door, he hopped out his side and did it for me.

After taking my hand to help me exit the vehicle, he did not move away. His eyes softened as did his expression when he spoke in a low tone with a hint of humor. "I suggest you not break down on the road anymore. I may not be in the area next time."

His comment sparked my curiosity. "Fitz," I concentrated my focus on the man who possibly changed my life forever, "why *were* you in the area?"

"I was en route to Lansing to check out a location for another bar. When I saw your blue car and your perilous situation, I had to get to you. It was nothing more than that."

"It was everything, Fitz. Again, thank you."

He gently took me by the shoulders. "You'd better get out of those wet clothes now. You wouldn't want to catch pneumonia on top of everything else you've been through today."

I nodded and made my way to the front door. Once in the house, I closed the door, but left it open just enough to watch Fitz get into his car and back out of the drive.

Friday at last! I love game night with Mayzelle and Gene. Games always helped me wash away the negativity that happened during the week. With Bluebell breaking down, having a petrified jackass accost me, and Fitz saving the day, it was a doozy! Except for the Fitz part, I hoped I never saw another week like that. But it was behind me. My thoughts flew to the row of dominoes in an exhilarating game of Forty-Two.

"Pass," Sherman began the bidding process of the game.

"I bid thirty," stated Mayzelle on Sherman's left.

"Thirty-one," I offered, smiling at Sherman whom I hoped had good dominoes to take tricks.

"Thirty-two," claimed Gene who called aces as trump. "It's too bad Mayzelle wasn't with you when you broke down yesterday, Riley." He placed the double ace on the card table.

"Why do you say that?" I asked, watching Gene take the trick.

"Because," Gene placed the one-six to open the next round, "she could have determined the problem with your car right away."

Before responding to Gene, I watched the play advance to the point of him taking another trick, after which, I addressed Mayzelle. "What, do you have some kind of magical vehicle diagnostic power?"

"No," Mayzelle laughed, "but when Gene and I got married, he taught me the basic workings of a car's engine and how to repair certain parts in case what happened to you, happened to me."

Gene led the blank-six domino on the next hand. "Have you gotten word on what caused the issue with your car?"

I watched Sherman play his six-five and finally take a trick. "No, not yet."

"Why were you even on that highway?" Mayzelle asked as she watched her opponent play the double deuce.

"Remember, I told you I had to run an errand for my boss, and that's why you and I couldn't have lunch together," I replied.

"That's right. Where were you going?" she asked.

"To Coral's agency in Lansing."

"Lansing?" Mayzelle showed interest. "That's where my sister lives. In fact, she moved there after losing her job from," she looked directly at me and smirked, "oh…" she cleared her throat and raised one brow, "Employment Opportunities for Tomorrow."

My attention stayed on my friend. "Who's your sister?"

Mayzelle raised her head. "Her name is Gertrude Delaney. She was the—"

"Receptionist," both Mayzelle and I spoke simultaneously.

The men were getting antsy at us women taking time away from the game to chit-chat but neither Mayzelle nor I cared.

"You knew her then?" asked Mayzelle.

I shrugged. "Not really. She was leaving when I arrived for my first day on the job. If I may say, she looked upset with her situation."

With her attention returning to the dominos, Mayzelle's disposition turned sour. "You would be, too, if having to put up with a boss who abused her employees like Coral Stevens did. Oh," she hesitated, and cocking her head mockingly, she glanced at me, "but Coral is your boss, now, isn't she?"

I saw nothing positive coming out of this conversation, so I tried to put an end to it. "She is, but I've experienced nothing like what you're talking about." My tone softened and became more sympathetic. "I'm sorry for your sister's troubles, and I can only hope she finds happiness where she is now."

"Hm," Mayzelle hummed, "time will tell. Riley, without a car, how did you get to work this morning?"

"Sherman dropped me off." The domino game resumed play. "Meredith had offered to take me when she picked up Kat, but it would be miles out of her way." I flashed a smile at my adorable husband who took another trick. "Besides," I assumed a coquettish grin aimed in his direction, "you didn't mind getting a little more sleep this morning, did you, darling?"

"No," he replied as he rearranged the dominos in front of him.

"Tell me again how you got to Lansing after your car died?" Mayzelle asked.

"The cutest old couple stopped and gave me a ride to the Lansing office where I called a mechanic to pick up my car."

"How nice," Mayzelle nodded. She focused on her dominoes again. "So, who brought you home after the incident?" Mayzelle asked.

"The office manager from the Lansing office graciously offered. She felt it was the proper thing to do since I broke down trying to get there." I watched Gene trump and claim the trick.

Gene laid the four-three down. "You're lucky that nice people stopped to help you, Riley." Without looking up, he issued a nod of satisfaction that his wife took the sixth trick. "There are deviants driving those roads. You put yourself in danger by driving alone on an open highway like that. Yes, you are a very lucky lady."

The seventh—and last—trick belonged to Mayzelle who played the double-five. She won her bid, assuring she and Gene received the first of seven tick marks on the score pad.

An hour and a half later, the game ended with Sherman and I losing five games out of seven. We were excellent Forty-Two players, so it confused me to have lost by that many. I played all the right combinations, so it wasn't *my* fault we lost. Sherman wasn't paying attention. I hoped nothing bad happened at work and he was keeping it from me.

The next day over a leisurely breakfast, I asked my husband about it. "Darling, you seemed to be off your game last night."

Sherman kept his attention on the financial section of the morning newspaper. "My poor performance," he turned the page, then snapped the two sides into adjustment, "was due to having bad dominoes, nothing more."

"Are you sure?" I rose from the table, went to the kitchen counter, and unplugged the coffeepot. Bringing it to the table, I offered to refresh his half-empty mug that sported green and blue Franciscan starbursts on it, but he waved me off. "Normally, you and I win more games than we lose." I refilled my companion mug with multiple-colored Boomerang designs, placed the pot on the counter, and returned to my seat. "Are you facing another crisis at work?" I took a sip. "I'm here to listen if you want to talk."

He abruptly folded the paper and thrust it onto the table. Visibly piqued, he looked me square in the eye. "There's nothing wrong at work, Riley. The only irritation I have is you badgering me about our game last night. I played the best I could with the few good ivories I had, so stop making a mountain out of a molehill."

My cheeks warmed to having to defend myself. "Fine," I threw my hands up in surrender, "sorry I asked." His change in demeanor disturbed me to almost probing further, but I thought better of it and chose to remain silent.

My husband was acting like an asshole and a damn good one.

Chapter Nineteen

*T*he weekend went quickly as they all seem to. Before I could quickly repeat three times the tongue-twister Danny Kay and Gene Kelly made famous— "Moses supposes his toeses are roses," it was Monday.

Since the mechanic had Bluebell, Sherman needed to take me to work. That was fine and dandy with me. I considered this an opportunity to get more morning love with my husband, but that didn't pan out.

Why does he seem angry at me lately? What have I done this time to make him mad?

Sherman rose and dressed at his normal early hour, then perused the morning paper over two cups of coffee until I came into the kitchen for my own caffeine fix.

"Good morning, darling." I smiled and walked over to kiss him. He did not turn his head away from the newspaper, so I ended up kissing his cheek. Better than nothing, I suppose.

"Morning," he mumbled.

That's all I got from him. Thank goodness for my one-year-old daughter. She and I had a marvelous conversation of squeals and gobbledygook words followed by tickling and giggles. I acted as though I understood everything she uttered.

Although I had no idea what Kat said on any occasion, Meredith did. On bringing Kat home one day, Meredith informed me that my sweet little girl had spoken the word *mama*. Hearing that pierced my heart with a sense of remorse. I wanted to be the first to hear Kat call *me* mama, not her babysitter. Then, to top it off, Meredith told me Kat took her first step.

Well, hells bells! I should have seen that.

I lost out on both major events in my daughter's life, but then that's what I got for handing Kat over to another woman to take care of five days out of the week.

This morning after Meredith arrived to sweep up my daughter and whisk her away, Sherman and I got into his car and started down the road.

Half-way to my office, he pulled into a filling station. "I have to pick up cigarettes. Do you need any?"

"No, I have a pack in my purse, but thanks."

"Be back in a minute."

Waiting for him, I people watched. A uniformed filling station attendant washed a vehicle's windshield while another checked the oil. I chuckled when seeing a woman in that car wrestle with her toddler to keep him from crawling out the open window.

Kids. What a joy and a handful at the same time.

My nose itched, and I sneezed. To prepare myself for another, I searched my purse for a handkerchief in case I lost the battle.

"Dagnabbit. I changed purses and forgot to put a hanky in."

In hopes of finding one in the glove box, I opened it and blindly rummaged around in the back of the compartment. Bingo.

I withdrew a handkerchief, but what I saw made me forget about any sense of nose discomfort. My mouth dropped open as I focused on a beautiful piece of cloth that didn't belong to me. For one, my assorted hankies were plain white and came from J.C. Penney, on sale to boot. This exquisite cream-colored, linen one with a purple accent embedded in one corner looked like a Bloomingdale's specialty. Two, I didn't wear the shade of red lipstick smeared across its fabric. So, who owned this mysterious piece of cloth and why did it occupy space in my husband's car?

Adding to my curiosity, I lifted the piece of cloth and detected a slight hint of perfume pressed within the woven threads. The fragrance seemed familiar, but I couldn't put my finger on where, or on whom, I'd smelled it. Then a frosty chill crept up my spine when the gravity of the situation hit me. Someone who owned this type of handkerchief—a similar one anyway—*did* come to mind. Coral.

I pressed the fabric between my thumb and forefinger and absentmindedly rubbed it as I recalled my first day at the agency where Beau played with a handkerchief in his mother's office. The telephone directory covered one complete side of the square material, so I never saw its entirety. Did the handkerchief Beau played with have lace with a purple accent in a corner like this one?

Digging back in time, I resurrected the image at Coral's New Year's Eve party when she grabbed my husband's balls, and Sherman did not flinch one iota when she did. Could this mean she and Sherman were having an affair?

I snickered at the insanity of the ridiculous notion. My husband was as loyal as a Bluetick hound sitting at his master's feet in front of a blazing fire. So, what explanation could he come up with to justify having such an item? I didn't ponder long because he opened the car door and slid into the driver's seat.

"Sorry," he quickly said. "There was a long line at the check-out counter." Putting the gear in reverse, he placed his elbow over the back of the seat and looked over it.

Before he got far, I placed my hand on his arm. "Uh, Sherman," I leveled my tone, "What's this?" Even though I wanted to spout off a long list of accusations, I intended to hear him out.

"What?" he asked. When glancing at me, he braked the car. His elbow came down and his expression softened, giving off an air of unsettled calm. "Well, it looks like a handkerchief, Riley."

"I know that, Sherman, but whose is it?"

His lungs expelled a deep breath, but not the kind released for doing something improper, but one of annoyance. "It's Gene's." He started the back-up process again.

His admission took me totally by surprise. "Wait, stop the car," I strongly urged.

"You'll be late if we don't get going, Riley, and I have a meeting to get to." He continued the backward movement.

"Stop this fucking car!" I stressed further, my voice threatening.

He did, out of hearing me profess such vulgar language. I was not one to swear aloud in normal circumstances. But I meant business.

"Who the hell is this Jean and why in God's name do you have her handkerchief?" I asked him.

He looked at me as if I had grown horns, which perhaps I did at that moment. "Not Jean with a 'J,' Riley, but 'G' as in our neighbor Gene."

My mind jolted in a doubletake. "Since when does Gene wear lipstick and carry a scented handkerchief?" But then I stopped. My eyes shot up and nearly bugged out of my head. "Are you insinuating Gene dresses in drag?"

He nearly came out of his seat. "What? No, for Christ's sake, Riley. Gene is a philanderer, and that belongs to one of his floozies."

Gripping the piece of cloth, I craned my neck. "Again I ask, what's it doing in *your* glove box?" I spat out.

Even though he tried to keep his voice calm, by the heaviness of his sigh, I could tell he was getting frustrated. "He and I were talking one day in his driveway when he pulled it out to brag about fooling around with this other woman. When Mayzelle approached us, he thrust it in my hand and told me to get rid of it for him. I shoved it in my pocket then later tossed it in the glove box. It's no big deal."

"No big deal?" It devastated me to learn a friend of mine was a bastard. And to hear my husband speak to the subject with ease, made my stomach turn. "I, for one, think it's a horrible thing for a man to do to his wife."

"As usual Riley," he lowered his head, "you are making too much out of this. Men do what men do. Some are as faithful to their wives as the day is long, but there are others who can't keep it in their pants. It's a fact of life, so put the thing back where you found it. We *have* to go. This outburst of yours has made us both late."

I replaced the delicate cloth and closed the glove compartment. Throughout the rest of the trip, I processed this upending information about our neighbor. Gene, a cheater? How sad.

Poor Mayzelle. The wife was always the last to know.

Two days later, I received two bits of news. Ignoring the awkward tension at our house, it thrilled me to get a call at work about Bluebell. However, instead of Fitz calling like he told me he would, the call came from Fitz's mechanic.

"Mrs. O'Keefe," the mechanic started. By the shakiness in his voice and how slowly he pronounced his words, I could tell he was an older gentleman. "Your vehicle broke down due to a split in the radiator hose that caused the overheating by allowing fluid to escape."

"Oh, my. What caused the crack?"

"Well," I could practically hear him scratching his head, "you know, I've worked with automobiles for many years, and I thought I'd seen everything. However, what I saw on yours bothered me."

"Bothered you how?"

"Mrs. O'Keefe, the damage on the hose was more precise than normal wear and tear. It looked like someone stuck a knife in the right place on the hose to allow the fluid to drip out."

"A knife?"

"Yes, ma'am. Have you or your husband noticed fresh fluid spots under the car?"

How would I even know? Neither Sherman nor I removed the unsightly stains from our home's concrete driveway left by the previous owner's vehicles. And when it came time to leave work, I wouldn't notice if I wanted to because of the dim lighting in the parking garage.

"I, um, well, no, not really."

He took a deep breath and moaned it out. "All I can say is, it's good you pulled over when you did. If you had run out of fluid in the radiator and kept driving, you could have destroyed your engine, and those things cost a pretty penny." He chuckled. "Yes, indeed, a pretty penny. I wouldn't worry about it now though. I replaced the radiator hose and gave the car a good going over. It's as good as new and is ready for pickup at your convenience."

"Thank you," I told him. "I appreciate your being so thorough. My husband and I will swing by for the car after work."

"He said it looked like a knife made the slit in the radiator hose that released the water," I informed my husband after we got home from reclaiming Bluebell. "Who would have done such a thing?"

Sherman seemed less than interested in the topic. "That mechanic has no idea what he's talking about, Riley. Anything could have made that hole, like a sharp piece of glass your tire kicked up. All that matters, is that nothing bad happened to you, and now we can get back to our normal schedules. Oh, and I talked to Gene earlier today. We're going over to their house on Friday to play Bridge."

"You and I both hate Bridge," I scoffed, putting the earlier incident behind me. "Can't we play something else? What about charades? You like charades, don't you?"

"I like it better than Bridge. I'll talk to Gene about it. When is Kat due home?"

As if on cue, the doorbell rang. Whenever Meredith brought Kat home, we always asked her in to visit so she could tell us what wonderful crafts Kat created that day. Today, Meredith produced a sheet of construction paper illustrating a turkey made from Kat's handprint. As with the rest of our daughter's masterpieces, I added this one to the collage of colorful pictures taped on our avocado green refrigerator.

On most days when Meredith deposited Kat on our doorstep, our little prima-donna raised a fuss when having to leave her babysitter, except on Fridays. That day of the week Kat slept over at Meredith's house since Sherman and I played games with Mayzelle and Gene. Kat got to spend more time with her favorite babysitter, and I received fun-time with our best friends.

Now, if I could only get some of that fun-time in the bedroom with my husband. Whatever "life crisis" Sherman was going through these last few weeks had put a dampener on our sex life. If the situation didn't change soon, I'd have to take a *hard* look at the *problem* and take it into my own *hands*!

The next day, I retrieved the mail from the squeaky-hinged, black mailbox attached to the wall beside our front door. Taking the letters into the kitchen, I stood at the counter and separated the ads from the rest of the correspondence. The last piece was an orange envelope that intrigued me. Whoever sent it, used construction paper. They also neglected to place a return address in the upper left corner of the envelope or on the back flap. My name and address were the only characters centered perfectly and typed in all capitals.

My mind flew toward an invitation to a party, but who was behind this creative piece of handiwork? Meredith had that kind of paper. Lord knew I had enough of my daughter's art projects on the refrigerator. Maybe Meredith was inviting Kat and me to a kid's party. Coral, too, had construction paper for her son to draw on, and perhaps this held an invitation to one of her spectacular soirées.

My joy of finding a card bearing pictures of balloons, or better yet, martini glasses, disappeared when looking inside. I withdrew a card all right, but it depicted neither a celebration for children nor an adult gala event. It revealed a cartoon someone meticulously cut out of a magazine and pasted onto a half sheet of white paper. The illustration showed a bride and groom cutting a wedding cake, but whoever sent this, cut off the original funny caption at the bottom. Instead, the new typed message read: "WHAT DO YOU CALL A MAN WHOSE WIFE HAS DIED? A WIDOWER."

Instantly, my heart dropped. I gasped when flinging both the envelope and its message onto the floor. Raising a clenched fist to my mouth, I backed away from someone's perverted attempt at telling a sick joke. This was anything but funny, and nothing less than a bold threat aimed directly at me.

Chapter Twenty

I sat on the couch and analyzed the piece of hate mail. Should I report this to the U.S. Postal Service? Surely, they would consider this act of aggression through their system as a criminal offense. I certainly did.

In the meantime, I thought about the construction paper. I could not entertain the thought that Coral or Meredith would do something like this to me. But then my hibernating idea about Coral and Sherman having an affair reawakened.

That explained the possible scenario about Coral, but what could Meredith's angle be? Was there one? I came up with nothing. She was Kat's babysitter *and* my friend. *Both* women were my friends. Not only that, but every craft store in the city sold construction paper, meaning any Tom, Dick, or *Harriet* could have bought it. In all honesty, I had no inkling who typed and sent the cryptic message.

The ringing of the doorbell interrupted my mental process. When I greeted Meredith at the door, she noticed a pallor to my face.

"Riley," she held Kat on her hip, "are you all right? You look like you've seen a ghost."

After prying my daughter's hands off her babysitter, I helped Kat transition to being home again. I stood in the foyer where the Tickle Spider attacked my daughter's ribs, and that broke the magic spell Meredith had over her. Kat loved *me* again. After I snuggle-kissed my daughter under her chin, I placed her in the playpen at the far side of the breakfast room where a new stuffed teddy bear awaited attention. Once she started baby-talking to it, I led Meredith into the kitchen where the offensive paper items remained on the linoleum. In silence, I pointed at them.

Meredith bent over and picked both up. "What *is* this?"

"Read it," I softly stated, trying to keep my voice from shaking, which it did, "and tell me what you think." I crossed my arms over my chest. Watching her face, I noticed she wore a dark red color of lipstick. That fact startled me even more. "Meredith, that's an interesting shade of lipstick you have on. I thought you only wore rose."

"I bought it recently to try it. I'm not sure it's staying," she stated, more engrossed in the note than discussing lipstick shades.

I watched her reaction in hopes of getting an indication if she was the culprit or not by what her body language revealed.

With furrowed brows, she looked at the picture and read the caption. Blankly staring at the note, she lightly tapped the side of it with her index finger. I then saw her gaze pass from the note to the floor as she struck the card with more effort.

Her actions confused me. Was she conjuring up an excuse, or did this whole thing concern her? In giving her some time, I opened the cabinet and removed two teacups, placing a teabag in each. Filling the tea kettle with water, I put it on the electric burner to heat.

"What are your thoughts?" I asked.

She ran her thumb over the envelope. On the first pass, she discovered something I obviously overlooked. "Were you aware someone mailed this from Lansing?"

My focus remained on her eyes as I moved toward her. "How do you know that?" I removed the envelope from her fingers.

She pointed at the imprinted circle at the top. "The postmark."

I could barely see the faint and splotchy image of the postage date stamp, but the city's name came through. I didn't know anyone in Lansing other than the couple of people I met when delivering Coral's package on the day Bluebell broke down. Mayzelle's sister lived there, but my introduction to her was too brief to be of any significance.

"This is not good, my friend." Meredith shook her head in dismay. "Looks like there's someone out there who is not keen on you being married to your husband. Any clue as to who it could be?"

Her answer (and body language) made me feel confident she had no part in this. As a result, I struck her from my suspect list.

That left Coral.

Before answering my friend, I started nibbling my thumbnail and paced across the floor while piecing things together in my mind. A year and a half ago, I saw Coral exit a phone booth in the building lobby at work a few minutes after I received the first hateful phone call from that nasty woman. Coral could have called me from there and spouted the vile demand.

Then I recalled the overly friendly crotch episode between Coral and Sherman on New Year's Eve. That could be something. Then Coral sent me on a that errand to Lansing. Did she send me there on purpose? Was she the one who poked a hole in my radiator hose? Did she want me out of the way so she could seduce my husband? And this envelope made of construction paper. Coral had plenty of that, including orange.

Another memory entered the picture; that of Gene's floozy's handkerchief. Did it really belong to his mistress or to Coral who had one almost exactly like it that her son played with?

I stared down at my hands. "Someone does come to mind, Meredith, but..." I stopped mid-sentence to talk out an idea.

"Meredith, let me ask you a question. You remember me telling you about the other episodes that happened to me in the past, don't you?"

"Yes," she simply answered.

"Could the same person have perpetrated all those and this one, too?" The possibility of this idea stimulated my analytical juices.

She pressed her red lips together and shook her head. "If that's the case, Riley, you're sitting in the bulls-eye of someone's target. What about getting the police involved?"

"And tell them what? That there's some deranged woman out there making threats against me? They'll ask who it is, and what do I tell them? 'I have no idea' isn't going to get me *or them* anywhere."

The loud shriek of the kettle's whistle made me jump. Steadying my hand, I poured the steaming liquid into two cups. I replaced the kettle on a different burner and removed the honeypot from the pantry. "Any other recommendations?"

Meredith took her cup and sat at the breakfast table. After putting a teaspoon of honey in my tea, I followed.

"Have you told Sherman everything?" she asked, taking a sip from the cup.

I closed my eyes and rubbed the back of my neck. "Not this one yet, but the others, yes."

"What's his opinion?"

I slumped in my chair, and with my hands clasped in my lap, stared at the deep brown liquid inside my white teacup. "He thinks I'm overreacting."

"Are you?" Her question reeked of skepticism with a tad of sympathy rolled up into one ginormous ball.

My head snapped up in shock that my friend would ask such a stupid question. "Not at all! The facts speak for themselves."

Meredith drained the rest of her tea and stood to leave. "Oh, Riley, I am so sorry you're having to go through this." She embraced me in a strong hug. "I wish I had some answers for you, but none come to mind." She cupped my shoulders with her hands in a gesture of support. With drooping brows and a heavy sigh, she shook her head. "It seems you're stuck between the devil and the deep blue sea."

"Yes." I hated to admit such a vile thing. "I suppose I am, and I'm quickly sinking to the bottom."

"Keep your chin above water," she encouraged

"I'll try. Thanks, Meredith. You're a good listener and friend."

Meredith placed her teacup in the kitchen sink. "Are you still going over to Mayzelle and Gene's house tomorrow for game night?"

I nodded.

"Okay, then." She caught Kat's attention, smiled, and waved. Kat held Meredith's gaze briefly, then went back to playing with the teddy bear. "I'll be by to pick Kat up in the morning."

Waiting for Sherman to come home, I paced, sat, and paced some more. Looking out the window, I licked my lips when thinking about my four mysterious occurrences spanning over the last year and a half. The vile phone calls, a knife in my car's radiator hose, a woman's handkerchief in Sherman's glove box, and a threatening note in the mail; I recognized Coral as the common denominator.

The anxiety this deduction generated made my insides quiver. If I didn't stop grazing on my nails and picking at my cuticles, I'd have none left.

Sherman, come home so you can help me figure out this dilemma.

It took my husband forever to arrive, and when he walked through the front door, I immediately approached him. "Sherman," my voice and fingers trembled, "look what I received in the mail today." I showed him the distasteful object.

He did not take it from me. "Can I at least put my briefcase down before you throw things in my face?" he scoffed.

Really? That's rude.

I pressed my lips and waited for him to place his briefcase on the floor of the foyer closet and hang up his jacket. Then I handed him the letter. It took him two seconds to read it. By how quickly he did, I doubt he even contemplated its meaning.

"It's nothing but garbage, Riley. All this means," he raised the note, "is that someone has too much time on their hands and you happen to be the object of their seeking attention. Throw it away." He thrust it back, then loosened his tie and walked into the kitchen to make himself a cocktail.

I stood aghast, watching his back as he disappeared through the kitchen door. His response to this latest vicious attack infuriated me. Instead of him wrapping his arms around me to make me feel better and kissing my trepidation away, he reacted like all those other times when he expressed his displeasure at my taking these events too seriously.

Where did that compassionate man I married go? Why didn't he recognize how much I suffered at the hands of this despicable person, or people?

His detachment of the situation made my viewpoint stronger about his involvement with Coral. But I had no proof. No evidence, no case. Without a case, I lost before starting, and I despised losing. My inner sleuth came slinking in. Going forward, I would carefully observe the attitudes of both my husband and my boss to see if my suspicion about them was correct.

Chapter Twenty-One

"**Riley, we'll be late if you don't get a move on.**" Sherman seemed anxious for our Friday night of laughter and drama; the fun drama in charades, not like what he and I experienced at home these days.

I placed plastic wrap over the warm brownies made for snacking between bouts of screaming out guesses. "I'm coming!" I yelled back. Then whispering to myself, "Jesus H. Christ, keep your pants on! Mayzelle and Gene just live across the street."

This was my first time seeing Gene in a new light—that of a cheating son of a bitch. It still saddened me that someone I knew and loved as a friend would do something so despicable. This would be an interesting night.

Charades was a boisterous game that afforded great stress relief. I became a different person when yelling out my opinion of who, what, or where the others silently described. As a result, my mind remained sharp, and my accuracy irritated husband and hosts alike. When you're good, you're good, and I'm terrific.

Before long, the mantel clock struck twelve chimes. That meant time for one more round. It was Mayzelle's turn and she drew a person's name. The game was even, and she could break the tie.

Anticipation swelled. Sherman tapped on the arms of his wing chair. Gene leaned forward in another chair. I stood behind my husband's chair, palms sweaty and eyes wide.

As Mayzelle stood in front of us, we could tell she mentally plotted her moves to prepare for acting out her character. Before continuing, she disappeared into her bedroom and returned, tucking the remnants of an object into her brassiere.

To begin her performance, she held up two fingers, meaning two words. Second word, first syllable. Wiggling fingers of one hand at ground level, she hovered the other hand over them. Gene guessed *fire*. Sherman guessed *hot*. Both, incorrect but close. Her thoughts led to another clue whereby she pretended to touch the wiggling fingers, then pulled back and grimaced. I guessed *burn*. Correct. Okay. Something *burn* something. Sherman yelled out George Burns. Wrong.

Next, she collapsed on the sofa to simulate a fainting spell. From her brassiere, she whipped out the hidden item and pressed it against her neck, after which she used it to fan herself.

I suddenly became light-headed. The spit in my mouth evaporated, and a pain pierced my brain. I forgot how to breathe, and when I remembered, my breaths were short and shallow.

"Sarah Bernhardt!" Gene yelled out.

"That's right!" Mayzelle screamed out, a brilliant smile across her face. "Very good, Gene! I thought for sure Riley had it straight away. What's the matter, Riley? Did you have brain freeze?"

Do I attack and accuse, or act as if nothing is wrong?

Not having more ammunition before firing, I chose the latter. "Gene beat me to the punch." My voice gave away nothing. "Good job, Gene."

In true dramatic fashion, Gene took a formal bow.

"Mayzelle," I said, "that's a lovely handkerchief." I approached my friend. "Where did you get it?"

Mayzelle fanned herself again. "It belonged to my mother. In fact, it's one of a set of four. You see the purple feature in the corner?"

Instead of shoving the cloth down her throat until she choked on it, I remained silent and merely raised a brow in acknowledgement.

"My mother loved that color," Mayzelle said, "so for her thirtieth birthday, my father had the purple lace embroidered onto four cream linen handkerchiefs and surprised her with them. The handkerchiefs alone cost my father a small fortune. Adding the lace made them one of a kind, and yes, I agree with you, it is beautiful."

I needed to confirm my hunch. "May I see it?" My hands shook, but I steadied them as best I could.

"Of course." She handed me the cloth.

My examination revealed the same texture as the one in Sherman's car. When lifting it to my nose, it sickened me to recognize the perfume engrained in its threads. Studying my soon-to-be ex-friend, I noticed she wore a bright red shade of lipstick, albeit faded over hours of conversation, drinking, and eating brownies. Come to think of it, she had always worn red lipstick. I just never gave it much thought. It meant nothing to me until now.

The truth produced an overwhelming hatred. In an instant, my mind traveled to a dark and scary place. I envisioned cutting off this woman's head with a razor-sharp meat cleaver and feeding it to a pack of starving dogs. The next image placed me at her tombstone engraved with the following inscription: *Here lay Lucifer's maiden who held the evidence of guilt in her backstabbing claws.* Though a pleasant thought, I hid my perverted desires with a gracious, yet fictitious smile.

Now, what about my husband? I'd have to have a heart-to-heart conversation with Sherman before I accused him of being a lying bastard. If he denied the part he played with Mayzelle, perhaps I'd break out that imaginary meat cleaver and wield it toward another deserving subject.

Sherman lingered to converse with our neighbors at their door, but not me. I made a beeline to Sherman's car in front of our house and quickly removed the handkerchief from his glove box. I shoved it in my pants pocket just as my husband turned to leave Mayzelle and Gene.

I unlocked the front door of our house and threw my small clutch onto the settee. My heart drummed furiously as I flipped on the kitchen light and strode to the sink. A shiver rushed up my spine as I looked out the window at the darkness outside. Even though my deep and rapid breathing nearly put me in a hyperventilated condition, I needed to calm down. The release of combustible anger would do nothing but bring the conversation to a quick and bitter conclusion.

Sherman by-passed the kitchen and stepped through the French doors into the living room, turning off the one lamp we left on to deter any night-crawlers—be they the multiple-legged or the two-legged type. "That was fun, wasn't it?" he called out to me.

Silence.

"Riley," he raised his voice, "did you hear me?" he called out, joining me in the kitchen.

I heard the building frustration in his tone, and it pleased me to no end. It did not, however, entice me to turn around.

"What's wrong with you?" his voice rose a tad. Still nothing in return. "If you're not going to say anything, then I'm going to bed." He turned to go.

"Sherman." I faced him with the heels of my palms resting behind me on the sink's cold, porcelain edge. "You and I need to talk." I remained calm on the outside while a rage simmered throughout every inner fiber of my being.

"About what?"

As smooth as silk, I opened the lower cabinet door where we kept the liquor. Sherman questioningly watched me grasp the bottle of Jim Beam and set it on the counter, then remove two highball glasses from the top cabinet.

"Riley, I don't want a drink, so don't make one for me."

Did he say something? Nothing I want to hear.

I opened the freezer, removed the aluminum ice tray and pulled its handle. With my fingernails, I plucked two ice cubes from the tray and plopped one in each glass. The suspense intensified as I used two shaking hands, instead of one, to pour the proper amount of amber liquid—plus ginger ale in mine—needed for the impending knock-down-drag-out fight. I took both glasses and walked into the living room.

He blindly followed me in. "Riley, what the hell are you doing? I told you I didn't want a drink. I want to go to bed."

"You need to sit down, husband," I urged, handing him his drink. My breath became stronger. I stood more erect, and my attitude reflected a tenacious power I had never launched in his direction before.

My use of the word "husband" and the staunch way it left my mouth took him by surprise. I'd never referred to him in such an odd way, and because of that, his eyes narrowed, and his body grew rigid. He insisted on standing.

"It's late, Riley," he countered and placed his untouched drink on the end table. "It's been a long night and I'm tired. If you can't tell me what you want to say in ten words, it can wait until morning."

"Sadly, Sherman, this matter needs tending to right now."

"Alright," he snorted and made a verbal grunt when sitting in his recliner, "fine." When I didn't follow suit, irritation took over. "Are you going to just stand there?" he asked, perplexed by my hovering beside him.

"At this point, it's best if I stand."

His eyes were cold and his jawline hard. By the way his fingers tightened on his knees, it was clear I made him nervous. "Look, Riley," he licked his lips, "you seem to be out of sorts, so why don't you come out with it. Did someone do something to upset you? Did *I* do something to upset you?"

Are you kidding me right now, Sherman! Hell, yes, you most certainly did, and you are not alone.

I started by taking a deep breath followed by a long draw of my Jim and ginger. "What did you think of Mayzelle's performance of portraying Sarah Bernhardt tonight?" Even tone, even disposition.

My question stunned him. His mouth fell open and his eyes squinted. "Is that what this is about? Sarah Bernhardt?" He quickly rose from his chair in a huff. "I'm going to bed," he growled. "This is ridiculous, Riley, even for you."

"Sit down!" I demanded. My authoritative tone brought him to attention. As a result, he unwillingly did as I demanded.

I walked to his other side and placed my drink next to his on the end table. "What did you think of the prop she used when putting on the fainting episode?" The control I projected amazed me.

He wrinkled his nose as if smelling something putrid. "The handkerchief?"

"Yes, the handkerchief. Did you notice anything familiar about it?"

"Like what?" His demeanor did not change.

I took a few steps and stopped in front of him, lowering my head in contemplation. I laced my fingers except for my index ones that remained straight to represent the barrel of a gun and pressed them to my lips. "Yes, like what?" I tilted my "weapon" toward him. "Did you even look at it?"

He shifted his head and eyed me. "I saw her fanning herself with one," he spread his hands out, "but what of it?" His face turned a light shade of red. "Riley, what is with the third degree?"

I cocked my head and stared at him. "Let's go over what Mayzelle's handkerchief looked like, shall we?"

"What the hell? Okay, fine," he leaned forward in this chair, "let's," he sarcastically jeered.

"First, it was cream-colored, right?"

"Yes, it was cream. Jesus, Riley, what is this?"

"Second, it was linen, correct?"

"I don't know. I guess." His face color deepened.

"Third, there was an embroidered purple accent embedded in the lace on one corner of it. Did you notice that?"

He closed his eyes and rested his head on two fingers. "Yes, Riley, it had purple on it."

"Fourth, and finally, *darling*," I mocked, "it smelled of Mayzelle's perfume. Oh, and Mayzelle wore red lipstick tonight. Did you notice that, too?"

That did it! He shot up out of the chair. "So what if Mayzelle's perfume was on the damn thing, Riley!" he screamed, trying to get me to back down, which I did not. "It belongs to her, so why shouldn't her perfume be on it? And who cares what color lipstick she had on!"

I removed the handkerchief from my pocket and slammed the cloth on the end table, which made him flinch.

"Does what Mayzelle used in charades remind you of anything now?" I raised my voice shy of yelling.

Sherman glared at the red-smeared cloth. "What has that got to do with anything, Riley?" His timbre evened out, but his eyes were wide open.

Oh shit! Does he not recognize it? Could I be wrong about this?

Self-doubt crept in. But I was too deep in kimchee to turn back now. I had to go ahead and see where it took me. "You told me, *that*," I stiffly pointed to the topic of conversation, "belonged to Gene's floozy, and that he gave it to you to dispose of."

I saw Sherman swallow hard and lose some of that red color covering his face.

Sherman lowered his tone, but frustration still rang through. "Yeah, so?"

"So, you are calling his wife a floozy." I had him dead to rights, or did I?

"Mayzelle? Of course, she's not—"

"A floozy?" I pressed my finger to my cheek.

Please God, don't let me be wrong about this.

Slowly, my eyes widened, and my mouth gaped with excitement. "Hmm. I've got it. What about a whore?" An eerie smile curled across my face. My ire escalated but staying composed was the key to a successful strike.

He opened his mouth to speak, but I threw up my hand. "Do you know what a whore is, Sherman? It's a woman who sleeps with a man who is not her husband." I hesitated briefly. "As I recall, you called Gene a philanderer. That's a man who is sexually unfaithful to his wife. Now, I think," I bobbed a loaded index finger at him, "no, I am certain you have it wrong about one of them. Gene is not a philanderer. Now *you* on the other hand…" I pointed both index fingers at him. If they were barrels of a gun, they would have fired point-blank at my husband's face.

Sherman reached his limit and turned to leave when I grabbed him by the arm. Finding the strength, I brought him around. "I'm not done speaking to you!" I snarled.

He ripped himself out of my grasp. "You may not be done with me," his tone was low and angry, "but I am done with you. This insane conversation is over!" He finished the watered-down drink then went into the kitchen where he shattered the glass in the porcelain sink.

"You are having an affair with Mayzelle, aren't you, aren't you?!" I shouted from the living room. My calm diminished, and hysteria seized control.

He stomped back into the room; hands fisted. He came close enough for me to see his chocolate eyes were piercing and icy. His mouth had spittle in the corners like a rabid animal. He scared me to the point of wanting to slither away on my belly. "You pushed me there, Riley," he accused, "so you have no one to blame but yourself!"

That shocked me out of any remorse or fear I suffered. "I knew it! You son of a bitch!" I raised my hand to slap him, but he caught my wrist. I jerked my hand away and backed up only to retrace my steps. "How can you think I am responsible for you having an affair, Sherman?! Did I thrust you into Mayzelle's arms? In her bed? No! You did that all on your own! I had nothing to do with it whatsoever!"

"You had *everything* to do with it, Riley. You badger me to death with your unreasonable demands. You throw out all sorts of ultimatums when it comes to our daughter. You claim to be a perfectionist, yet you can't even make a meal worth eating. Not to mention you are the worst fuck I've ever had!" He moved closer until he came nose-to-nose with me. "All you do is take, take, take. I give you everything you deserve when it comes to sex. But not *once* have you tried to go down on me because it disgusts you to even think about it. Oral sex for *both* partners is a natural act, Riley, so get over whatever phobia you have about it!"

*How **dare** he speak to me this way?!*

"The worst fuck you've ever had?" I erupted. "Who instructed me in the art of lovemaking, Sherman? You! So, if I'm the worst fuck, then you are a horrible teacher," I yelled. Tears welled in my eyes but refused to fall. Chills invaded my skin to where my hands felt ice cold. My body shook as if an earthquake rattled the wood floor beneath my feet. But I would not cave in. Not now, not ever.

He ignored my response and started to walk away, but then spun around. "And don't think you are free from scrutiny under the microscope, *sweetheart*," he spewed. "What about the extracurricular activities you have with your boss's husband?"

I stood my ground and fought back. A deep breath filled my lungs. My nostrils flared, and I gritted my teeth. "I have never had extracurricular activities with Fitz, so stop trying to turn this around on me. By your own admission, *you* are the one having a fucking affair!"

"Bullshit!" he exclaimed, then stomped around to the backside of the couch. He spread his hands on the sofa's back and lowered his head and his tone. "You know, Riley, I can't do this anymore.

You know what else," he eyed me, "I'm glad it's all out in the open because now I don't have to pretend I care about you or your goddamned feelings."

His declaration bore a hole so far through my heart, you could see my lungs.

Not able to suffer this torment any longer, I played my hand with a final remark. It took everything I had left in me to control the shaking that ravaged my body. "If you're not happy," I sneered, "then do something about it." I pointed toward the front of the house. "You know where the door is. Use it."

I spoke this way to the man I loved; to the man I trusted more than anyone on this earth; to the man who I thought cared about and loved me like no other.

Fucking wrong again, and again, and again! Goddammit!

The remaining chamber of my heart liquified when he issued one last spiteful glare, grabbed his keys, and left the house. The slamming door behind him rattled the side windows.

I stood in silence; my hands at my side, and my heart beating ten times its regular speed, breaking just as fast. The lump in my throat the size of a baseball prevented me from swallowing; not that I had any spit in my mouth.

His words reverberated in my head, and I analyzed each of his accusations. *Do I put forth the effort to improve my shortcomings in the culinary realm? No, but he never complained about it before. Maybe if he had I could have worked harder at it. Am I a bitch in wanting everything my way? Yes, but most often my way is the correct way; but obviously he sees it differently. Do I have a phobia about oral sex? Absolutely, but come on…I can't be the only woman on earth who won't do that.*

It's a hard thing to admit my choices added to this fiasco. But the one thing I never did, as he accused me of, was stray. Sherman did. He saw an out and took it.

Coward.

The more I thought back to Sherman's and my conversation, the angrier I got. His actions were a million times worse than anything I did or didn't do, or whatever the fuck he thinks I did or didn't do.

Not able to sit still, I walked all over the house. Ringing my hands, I stewed over this situation for an hour thinking it could not end with me as the villain. There had to be a solution to turn this around. But what? My brain stopped working on that dilemma. Instead, it ventured down a different road—a vengeful one. It didn't just take two people to destroy this marriage. It took three. Someone else tampered with its demise, and she would not get away unscathed.

Chapter Twenty-Two

'*H*ell hath no fury like a woman scorned.' I would test that theory. It was two o'clock a.m., but that didn't matter. I marched out of my house and barreled across the street. On this moonless night, only the soft glow from the corner streetlight at the end of the block illuminated my path. Making it to the other side of the street, I stopped and checked my emotions at the curb. It served no purpose going in like gangbusters, shooting from the hip. Better to take it nice and easy and make Mayzelle suffer a slow death when I confronted her.

I took deep breaths before continuing up the walk to my neighbors' front door. After ringing the doorbell several times, I waited. It took two more times before I heard Gene's irritated and muffled call to, "Keep my pants on," as he made it to the front of the house. How ironic. If only Sherman had kept *his* on, I wouldn't be on this doorstep and he wouldn't be wandering around town God knows where.

Gene opened the door, half asleep and pulling his robe closed. "Riley, what's wrong? Did something happen to Sherman?"

"You might say that," I said, masking my animosity. "May I come in, Gene?" He stepped aside and allowed me into the small foyer. The interior of the house lay dark and silent. "Where's Mayzelle?" I asked.

"Asleep."

"Go get her, Gene. You both need to hear this."

He was fully awake now and confused with my demand. "Can't whatever it is, wait, Riley? It's two o'clock in the morning."

"Yes, it's late, Gene, but this is too important to wait. Give me a chance to explain, and then you'll understand."

Visibly aggravated, he turned on a living room lamp. "Do you want to sit down? It might take a minute for Mayzelle to join us. She's a sound sleeper."

Guess it depends on who she's sleeping with.

"No, I'm fine right here," I replied.

Saddened by the memories, I stared into the now lit room where a short time ago the four of us were laughing and enjoying each other's company. How things changed on a dime.

When Mayzelle entered the room, my temper rose. I hated her.

"Riley?" Mayzelle asked. "Gene said you wanted to talk to us." Smiling, she attempted humor. "Isn't it a little late for a tête-à- tête?"

My first impulse was to scratch her eyes out and shove them into that mouth that no doubt had caressed Sherman's dick, but I kept composed. "This won't take long, Mayzelle." An avenging smirk crossed my lips. "I want to return something that belongs to you."

"Oh? What did I lose?"

From my pocket, I pulled out the lipstick-stained handkerchief by the corner and dangled it in front of her. Horrified at seeing it, her eyes widened, and the sleep induced rosy cheeks vanished.

Gene didn't notice the change in his wife's complexion. "That's one of your mother's handkerchiefs, Mayzelle," he declared. "I wondered what happened to the fourth one." He faced me. "Did she leave it at your house?"

Oh, Gene, I am about to add a very large pit to your cherry pie life.

"Not exactly."

Beads of sweat formed on Mayzelle's forehead. This time, Gene noticed. "Mayzelle, are you okay?" he asked. His focus shot to me. "Riley, enough with beating around the bush. If you have something to say, say it. Whatever this is, is upsetting my wife. Does it have to do with that handkerchief?"

"She *does* look unnerved, doesn't she, Gene," I offered with gluttonous vindication in my tone. "It would tickle me pink to explain. Let me start out by telling you a little story." I took a deep breath. "Once upon a time, my husband accused you of being unfaithful to your wife. He even called you a philanderer and told me *this*," I waved the handkerchief in front of him, "belonged to one of your whores. However, the truth of the matter is, my husband is that culprit, and your wife is the whore. You see, Gene, my husband and your wife have been intimate behind our backs."

Shocked at this information about the woman he loved, Gene's eyes flew open. "What are you talking about?" He glanced at his wife who had tears welling in her eyes. He approached her and wrapped his arms around her shoulders in consolation. "Riley, how can you make such a vile accusation against your best friend? That's a cruel thing to do. You need to leave."

"Not until *my best friend*," the words left a nasty taste, "admits her sin against me and against you, too, Gene." I faced Mayzelle. "It's true, isn't it Mayzelle?" I turned back to Gene. "Tonight, after Sherman and I got home from your house, we had a big fight that resulted in his confession about his and your wife's affair."

Gene swallowed hard. His face lost all color, and his brows furrowed. Releasing his wife, he took a step back. "Tell me there's no truth to this, Mayzelle," he appealed to her. "Tell me Riley is lying."

With her secret open for the world to see, Mayzelle wiped away streaming tears before grabbing Gene's arm. "It was only a minor fling," she sputtered. "I made a terrible mistake, and I…I'm very sorry for doing this to you." Heaping sobs garbled her words as they ran together. "You…you're the one I love, Gene. Sherman meant nothing. Nothing. You have to believe me! Please, Gene…" Desperation pitted her voice.

Gene jerked from under her grasp and rushed into his bedroom, leaving me to wonder what he was doing. Thinking of my next statement, I glared at Mayzelle, but her eyes never met mine.

Before I said another word, Gene returned fully clothed, albeit untucked here and there and forgetting to put shoes on; his slippers remained on his feet. "Where's your bastard husband, Riley? He and I have a score to settle, and I'm going to settle it right this Goddamn minute."

Gene was no match for Sherman and Mayzelle knew it. As he started for the door, she grabbed his arm. "No, Gene!" she yelled, "please don't do this! I won't let you get hurt!"

"It's too late for that, Mayzelle, but now it's my turn to dish out some pain of my own." He faced me. "Where is he, Riley?!"

With a lack of concern, I shrugged. "Good question, Gene. After he stormed out of the house, I can't say where he went. To Hell, I hope."

Out of frustration, Gene slammed one fist into his other palm. "Goddammit!"

Ah, what a lovely day of reckoning. "Well," I let out a long, audible breath, "I suppose you two will have a tête-à-tête of your own, so I'll be on my way." I turned to go but stopped mid-stride. "Wait," I changed direction, "there is one more question I have for you, Mayzelle. Are you the *bitch* who called me at work, too? Whoever has been threatening me uses a cloth to disguise her voice, and well," I held up the handkerchief, "this is a cloth, now isn't it?"

Mayzelle's neck stiffened, and the veins stuck out as she vigorously shook her head. "No!" she spouted in a loud and quick response. "I'd never do that to you! It was Gertrude!"

That set my ears to burning. "Your sister, Gertrude?"

"Yes!" Mayzelle had no difficulty throwing her blood relative under the bus. "I told her about my affair and mentioned how it would be much easier if Sherman was single. It didn't come across maliciously, Riley, but in a wishful thinking kind of way. How was I to know she would take it upon herself to act on it? She just wanted you to kick him to the curb so I could have him to myself. She did it to make me happy!"

Gene's mouth slacked in disbelief as his gaze pierced his wife.

"What about stabbing my radiator hose with a knife?" I queried further. "With your familiarity with cars, you would know exactly where to puncture a hose to inflict the most damage. Are you guilty of being that hateful to put my life in danger, Mayzelle?"

Mayzelle's legs no longer supported her. In her distress, she fell into a heap on the floor, covered her face, and sobbed uncontrollably.

If she thought tears would soften my disposition and dispel the new onslaught of questions I had, she had another *think* coming. Determination overtook me as I squatted down to get her attention. "Answer me, Mayzelle," I urged in a not so kind way.

"No, it wasn't me," she sputtered, eyes glued to the floor. "Gertrude did it, and the cartoon that came in your mail…she sent that, too."

But then as if struck by lightning, Mayzelle's head shot up. Her reddened, moisture-filled eyes flew open as she wailed and forged a fierce campaign to denounce any participation in the terrorizing threats. "But I…but I didn't know anything about what she'd done until recently! Gertrude had laughed…when confessing it, thinking I'd find it humorous. But I didn't find it funny at all, Riley! I didn't! I told her she should never…have done such horrible things to you. She even gloated about more threats she had in place for the future to ensure you and Sherman split up. I begged her not to go through with them!" She nodded her head and tightly closed her eyes. "Yes, I admit having an affair with Sherman," she grimaced when balling her fists and keeping them close to her chest. "But...but not of anything else!"

What a pitiful display from a dramatically pathetic person. Even when groveling, she did it with a dynamic flair.

I softened my tone in understanding. "Somehow, Mayzelle, I believe you. Not sure why, but I do." And I honestly did.

I rose and stood above this sorry excuse for a friend, feeling nothing but disappointment and disgust. "There's one more thing, Mayzelle, and then I'm done with you."

She looked up at me with blood-shot eyes. "Anything, Riley," she sobbed.

"How did you do it? Sherman left for the office at the crack of dawn and came home shortly after I did. He and I were together on weekends, so, when did you two have time to arrange these sexual playdates?" About to discover the coordination of her and Sherman's multiple rendezvous kept me calm on the outside but erupting on the inside.

Deflated, Mayzelle shamefully hung her head. "I would make up excuses for Sherman to come over and help me when Gene ran errands for me."

"Like moving furniture?" I asked.

Mayzelle merely nodded. "Also, after leaving your house every morning, he drove to the pastry shop on First Street and waited until," she glanced up at her husband, "Gene left for work." Her eyes drifted back to the floor. "Sherman knew Gene's schedule because I told him," she continued. "Then, Sherman came back and sat in his car around the corner until he saw Gene's car pass by. When the coast was clear, he'd walk to my house, enter through the back door, and stay until eight o'clock."

*Oh, Sherman, you son of a bitch. Why did you fuck up our lives? Were you **so** unhappy that you resorted to adultery with our fucking best friend who lives across the fucking street?*

Yeah, I was angry.

And hurt.

And devastated.

Mostly, sad, but no less determined to get revenge.

"Well, well, well. Until eight o'clock, huh?" I smirked at the information. "That's quite the arrangement, isn't it?" Such was the secret life of Sherman and his round-heeled hussy. I then remembered, during one of her phone calls, Gertrude had asked if I knew with whom my husband was having lunch and fucking afterward.

"And what about lunchtime Mayzelle? Did you see him then?"

She replied with a nod.

My lungs filled with oxygen, and I exhaled it with satisfaction. Turning back to Gene, I looked at him with sympathy. He and I were both victims here. "I'm sorry our spouses let us both down, Gene," I offered, then addressed the pile of shit on the floor. "And, Mayzelle," the woman shrunk when looking up at me, "for future reference," I squinted at her, "you should be more careful when leaving incriminating evidence lying around." I dropped the handkerchief at her feet. With shaking hands, I opened the door and walked out.

Sleep escaped me for the rest of the night. My emotions were all over the place, preventing me from relaxing. Instead I fumed over my hatred for Mayzelle and Sherman and what they had done to me.

In a fit of rage, I threw decorative sofa pillows across the living room, avoiding the breakables, of course. Oh, I wanted to shatter something all right, but Sherman wasn't there. I wanted to smash his face like he smashed my heart. The beast in me begged to fracture his cheekbones, knock out every tooth, and crush both eye sockets. Too bad I'd never get the chance to fulfill my desire.

When the sun rose, and the clock chimed eight, I crawled out of bed, still in the same clothes I had worn the night before. Phoning Meredith, I asked her to keep Kat a little longer while I ran a few errands. She agreed without hesitation.

I first stopped at the police station where I filed a formal complaint against Gertrude. The only charge that held any grit was endangering my life by shoving a knife into my radiator hose. The other incidents showed malice but would fall short of going anywhere on their own. While there, I called Gene and asked him to provide a statement about his wife's disclosure about her sister. He willingly obliged.

Next, I visited the local hardware store and bought a new lock for the back door and a locking screen door that went in front of the front door. I hired a professional to install both.

The last task was to retrieve my daughter from Meredith. Done, done, and done.

It took a week for Sherman to contact me. When he did, he never apologized for his indiscretion or vicious remarks, and I didn't ask for them. We spoke briefly about Kat, and he told me that if she or I needed anything, our joint bank account would never lack for funds.

How sporting of the asshole.

He and I also set up a schedule to where he saw Kat regularly.

Good God Almighty! What a fucking mess my life has turned out to be!

Chapter Twenty-Three

*T*he rumor mill circulated the news of my separation. I should have guessed that Coral would catch wind of the story. Gertrude *was* her sister-in-law. It was only a matter of time before Coral's brother spilled the beans about what happened. On a positive note, Coral took my side from top to bottom. She always considered Gertrude a bad seed, and this proved it beyond a shadow of a doubt.

It took a few days before informing my mother about my new situation with Sherman. Her response shocked the hell out of me.

"Oh my dear, dear daughter," she sobbed over the phone, "this is terrible. I am so sorry you had this little tiff, but I know you will right the ship in quick order."

What?! Right the ship? Me?

"Mother, did you not hear it was Sherman who had the affair with my neighbor, not me. Why in God's name would *I* be the one who 'righted the ship' as you call it?"

She cleared her throat. "Because that's what wives do, Riley. Husbands are irresponsible sometimes. As a result, they destroy our trust in them, but never to the point of no return."

"You know this how, mother? Did…dad cheat on you?"

"Men do what men do, dear, and—"

"Oh, great!" I yelled. "There's that phrase again! Men having affairs is more than irresponsibility, mother, it's breaking a vow between two people and God."

"You are correct, Riley. It will take time to sooth your temper enough to see what is important. It took me a month to realize being married to your father was a higher priority than his indiscretion."

I swore my mother lived on some other planet.

"Oh, I'll take time, mother, you can count on that. And my only priority is my daughter. Sherman can go to hell as far as I am concerned."

"Riley!" she admonished. "Watch your language! You are a lady, and ladies do not utter such vulgarities."

She'd disown me if she knew how vulgar I was with Sherman.

I never knew my mother suffered what I was going through.

*My father cheated on my mother. How could he? He was perfect. My mother **is** perfect. Both were the perfect couple. Dear God. That just goes to show no one knows what happens behind closed doors.*

It took a month to settle into a new routine. The nights of screaming into pillows so Kat couldn't hear, gnashing my teeth, and crying my eyes out were over. A new phase began in my life, and I needed to put on my big-girl panties and deal with it.

Terminating game nights on Fridays depressed me. But there was more to life than dominoes, cards, and charades. Meredith continued to keep Kat those nights while I ventured out to dinner or to a movie with Hazel who bolstered my confidence as a "single" woman now. Or I'd stay inside cuddled up in my chair, reading a good romance novel, eating buttery popcorn doused in extra butter, and drinking wine.

One Friday night I did something different. After work, a group of us girls, including Coral, agreed to meet for drinks at The Midnight Lounge. I explained to those other than Coral, the situation of prostitutes working there, but it didn't seem to matter. In fact, Babs had never seen one and was curious what they looked like. Our male co-worker, Brendon, offered to come along as our protector. With pleasure, we accepted his voluntary sacrifice.

With five minutes to go before the office closed, Hazel bounded in with a grin as wide as the state from which she hailed. "Are you ready to boogie tonight, darlin'?" she asked me.

This Texas twister tickled me pink. Her accent would gain attention from the patrons at the bar, meaning we should expect a few men showing up at our table.

"I am. Are the other girls and Brendon putting their client accounts to bed for the night?"

"They already have. Coral told them to start the process fifteen minutes ago, so let's giddy-up-on down the road!"

"Speaking of our boss," I said, "let me check if she's ready. While I do that, tell everyone to meet in the client parking lot and we'll caravan to the bar."

When Hazel left my desk, I buzzed Coral to let her in on the plan. She said to go on and that she'd meet us there.

When everyone was in their cars, we left single file and stayed close together until pulling into The Midnight Lounge parking lot. I looked for a little red MGA roadster. Not there.

Damn. No free drinks from Fitz.

Ten o'clock rolled around, and the girls left one by one. That left Hazel, Babs, and me at the table with Brendon. Coral never did show up. I hoped nothing serious kept her.

In the middle of a deep conversation with my friends, a man approached our table and asked Hazel to "Twist and Shout" with him. Our mouths drooled at the handsome tall drink of water.

Making goo-goo-eyes, Babs attracted a gorgeous guy across the room. With a turn of her head and a graceful swoop of her hair, she watched him move our way. Two minutes later, they wandered onto the dancefloor. Brendon kept looking at his watch.

"Brendon, you can go if you want do. I'll be okay."

"And leave you alone at this table for these men to ogle or worse? Not on your life, Riley."

I smiled at this kind man.

Sherman used to be kind like that, but now he's a son of a bitch.

The music kept me moving and swaying until someone tapped my shoulder. "Why don't we take those moves off of your chair and put them where they belong, good-looking."

That deep, sultry voice raised my spirits. My pearly whites sparkled when seeing Fitz standing there in his classy sports jacket with his hand out. "I hope that means dancing with you, handsome," I returned the compliment.

Impishly, his mouth crooked up as did one brow. "Did you have something else in mind?"

I clasped his hand. "You're incorrigible, Fitz." I turned to a grinning Brendon. "You can go home now Brendon. Thank you for being our watchful angel tonight."

Fitz swept me around the dancefloor with every song. He oozed finesse when dipping, turning, swaying, and swinging. When a slow dance played, the splay of his hand caressed my back, guiding me in the proper direction with gentle pressure. To follow his shifts, my pelvis pressed against his, helping me feel the rhythm and movement. His other hand possessed mine with a tenderness allowed a baby. I deeply inhaled the heady scent of his cologne that filled my nostrils and weakened my knees. He held me so close, the tips of my breasts flattened against his chest. The song may have been music to my ears, but a whole different tune reached my vagina. I wanted him to want me, yes, in that way.

During a swing dance with Fitz, I saw Hazel and Babs wave their goodnights from across the room. Now just the two of us, Fitz led me to a two-person table in the corner, away from everyone.

"I feel for you, Riley," he proffered. "Separation is a hard pill to swallow." His lips turned into a naughty grin. "But with water, it slides down with ease. What I mean, Riley, is if Sherman hadn't had an affair, I wouldn't be here with you right now."

Ouch. That double-edged sword left a jagged mark. He raised his glass of bourbon. I raised my gimlet, and we toasted to infidelity.

Closing time was at hand. "Can I walk you to your car?" Fitz asked. "It's best you escape early to avoid the demolition derby that always takes place in the parking lot."

I loved his gentlemanly manner. More than that, I wanted him to kiss me. I sure as shootin' wanted to kiss him.

Oh, no. Hazel's Texas lingo has rubbed off on me.

I wanted his and my tongues and mouths to meet in a sensual dance, weaving, sucking, releasing, dodging. My heart pounded with an erratic flutter like it housed a thousand butterflies.

But he belongs to Coral. If I participate in what I want from Fitz, I'll be just like Mayzelle—a floozy, right?

Fitz escorted me to my car and ran his hand over Bluebell's fender in the same way I imagined him running his hand over *mine*. Strong fingers stroking over the metal of a car. Strong fingers stroking up my inner thigh. Same thing. *Lucky Bluebell...Poor, pitiful me.*

"She looks great. No more troubles I take it." His statement came across as sincere.

I shook my head. "You can't see the radiator hose from here, Fitz, but no more problems. Your mechanic took good care of Bluebell, and my saboteur is as far away as possible."

"You were right."

I cocked my head. "About what?"

"The way Coral reacted when hearing what happened to you on the highway. She feels a sense of responsibility because of her relationship with Gertrude. My wife is aware how mean-spirited Gertrude is and thinks she should have been more perceptive when your troubles started."

"You told her, then."

"Couldn't help it. A lady in the Lansing office called and filled her in on the story, so she asked me what part I played."

"It's not Coral's fault. What happened, happened because a deranged woman had strange ideas on how to make someone happy, that's it. Please tell your wife not to lose sleep over it, okay?"

He stepped into my personal space. "I'll tell her." He caught me staring into his eyes. "You look fantastic."

"Yes, I know," I smirked.

He threw his head back and belted out a drawn-out laugh. He was sexy as hell when he did that. I'd love to see him do it more often, but…I heaved a sigh.

He belongs to Coral.

"Well," he slid in half a step more, "I'd better let you go."

The short distance between us ignited my sexual appetite. My palms moistened, and my *down-under* pulsed. In that moment, my depraved mind wanted him to put his arms around me. My sex drive pleaded for him to pull me close and hold me tight to where I heard his heartbeat drumming against me. I wanted to hear him whisper naughty things in my ear. I yearned for his lips to caress mine. I craved for him to trace every inch of my body with his hands until he reached the goal of my complete seduction.

Just because Sherman wasn't in my life didn't mean I had to give up the joy of sex. *Hell no!* My libido may have dimmed when dealing with my separation but skyrocketed with Fitz standing here in all his Adonis glory.

But he belongs to Coral, you fool!

He stepped back and placed his hands on my shoulders. His gaze drifted away from me as he leaned down and kissed me on the forehead. "Drive home safely," he said above a whisper.

My resolve weakened. "Okay," I sputtered.

He opened my driver-side door and waited until I slid into the seat before closing the door and stepping away. I started Bluebell's engine, pulled out of the parking space and away from the building. In my rearview mirror, I saw him standing there, hands in his pockets, as I turned the corner.

That image of Fitz stayed with me. I tried to tamper down the unlikely scenario inundating my mind. I focused on something entirely different like adorable, cuddly puppies scampering over each other on shaky legs.

Strike one.

I moved on to soft, furry kittens nuzzling their mother to get attention.

Strike two.

Last, but not least, I pictured my rose garden in the spring with tender buds expanding into full blossoms, sweet and colorful.

Tender buds expanding into full blossoms? Are you kidding me? No, stupid brain.

Strike three!

This unrest allowed a hot and steamy war to rage in my genitals. The blood rushed to my face creating an instant headache. Aching above…aching below. I had only one way to resolve my predicament. Fitz needed to make me forget Sherman; to be in my bed; to screw my brains out.

Okay, that's three ways.

Musings spiked as did my sexual fever.

Did I forget he belongs to Coral? No, but do I really care? YES!

The more I fantasized about what Fitz could have done—should have done—to me, I reached a threshold where the pulsing between my legs grew stronger. I willed the throbbing to stop, but without a working brain, my body ran amok. If I entertained one more erotic notion, I'd convulse.

At home, I quickened my pace to the bathroom where I splashed cold water on my face to jolt me out of this romantic fantasy. The medicine cabinet mirror reflected the conflicted woman I had become. Where was my moral compass? Stolen by Lucifer's butler named Lust who hungered for my virtue.

All I wanted was for Fitz to slather me with sexual attention. Every inch of skin needed caressing, tasting, exploring with his fingers and tongue. I craved to have him go down on me and lay claim to the safeguarded jewel God created for my sexual enjoyment. That fleshy nub cried out for his fingers to fondle it, his tongue to stroke it, his lips to nibble and suck it any way imaginable.

My version of lust sped in one direction and I enjoyed the ride. But I had a relentless brain that had been screaming at me all night that Fitz belonged to Coral.

Coming to grips with that reality, I heard the doorbell ring. It was three-fifteen a.m. I smoothed my hand over my skirt out of nervousness and cautiously approached the foyer lit only by the full moon's radiance streaming in the glass-shelved windows on either side of the front door. I strained my neck to peek through one of the narrow windows. Lo-and-behold. There, in all his unholy glory stood, not the devil's butler, but Lucifer himself.

Fitz.

Chapter Twenty-Four

I **threw open the door.** Unlocking the screen, I grabbed Fitz's jacket collar with both hands and dragged him into the house with my lips claiming his and vice versa.

Morality be damned! Sorry Coral. I can't help myself.

Without a word, he pushed me against the foyer wall and kissed me with the same fervor I visualized on my way home. My leg raised to sidle up his. He grabbed it with strong fingers in his desire to bring it higher. Then he slipped his hand beneath the hem of my skirt and up the contour of my outer thigh. The garter belt stopped him, but two shakes later, his palm moved over it, across, down, and under. Beneath the obstacle, he found warmth where warmth should always be in times like this.

Breaking the kiss, Fitz swept me into his arms. Wanting more of his lips, I recaptured them, biting and sucking as he carried me to the living room where he flung me on the couch. I drew myself up and reached to keep him in my grasp, but he grabbed both my wrists and shoved them and me back down. Keeping my hands secure, he straddled my torso and wedged one knee into the crease where the cushion met the couch back. He leaned over me, keeping his head close to my mouth without making contact. To gain traction, I raised my knees behind his back and kept them there.

"By your actions, Riley, it seems as if you want me to fuck you." His words rolled off his lips and onto my body with pinpoint precision. I nodded with enthusiasm. "So, I am not misinterpreting what I see," he hissed with primal need. He bound my wrists within his hands. "Let me hear you say it." His voice was urgent, he recognized the crazed look in my eyes that begged for him to take me. "Tell me how much you want to scream in pure ecstasy when I plunge my cock into your pretty, wet pussy." His grasp tightened on my wrists.

His vulgarity taunted me. Excited me. Aroused me. I tried to free myself so I could tear the clothes off his body. I never knew this raunchy side of me existed, but I liked it! I could not get enough air in, and I could not blow enough air out as I matched his hunger. All this body heat morphed me into a beast whose sexual desire drove me into a crazed frenzy.

"Yes!" I screamed. I arched my back as best I could with his weight bearing down on me and closed my eyes. "I want you to fuck my brains out, Fitz! Now! Do it now! Rip off my panties and thrust your cock in me! Fuck me, Fitz! Fuck me good and hard!"

Who am I?!

Certainly not subtle old Riley. Not the woman who tried to keep her foul language inside her mind, and most definitely not begging a man to fuck her!

His lips crushed mine. With nimble fingers he reached beneath my skirt and entered the underside of my panties. A slight movement to the left and he found my gateway to Heaven ready for him.

I gasped when he raised his body to yank my underwear down. He found resistance from the garters holding up my stockings. Never hesitating, he reached higher to the garter belt, unzipped the side zipper, and pulled the belt, stockings, and panties down over my knees. In his haste to remove the interfering underthings, he only drew them over one foot and left the rest jumbled around my other ankle. Then he stopped.

"Well, I'll be damned." He ran his fingers lightly through my pubic hair.

"What?" My voice was raspy at the interruption.

"You're a true redhead."

"What did you expect? That I dyed my hair this color? Now, shut up and put your attention where it belongs, Fitz!'

He spread my legs farther apart. On his knees, he unbuckled his belt, unzipped his pants, and pulled his underwear flap apart to release the rock-hard serpent.

Shoving my skirt higher, he grabbed my hips and raised them to the correct angle for entry and drove deep inside me. It all happened so fast, I let loose an electrifying cry at the enormity of his member. His hold on my hips kept me steady as he set the pace.

My lungs strained with every breath as I pawed at his jacket, taking handfuls to keep me anchored and available. When he pushed forward, I shoved my hips stronger against him to receive his bulk. With every thrust, both of us groaned louder until the whole room filled with primordial cries of unhinged, sexual mania.

Lightning fast, Fitz pulled out, and with one more ferocious grunt, he spilled his seed over the front of my knitted garment.

Damn, this is my favorite sweater!

Fitz rolled off me and went into the kitchen where he turned on the faucet. When he came back, he held a wet cloth and gently pressed it against my swollen vaginal lips. The warmth of the soft terrycloth soothed the irritated flesh. The relief it provided made me close my eyes and savor the comforting display of attention. He then moved up to my sweater and wiped his semen off as best he could. Only then did he rub the sticky fluid off his member. As ferocious a lover as he was, this act proved gentle, sweet, not at all what I expected.

He had time for one more sexual tryst with me, but not on the couch. Slipping my lingerie off my other foot, he helped me to my feet, and hand in hand we went upstairs to my bedroom.

Once there, he stood me against the bed and took his time in removing what clothes remained on my body. The sweater came first. Skilled hands unfastened the pearl buttons, slipped the knitted garment off my shoulders, and let it drop. That left my breasts trapped in a bra that lifted and separated. Red splotches indicative of my heightened libido covered the plump swells.

Moving his hands around to my back, he captured the bra hooks within his fingers. One by one, he freed them, then slipped a finger under each strap and lightly drew the bra off my arms and tossed it on the floor.

My breasts are bare. In front of Fitz. Oh, my God. What? I just fucked the man. It's too late to be timid about exposing my body.

My anticipation grew. The only thing I needed from him to help me get through these next few minutes was his mouth upon mine. His lips were the receptacle by which I would draw strength, so I leaned in for that comforting kiss. He stepped back, not allowing my touch. His action baffled me. The steamy look in his eyes stayed the same, but his moving away concerned me.

"Not so fast," he whispered when cupping my cheek with a warm palm. I closed my eyes and let my head fall into the light embrace of his hand. "Patience is a virtue, and I am one virtuous son-of-a-bitch," he cooed. "I am going to work you until you are putty in my hands." He leaned down and put his lips over my rock-hard nipple, covering it with the cavern of his mouth. The tenderness he displayed in savoring its shape and firmness allowed a swell of quivers to escalate from my chin to my knees.

Now for my turn. With my focus on removing his shirt, I reached for the top button, but he clasped my wrists and placed them to my side. He kept his softened gaze on my surprised eyes then pressed one finger to my lips. It became clear I was not in control.

Unzipping my skirt, he thumbed the elastic waistband of my slip and glided both pieces of clothing to the floor in a puddle around my feet. I now stood buck naked except for the flushed patches on my skin unmasking my wanton desire. It was wrong, but I needed this right now, with Fitz.

Our movements were slow, deliberate. I kept a level head, but not so level a heartbeat. It raced again and I couldn't slow it. My loins pulsed, and my brain cells ignited, creating new and vivid images of scenarios I had never imagined before.

Every move he made going forward was erotic. Demanding my unwavering attention, he kept an eye-lock with me when picking up where I left off on removing his shirt, except he started from the bottom up.

Using two skillful fingers, he pushed the bottom button through its hole with precision. Then on to the second. Reaching out, he cupped my chin and leaned in as if to kiss me. I closed my eyes to receive the caress, but then he let go of me. When I raised my lids, he slid his tongue over his top lip and smiled a wicked smile before slipping the round button through its threaded counterpart. Number three, four, and five came next, leaving number six as the final act. This teasing game was as erotic as hell. My vagina screamed for mercy.

My eyes clung to his every move. He reached up to attend button number six. Heightening the effort, he stopped then shoved it through. With his task complete, he left his shirt draped open and stood staring at me as if he expected me to do something. I didn't know what *he* wanted, but *I* wanted to rip the garment right off his fucking body!

Trembling with anticipation, I drew toward him to finish the task. He clasped my wrists, but this time, held them in front of me. He bore into my gaze as he lowered my hands to my side. Parting his shirt, he pulled it off. Slowly. Lustfully. One sleeve at a time and tossed it next to the clothes laying on the floor.

Holy hell, what a performance.

Crossing his arms, he grasped the bottom of his T-shirt and drew it up to reveal chiseled muscles no doubt fashioned by extensive workouts. When raising it higher and over his head, he uncovered the sharp design of his shapely and impressive chest. Smooth and well-defined pectorals glistened in the light of the only illuminated lamp.

Now came the removal of his pants. This act received as sensual a disposal as the previous pieces of his clothing. Still focusing on my face and the rosy glow beaming over it, he slipped thumbs beneath the band of his pants and elastic of his underwear. Together, he slid them down, revealing a swollen cock-a-doodle-doo, ready to crow at the slightest touch. Soft, dark hair blanketed powerful thighs and well-developed calves. What hair he lacked on his chest, he made up for on his legs and around his balls. With his pants off, he tossed them aside, adding another element to the existing heap on the floor.

My God, he was gorgeous as he stood naked in front of me. My eyes returned to his straight, super-charged phallus that stood erect and at full attention. I felt compelled to salute.

Not even the true Adonis could lay claim to this many heavenly parts on one male body.

Chapter Twenty-Five

Fitz manipulated me with his eroticism. I could have climaxed without so much as him touching my crown jewel or getting near its hollow companion. But what fun would that be? My female God had gifted this man a hotness to the Nth degree, and Fitz knew how to wield it.

I stood before him in my birthday suit, anticipating my coming together with fever high and will-power low. After lifting me in his powerful arms, he sprawled me out on the bedspread then straddled me. Our eyes locked; his were a deep blue filled with hot passion; mine were wide and wanting, the color of lust, whatever color that was. He cupped my breasts with his thumbs traipsing over my nipples while his mouth occupied mine in potent kisses. He was extra careful to caress my lips with care so as not to broaden the pain from overzealous teeth.

Without breaking the kiss, Fitz smoothed his hand down my abdomen to my thighs where he then pushed them apart. As he captured the crux of my womanhood, I drew in breath and grabbed my hair, yanking on my locks when advancing to the plateau on a sexual plane.

With my being in a state of arousal, the blood filled every nook and cranny of my head, causing it to feel twice its size from the rising power of the intense orgasm. It took only seconds for my final shriek to pierce the room when Fitz brought me to relief. Once he did, he slipped inside me. Each thrust topped the one before as he buried himself in the slick cavity. My legs wrapped around his torso like a vice. I crossed my ankles and clung to his back as the ride continued. Animalistic groans left his mouth as his crescendo escalated.

Before reaching his climax, he pulled out. With one last strained moan, he again rested his manhood on my stomach where the orgasm concluded. Immobile for a moment, he then lowered himself on top of me where we lay frozen, except for deep breaths.

My wish to experience shameless sex came true. Fitz enlisted the senses that brought about a glorious, proper, and utter ravaging of my body, inside and out.

Fitz, too, had his wish granted; I became putty in his hands.

Fitz and I lay in bed together, his leg resting over mine. When admiring his physique—over and over again—I noticed a small brown tattoo on the upper part of his shoulder. His eyes remained closed in sleep. In that moment of silence, I softly traced what resembled a crescent moon with a star poised above it.

No sooner had I done that, I ran my fingers lightly up and down the peaks and valleys of the exquisite muscles in his upper arm until he stirred. Barely opening his eyes, he saw me relaxed, and my face bearing a brilliant look of contentment.

He reached over to gingerly brush across my lips with his index finger. "What's that smile for?"

"I'm happy, that's all," I whispered. "Truly happy."

"And what is making you so happy, Riley?" he muttered.

Triggered by the romantic interludes, my face, neck, and ears warmed as an involuntary blush arrested me. I lowered my eyes. "You," I confessed. "Being here with you is making me happy."

He reached his hand to the back of my head and drew it forward for a brief kiss. "As much as I hate to, baby cakes," he removed his leg from over mine and rolled out of bed, "I have to go."

I turned on my side and furrowed my brows. "Baby cakes?"

He threw the blanket onto the floor, baring my naked body. He did not allow me time to utter one word before he thrust one hand into the tangled locks on my head. Grabbing a fistful of hair, he kissed me while rubbing my bottom as if a genie would appear and grant him three wishes. "Yeah," he uttered, rubbing my behind, "soft as a baby's butt."

I didn't expect that but received the act, and concept, with the spirit in which he meant it. Licking my lips to gather the very last drop of how he tasted, I lowered my tone. "Why can't you stay?" I whimpered.

He looked at me sideways with a raised brow and sly expression. "I have a wife, remember?"

His statement brought all those whoring beliefs back to plunder my mind. What he said threw me into a fit of self-condemnation. I supposed I was no better than Mayzelle.

Damn it! But what does that make him? A man-whore? Yes, and a very good one at that.

"Won't Coral wonder where you've been all this time?" I asked.

He drew his foot through a pant leg. "No. Not as long as I come home."

"By your own admission of the pact you and she have, don't you have to confess your whereabouts?"

"If she asks, I'll tell her I was with another woman. She doesn't ask questions, and I don't offer information."

What an odd relationship these people have. No secrets, and no kiss and tell. Un-fucking-believable! And here I am, right smack dab in the middle of it. How many women does he have on the side? Does

*Coral know about all of them...any of them...me? Was Fitz **that** good sexually to have multiple affairs?*

My one-time fling revealed an unquestionable, yes. Was I delusional? Perhaps. Did I care? Not anymore.

I stepped aside from the absurdity of his way of life and watched him dress. "Fitz, where did you come up with the idea for your tattoo?"

He shot me an inquiring glance. "I don't have a tattoo, Riley."

"Yes, you do, silly," I grinned at what I considered playful banter, "the one on your shoulder that looks like a celestial night scene."

"A what?"

I sprung out of bed and stood before him. His pants were on and he was about to slip his t-shirt over his head when I stopped him. "This one," I whispered, then gazed up at his handsome face peppered with a five o'clock shadow that looked more like coffee grounds than whiskers.

He stepped back to finish putting on his undergarment then slipped on his shirt and buttoned it. "That's not a tattoo, it's a birthmark."

His socks went on next. "My father has one almost exactly like it," one shoe went on and he tied the laces, "as does every man in my family on my father's side. It may be in a different place, but the shapes and color are similar." He affixed the other shoe.

"Hmm," I crossed my arms over my breasts, "interesting. You've shared nothing with me about your family. Perhaps one of these nights, you can fill me in."

Shrouded in layers that masked his perfect body, he uncrossed my arms and cupped one of my breasts. "Maybe." He licked the areola and blew air on it. This act made me close my eyes and shiver in his hands. "But for now..."

Fitz captured a protruding tip on a fleshy swell and lightly bit down until I arched into him. When I did, he flicked his tongue over it, causing me to utter a guttural version of his name.

Backing away, he left me hanging in sexual limbo. "I have to go," he said with a smirk on his gorgeous lips.

As if shocked by a cattle prod, I lurched when coming out of the intoxicating splendor of his touch. "What! You're leaving me like…this?!" I crossed my legs while standing there to prevent any building lubrication droplets from dribbling down my inner thigh.

He laughed. "You'll survive." Turning on a dime, he grabbed my hair again and pulled my head back. Nose to nose, he gazed into my eyes with a wanton lust. "I'm leaving you with," he grabbed my hand and pressed it against his loins, revealing a firm bulge in his pants, "how much you make me want to stay. But if I have to leave this way," he thrust his fingers into my hollowed grounds, "then so do you." Before he removed his hand, he kissed me with deep purpose. "See you later, baby cakes." He reached around and gave me a quick spank on my butt.

I wanted to break every one of those fingers he used to throw me off a sexual cliff. Instead, I threw on my peignoir robe—useless in covering anything—and walked him to the front door. Bidding him goodnight, I kissed him one more time, then closed the door.

Through the side window, I watched as he walked down the front porch steps. When reaching the sidewalk, he turned back and saw me peering out the window, whereby he saluted before disappearing down the sidewalk.

Hold on a minute. Where is he going, and where the hell is his car? How odd.

My coffee tasted ten-thousand times better, even though I drank it sitting at the breakfast table very much alone. Fitz had left my house around a quarter to four this morning. I hadn't wanted him to go, but both of us knew he would. Coral expected him home every night. Though not considered *night* anymore, the darkness counted. Their whole arrangement of sleeping around still confounded me but eased the guilt I once harbored when contemplating—and having—sex with him.

Waiting for Meredith to bring Kat home, I rationalized my recent behavior. Once upon a time, my extramarital involvement with Fitz put me in the same category as Mayzelle—cheater, cheater, pumpkin eater. Now, the circumstances were different.

Of course, they are.

My acting out a fantasy fling with Fitz was a onetime thing, not an all-out affair like what Mayzelle had with my husband. As a result, my soul was clear.

Chapter Twenty-Six

*M*onday morning brought a sense of trepidation. Did Coral ask any questions? Did Fitz confess anything about his and my romantic interlude? If he did, would it matter to his wife? It mattered to me that I slept with my boss's husband. Surely, in anyone's book, that is not a good thing—morally or career-wise. I believed that could result in her firing me.

Seated at my desk and working on a supply order, I received a buzz from Coral to join her in her office. Her tone seemed tense, making me nervous. I feared sweating bullets would do no good, but a handgun with bullets in it might be a useful weapon for Coral to use on me. I knocked on her door and she called for me to enter.

"Riley, please sit down." Coral waved me to take a seat in a chair opposite hers. She remained seated at her desk where a plain mustard colored clasp-envelope lay on top.

By her lax yet unwelcoming body language and voice devoid of emotion, I sensed trouble. "You seem upset, Coral. Is something wrong?" I feared the answer.

Only then did she stand. But instead of facing me, she stood with crossed arms and looked through the open, wooden blinds covering the window. "There could be," her tone turned authoritative, "and it concerns you and my husband."

Oh, dear God. Here it comes.

I pictured myself blindfolded and tied to a pole in front of a firing squad, except this "squad" consisted of only one person—Coral Kingston. My courage waned but pressing my knees together and sitting up straighter helped compose it. "What about us?"

She didn't move. "I meant to join all of you last night at the bar."

"Yes, it disappointed us when you didn't show up."

"I appreciate that, but there was a specific reason I never made it." She turned toward me but continued to stand with her arms in the same position as if putting a protective barrier between us. "How well do you know my husband, Riley?"

Crossing my legs seemed a casual gesture as I prepared to whip out a bold-faced lie. "Not very."

"You didn't know he's the president of a financial institution here in town?"

Wait, what? He's not solely the proprietor of a bar?

I visualized him sitting behind an ornate desk stacked with a mountain of hundred-dollar bills. It calmed me in one way but excited me in another. I would love having sex with him under all that dough.

"No," I tried not to give myself away, "I had no idea."

She slowly nodded her head, which did not help me determine if she believed me.

Coral placed her hand on the back of her chair. "You are an intelligent woman, Riley, and an attractive one, too. I imagine, since you and your husband have separated, your nights are lonely, and you have found solace in the arms of another man."

Did my heart skip several beats?

In twisting the truth, I squared my shoulders and raised my chin to prepare for the first bullet. "To be honest, I haven't dated since Sherman and I split up." Lying to her was difficult, but necessary.

She cocked her head. "You haven't? There has not been even one gentleman who has caught your eye?"

I raised my brows without blinking, pressed my lips together into a tiny slit of a mouth, and slowly shook my head.

Can she sense the fingers of fear wrap around my throat, squeezing off my air supply?

She returned to her seat and interlaced her fingers atop the envelope. "There is a subject I'd like to discuss with you," she began, "and if you feel uncomfortable, we'll stop and go our separate ways."

Separate ways? Jesus, please make Coral stop torturing me and move on to the execution.

Though falling apart inside, I appeared unruffled. "Of course, Coral. I'm all ears."

"I've been watching you lately and have discovered something disconcerting." She picked up the clasped envelope and unwound the crisscrossed string from the two circles, extracting a large photograph and staring at the print.

What was she looking at? My guilt made me forget to blink, swallow, or breathe. Had Coral hired a private investigator and had evidence of Fitz and me in a compromising position at the bar perhaps?

Coral hurry and accuse me of sleeping with your husband. I won't deny it. Then you can use those designer alligator pumps to kick me in the ass all the way to the unemployment line.

She replaced the picture in the envelope. Without looking at me, she slid the envelope across to my side of the tabletop using two fingertips.

"Would you mind looking at that picture?" she asked without reservation. "I would love to hear what you have to say about it."

Perspiration coated my armpits. My hands trembled when staring at the object. Before touching it, I dragged my open palm down my thigh to allow the dress material to blot away the accumulated moisture.

I drew the photograph out while focusing on Coral. Only when she nodded and lifted both brows in urging me to view the black-and-white image, did I dare lower my eyes.

My breath caught when seeing the picture. It was not of Fitz and me, but of a striking female model posing in an exquisite tailored Christian Dior day-dress like the style Jackie Kennedy would wear. Stupefied, I peeled my eyes off the photo to see Coral sitting anxiously, waiting for me to say something.

"You're shocked, aren't you?" she asked. "I wasn't sure how to approach you with this, so I tackled it with a visual aid." Coral's expression lost its severe features and her attitude softened to a thoughtful one.

Rising from her chair, she rounded the desk to lean up against the front of it, facing me. "Riley, dear, you need to move forward and try to find yourself, and to do that, there are certain things I can suggest. For instance," she leaned toward me, focused on my hair and smoothed it with her hand. "If you change your hairstyle," she then lifted my chin, "choose a different shade of lipstick, and," she straightened her posture and gave me a once-over, "update your wardrobe, you might discover how much more appealing you would be to the opposite sex."

I sat stunned at my boss's statement. *This* is what she wanted to talk about? My image? Without intending to, I broke out laughing and couldn't stop. I swear, tears ran down my cheeks before I got ahold of myself.

"Riley," Coral's brows narrowed at my outburst, "does your reaction mean, 'Oh, Coral, you silly woman, there's not a chance in…well, you know where…that I would consider such a thing,' or is it, 'Oh, Coral, what a great idea, and I can't wait to try this'?"

She had to give me a minute to reorganize my thoughts and reduce the tension in my chest that nearly gave me a heart attack. "It's the second one, Coral, and I agree that I might have let myself go a little." I hadn't, but if she wanted to consider me slovenly, I'd let her. Whatever made her happy, made me happy, too.

She clapped her hands. "Wonderful!" Her demeanor changed to one of excitement at her own relief. "I had worked myself into a dither worrying how you'd receive this. I even sought the advice from one of my friends," she pointed to the picture, "who happens to be the model in the picture there, on how to address this with you. That's where I was last night."

She heavily breathed out and wiped her fingers across her forehead. "I am *so* relieved. Now," her tone turned serious, "to my husband. In his position as president, he travels in an elite circle. There are several men in that fraternity of upper-crusts that would love an opportunity to take you on a date, but for that to happen, you need to look less cube," she hesitated and raised a brow, "and more hip." The sparkle in her eyes gave away how much she enjoyed this. "I hope you don't mind my candor."

The wind was back in my sails, lifting my spirits and forging me full speed ahead. "Not at all, Coral, not at all. Since you're good at this kind of thing, do you have any suggestions how I go about this transformation?"

"I do indeed, my dear. I have two girlfriends who would love to get their hands on you. They can be persnickety, but their sense of style is impeccable. Would you be up for a make-over day filled with shopping and beauty treatments?"

I stared back at her with a smirk on my face and bobbed my head up and down like a dancing hula girl dashboard doll.

The next weekend, Meredith babysat Kat while I shopped with Coral and her two sidekicks who had many ideas on how to create a swan out of, I guess what they considered an ugly duckling.

We stopped first at an exclusive salon where they told the hairdresser I wanted a style that embodied the 1960 symbolic representation of social change—whatever that meant. My Marilyn Monroe curls were out, replaced by the high-towering beehive with soft, curled tendrils cascading down the side of my face. With all the teasing involved, it looked more like a rat's nest than where bees lived, but overall, it wasn't so bad. On the plus side, I appeared taller.

Next came a boutique where I purchased two tailored suits that reflected the new skirt style of just-above-the-knee hemline. Knees were the ugliest part of a woman's leg, so why would anyone want to see them; not me, but I had no choice. There were three eagles with their eyes on me who plunged me into 1960 knees first.

Our last stop was the cosmetic counter. I kept my winged liner, but this new age of the gentlewoman demanded more. Lashes now received an abundant amount of mascara on upper and lowers; lids celebrated a new pastel palette of eyeshadow; and lips vanquished the red in exchange for a pale shade of lipstick—even lilac! By the time they finished with me, I had no idea who stared back in the mirror.

It had better be worth the outrageous amount I spent for my new look. Thank goodness I had my checkbook. The amount of cash in my purse was nowhere near enough to cover the cost. With a sigh, I gathered my shopping bags and went home.

When recalling myself all dolled up in gorgeous dresses, the way my hair looked all sexy in its giant poof, and the soft-dazzled softness of my face, this excursion wasn't a waste of time after all.

Watch out world. Foxy Riley is on the move!

Chapter Twenty-Seven

he newly improved Riley O'Keefe made a splash with the office. No one could keep their eyes off me—especially Brendon—when Coral paraded me around the inner office like a prized tiger with top billing in the circus. My hair did not look as bee-hivey, but poufy enough. The new couture style of the violet colored A-line dress made me feel chic and elegant. I had to admit, I liked it.

Fitz had the most difficulty with the enriched me. He came into the office to take his wife out for lunch and almost tripped over his feet at seeing me behind my desk.

"Excuse me," he mocked, "does Riley O'Keefe still work here?"

I followed his lead. "She did but went missing when little green women from outer space snatched her and changed her appearance."

"Well, all I have to say about that is," he whistled a catcall. "Stand up and let me get the full-body view."

With the warmth of a blush rising, I rose and strutted around my desk. Stopping in front of him, I glanced at the connecting door to make sure no one was there, then placed one hand on my hip, one behind my head and struck a pose.

"Turn around, slowly." He gave the impression of a lion assessing his prey before devouring it. "Mm, mm, mm," he murmured, "this is something I could get used to."

I returned to my desk. "Don't. You and I will not be *that* friendly again."

He leaned his elbows on the desk's glass shelf as he raised one eyebrow and glowered at me. The look he gave me made me nervous.

"What are you doing?" I asked.

"I'm imagining what the lingerie underneath looks like, so I'm undressing you with my eyes to get a glimpse of those firm and supple—"

At that moment, Coral walked through the door. "Oh, good, you're here, sugar," she greeted Fitz.

Saved by the wife!

To cover for my discomfort, he came to my rescue. "I was admiring your new Office Manager."

Coral's grin widened with the statement. "She *is* stunning, isn't she? Now it's your turn to fulfill your end of the bargain, Fitz, and fix her up with one of those wealthy friends of yours. Not the stuffy ones, mind you. Someone who will show her off and treat her like the proper lady she is. Okay, we've talked enough, let's go. I'm as hungry as a tigress on a vegetarian diet."

Coral looped her arm through her husband's, and as they walked together out the office door, Fitz discreetly glanced over his shoulder and winked at me.

Later that week, Coral called me into her office and announced Fitz had arranged a blind date for me with his mortgage processor.

I took on the role of a naïve, jilted wife. "Coral, why do you think it is all right for me to date while I am still legally married?"

Her answer explained the question I neglected to ask about a statement she made a long time ago. "Remember my telling you on your first day here that I have an unconventional way of thinking concerning the mental and physical actions in my life?" she asked.

"It was a curious statement, so yes, I remember it well."

She rose from her desk and walked around to lean against it. "I was referring to extramarital affairs."

Did she just see the blood drain from my face?

"Don't look so astounded, Riley," she reached down and rested her hand on mine. "I consider affairs as lessons. I've had two or three of my own and know Fitz has had many." She then sat in the chair beside me, gracefully crossed her legs and twisted to face me head on. "He and I both consider them a constructive way of maintaining a healthy and sexually stimulating marriage." She softened her expression and gently placed her hand on my shoulder. "This may surprise you, but Fitz has told me he added you to his list of bedded women."

Holy shit! Now my brain cells are escaping. What's next?

At her disclosure, the blood in my veins instantly turned to ice, causing chills to prickle the entirety of my body. I had to urge my heart to keep beating so I wouldn't fold over and faint dead away on the floor.

"Um, I, uh, I mean, he and I, uh…" Not a single sentence came out of my mouth.

By hearing me stumble over my words and watching my eyes nearly pop out of my head, she recognized panic when she saw it. "Don't fret, dear," she beseeched, "I don't mind. In fact, he has picked up on your softer mannerisms that have taught him to be a more compassionate lover, and for that, I thank you. To be honest, Fitz and I are quite…rough with each other from time to time, and you bring out a different side to him that I'm finding quite enjoyable."

Oh, my God…oh, my God…oh, my, God!

Coral thanked me for having slept with her husband. I had no idea what she meant when saying her husband learned from me. What the hell could *I* teach a man like Fitz. What planet did Coral and Fitz hail from because this was *not* how life worked on Planet Earth!

"Anyway," Coral took my clammy hands in hers, "getting back to your dating. If the roles were reversed and one of Sherman's friends set him up, you can bet your bottom dollar he'd go."

Come in for a landing, Riley. Breathe.

"Uh, yes, knowing what I know about him now, I suppose he would." I skirted that conversation and moved in a different direction. "So, what's this mortgage processor's name and when will he contact me?" I asked with a newly formed interest.

Coral shrugged in releasing my hands and rose from the guest chair to start back to her own. "I didn't think to ask Fitz about the man's name, so let's call him," she stopped in her tracks as her lips turned up, "Yahooty."

Sweeping by the edge of her desk, her movements displayed elegance like the poised goddess she constantly portrayed. "It's up to you to discover his identity Riley. But anyway," she picked up a pencil and lightly tapped it against her palm a few times, "Yahooty will pick you up on Friday at eight o'clock and take you to the country club for dinner. Oh," she opened her lap drawer and carefully placed the pencil in its proper slot, "and something else," she offered as an afterthought, "Fitz made me promise to deliver his instructions."

At that, I lowered my brows and smirked. "What kind of instructions?"

"It's ridiculous really," she sat in the comfortable black desk chair and looked at the wall while scrunching her eyes, "Now, let me see if I can remember correctly." Nodding, she smiled. "He wants you to end the date if it's not panning out for you. You are to tell Yahooty that your stomach is queasy, and you need to go home," she waved her hand, "or some such nonsense. But honestly, dear, you don't need prompting by anyone on how to get out of an uncomfortable situation."

I could use that someone right now!

Forget Coral's acceptance of my having a romantic romp with her husband, the rest of this verbal exchange seemed as wacky. I didn't know my date's real name; he was not going to call before showing up at my house; and I had an escape plan if things didn't go well. Life was about to get interesting.

Friday night came, and by nine-thirty p.m., my date had ended, and I sat tucked alone at home. The excuse I gave Yahooty—not worth remembering his real name—came during our meal. It seemed the food I ate was too rich for my stomach, and if he didn't want to see my dinner in a different form, he should drive me home. He most definitely got the message and paid the bill.

While walking me to my door, he invited me out again. To back up my earlier claim, I grabbed my stomach and acted as if I was going to hurl on his shoes. After that, he hastened down the road and disappeared from my dating card.

Thirty minutes later, I donned my pastel pink baby doll pajamas. Planted in front of the television set with a glass of wine in my hand, I was ready to watch a police drama that would bore me to the brink of falling asleep.

The show did the trick. An hour and a half later, I woke to the Indian-head test pattern that came on after the channel went off the air. I turned off the TV, swallowed down the remaining wine and started upstairs to call it a very wasted night.

Halfway up the stairs, I heard a faint knock on the screen door. Carefully creeping back down each step, I steadied myself on the last one and peeked around the wall to see out the front door's side window. My porch light was off, but the existing moonlight allowed me to make out the silhouette of a man.

Oh, please don't let it be Yahooty coming back to check on me.

If I stayed quiet, the person would go away. Another knock sounded followed by the person softly calling out my name. Cushioned petals of disquiet gave way to needles of irritation when it hit me who stood on my doorstep.

I descended the last four stairs of the landing, flipped on the porch light, and opened the door but kept the screen locked. Illuminated in the faint glow of the single lightbulb, stood the statuesque form I knew so well. Summer nights allowed him to wear a white, crisp shirt rolled up to mid-arm, and casual slacks creased to perfection. Suede lace-up oxfords costing more than what I made in a month, provided a soft cover for his feet. All these images flashed before my eyes in seconds.

But then, my attention flew to his face. Cobalt blue eyes smiled sheepishly as did the curve of his kissable mouth as if harboring a secret. There was a secret, and his hands hid it behind his back.

My curiosity got the best of me. "Fitz, why are you showing up at my house now? Are you aware of the time?"

At my question, he smirked. "I know exactly what time it is, but that doesn't matter right now. What *does* matter is that I brought you something to make your tummy better." With his announcement, he grinned from ear to ear and brought that *something* around so I could see it. "Voilà! Chicken soup."

My God. Even holding food, he was as sexy as hell, but I held my ground. "Why would you do that?" I blurted.

He raised his shoulders in nonchalance. "Because a little bird said you were in poor health."

"Who told you I was sick?"

"Your date."

"My date!" I pressed my hand to my chest with fingers splayed as my eyes nearly flew out of my head. "When did you talk to my date?"

He looked at his watch. "Oh, about an hour ago."

Forgetting I practically had nothing on, I thrust my hands on my hips and cocked my head. "You are a crazy person, Fitz. And not only that, you know darned well I'm not out of sorts." I pointed an accusing finger at him. "It was your idea to tell him this cock-and-bull story if I didn't like him."

His grin expanded. "So, he wasn't your cup of tea?"

"Not my cup of tea or anything else for that matter. Why would you set me up with an egotistical jerk like that in the first place? I thought you liked me."

His tone turned sly…and dangerous. "Have you forgotten how much I like you? If you let me in, I can rekindle your memory."

"Go home, Fitz," I sternly told him. *No, Fitz, please stay.* "Take your soup and get back in your car." I glanced over his shoulder and only saw Bluebell. "Where *is* your car?"

He pointed his thumb over his shoulder. "I don't want to tarnish your impeccable reputation, so I parked it around the corner."

"Thank you at least for that, but having you standing at my door does not appear proper should someone drive by and see us talking like this."

"You are absolutely correct. That's why you need to let me in. You shouldn't have to explain why you were talking to a man through a screen door, wearing nothing more than your PJ's. Besides, the soup is getting cold."

A growl rumbled up my throat as I unlocked the screen and stood to the side. Glancing over his shoulder to make sure no one was watching, he opened the screen and closed both doors behind him.

Before moving any further, I thrust my index finger at the floor in front of him. "You wait right there, mister," I demanded. I ran up the stairs and into my bedroom where I yanked the sheer robe of a peignoir set off its hanger and wrapped it around me.

Watching me come down the last four steps, Fitz grinned, but then wiped the lascivious gaze away. "That's so much better, Riley," he mocked approvingly. "I can't see a thing now."

I pulled the two sides of the robe tighter to bring the opening closer together. "You are such a comedian, Fitz." To protect my breasts from his penetrating glare, I crossed my arms. "Now, what type of soup did you say that was?"

His satisfied expression returned. "Chicken with vegetables and noodles. There's enough for two if you want to share."

"Fine," I harshly replied and began walking to the kitchen, "I'll get us each a bowl." Then I abruptly stopped as did he. Turning around, I made a point very clear. "But there will be no monkey business, do you understand?" I insisted.

He fingered an "X" over his chest. "Cross my heart and hope to die, stick a needle in my eye."

I avoided the urge to laugh and kept my staunch air. "Okay, then, come on."

The soup had no taste, but the company made my mouth water. The way he sipped the soup off his spoon sent my stomach into a frenzy of butterfly flutters. When he dabbed his lips—those tempting lips, beckoning lips—with a napkin, it made me crave to be that piece of cloth. I had no taste for anything but the man sitting across from me.

When our bowls were empty, Fitz washed and dried them, after which I opened the cabinet to place them on the shelf. Reaching up with my back to him, I felt two arms encircle my waist. I remained strong until teeth touched the flesh of my neck and tenderly started to nibble.

"Fitz," I reprimanded, "that constitutes monkey business, so remove your arms and lips this minute!" *No, keep doing what you're doing and never stop!* He must have overheard my silent plea because he did not stop, but instead started licking as if savoring me. "Fitz!" I spoke louder and with more intensity. "Stop that!" It became impossible to stay strong, and by his front pressing into my backside, something else amazingly hard pressed up against me. "What are you doing?!"

His throat rumbled as he moved to my earlobe while caressing my shoulders with skillful hands. "I'm having dessert, and you, my dear, are delectable."

When it came to Fitz, my emotions lay as bare as how I wanted our bodies to be. At his touch, my skin goose bumped, and my brain froze, numbing any modicum of morality I had left. The more I stood helpless to his charms, the more he took advantage of that weakness.

Concentrating on his desire to taste my neck, I felt his hands glide from my shoulders. Fingers pressed alongside my waist, over my hips, across my belly and down to my—

Holy crap! There are too many monkeys doing business in this jungle!

The solid weight of his body pinned me against the countertop, preventing me from shoving his hand away. At the firmness of his penis poking me in the back, I felt my heart soar knowing I turned him on that much for him to be *that* hard.

This had to stop before I lost control and gave in to my own sexual desire that loomed inside my brain and between my legs. There was only one way to get me out of this precarious position. I wiggled until turning around in his arms which ended up being a huge mistake. *No, not really.* The action brought his hands back to his side but left me nose to nose with him. The way he looked at me penetrated my soul with enough power to make my knees wobble, but I needed to resist this man's advances. *No, I didn't.*

He placed his hands on the edge of the counter with me trapped between them. My heart beat itself silly. My body quivered with his being this close. My chest deeply rose and fell. I felt the rise of heat to my cheeks from a rush of sexual desire. There was little doubt about the lustful craving I displayed. In the forefront of my mind, I wanted him to lavish me with the banquet offerings I rightfully deserved.

His sizable hand, powerful yet soft as if never doing a lick of manual labor, cupped the side of my cheek. I closed my eyes and swayed. Covering one butt cheek with the expanse of his other *monkey paw*, he pulled me closer, allowing his erection to press into my stomach. The entirety of my resistance surrendered in allowing my head to fall back and expose tender flesh.

Accepting my abdication, he placed his lips at the top of my ear. With the tip of his tongue, he leisurely traced along the inner curve of it, massaging the high and low points seductively.

Oh, he is good.

He knew exactly how to strip me without removing one piece of clothing from my body. What little I wore would soon find a place on the floor somewhere in this house.

Falling into the lap of external seduction, I stretched back to grant him more options. As an expert in using his mouth to cajole and manipulate, he scorched the flesh of my jawline like smoldering embers awakening to a breeze.

*Oh yes, he is **that** good.*

I placed my hands on the countertop for support as his lips moved up to the tickle spot under my ear that kindled heat against my skin. His mouth captured mine. The animal in me came alive, and I threw my arms around him, digging my nails into his back. With urgency building, our kiss intensified. His hands wandered once again, making my mind sluggish and libido ferocious.

His hand drifted between my legs and stroked the material barrier protecting my swollen bead hidden beneath. And I allowed it. Completely. Utterly. Unabashed. Unashamed.

His fingers breached the top of my panties and snaked through the curls that covered my sex. Two fingers parted the soft folds, and the third uncovered the sensitive nub. I arched my back and gasped for more air. My juices flowed, giving him lubrication to swirl his fingers around my swollen bead, and then…and then…*Oh God in Heaven*…one finger entered me. In it went, then out and over my clitoris, repeat…repeat…repeat.

Quicker.

Faster.

I orgasmed seconds later.

Completely. Utterly. Unabashed. Unashamed.

Chapter Twenty-Eight

For the next six months, I spent most every Friday night with Fitz. Most times, he'd come to my house. Sometimes we'd meet at The Midnight Lounge and sit at a corner table, drinking and laughing, but nothing more other than playing footsie under the table. We would then leave the bar separately and rendezvous at a hotel on the north end of town.

The first time at that hotel made an indelible mark in my brain. Fitz had clutched my clammy hand as we stood before the lobby door. "Don't be nervous, baby cakes," he whispered before bending over and placing a light kiss on my lips. "This hotel enforces a strict discretion policy."

My eyes widened as they raised to meet his. Thank God he couldn't feel my heart about to burst through my chest. "What do you mean? What kind of discretion policy?"

"You'll see."

My legs shook with every step as we approached the registration desk. The clerk acknowledged our presence with a nod and a sly smile. I assumed Fitz would sign us in under an assumed married name, but the clerk never took our names, asked for identification, or made us sign the register. He just slid a room key across the counter to Fitz and bid us goodnight.

I glanced at the key, the clerk, then Fitz. Confusion overtook me, but before I could ask a question, Fitz lightly placed his index finger over my lips to prevent me from speaking. At that moment, the lightbulb went off in my brain. The hotel's "discretion policy" meant turning a blind eye to its regular guests, and Fitz was probably one of the best ones they had.

That bothered the hell out of me. I had become one of Fitz's women he brought here. I couldn't go through with this. Could I?

Fitz lowered his eyes as if reading my mind. "Don't look so shocked." He caressed my cheek. "Your identity is safe, so there's no need to worry."

I didn't want to make a scene in front of the receptionist, so I fixed a cement smile on my face and turned around. Fitz slipped his arm through mine, and we strolled to the elevator.

Once in our hotel room, Fitz encircled his arms around me, but I pushed back. "How many women have you brought here before me?" I demanded, crossing my arms over my chest in protective mode. "How many will you bring after me?"

He stepped forward, I stepped back. "You know what *they* say," he whispered, 'if you can't accept the answer, you shouldn't ask the question'."

I placed my hands over my ears to make sure my head still clung to my neck and hadn't fallen off somewhere like my principles. Jesus Christ! Was this the new me? Did my infatuation and lust for Fitz kill off that decent young woman I used to be?

Fitz stood still, arms hanging motionless at his side. I took a hard look at my lover and realized he was right as rain. I didn't want to hear anything about his other women. He chose to bring *me* here tonight, not someone else. He was about to have sex with *me* tonight, not someone else. I lowered my head. This night would be about us…him and *me*…not someone else.

The workweek marched on. At home, Kat entertained me by learning the word, "bird." Now anything that flew she called a bird—airplanes, bumblebees, and even flies.

I adore her.

Speaking of Kat, my mother called me one evening and asked if she could be present for Kat's second birthday the following week. I had seen little of my mother after she helped when Kat was two months old, so I agreed to go upstate for a visit. I had a week of vacation coming.

Coral had been after me for a long time to visit my mother. "I am delighted you are finally taking my advice, Riley," she announced when I asked for the time off. "No one knows better than I that mother-daughter-grandchild time is precious. I wish I had had more time with my own mother, but death takes what death wants."

No one could ask for a better boss than Coral. Even under unbelievable circumstances concerning Fitz and her uncanny relationship rules along with Fitz and *my* relationship, she and I remained friends. All was fair in love and…more love.

It was strange entering my parents' home again because nothing looked the same. My mother explained that after my father died, she hated the memories the furniture raised, so she sold it all and replaced it with more updated versions. It looked nice except for a pair of wing-backed chairs imprinted with bright pink owls. My mother had quite an unusual taste.

My mother went all out for Kat's birthday. Colorful streamers draped across the ceiling with just as colorful balloons hanging from them. We celebrated with chocolate ice cream that complimented a white cake with bright pink frosting. And the presents! I'd never seen so many clothes and toys for one little girl in all my days. You'd think my mother would never see her granddaughter again.

That was exactly why my mother wanted us to come up. Her cancer had returned and this time doctors had nothing else to give her to fight it. They told her she might have six months to live, but there were no guarantees.

I could only describe myself as devastated with a capital "D." No, that wasn't all together right. Guilty came to mind, too.

All the times I should have brought my daughter to see her grandmother, I found excuses not to. I told my mother I was too busy at work, or that Sherman had Kat on the weekend in question, or I was sick, or Kat was sick. None of which were true. It came down to my not having the desire to see my mother. I knew she would try and tell me how to raise Kat, and I didn't want to hear it. I had my own ideas and my own ways of doing things. My mother molded me into the woman I became—smart, determined, and thoughtful—and I wanted to be the one who sculpted Kat into that kind of woman.

But now cancer would claim my mother's life. These days surrounding Kat's second birthday would be the only recent memories allotted the woman who gave me her last name when adopting me at birth and who still cared for and loved me today. And what did I do to repay her? Ignored her. Stole time away from her getting to watch Kat grow up.

Guilty as charged.

The day Kat and I returned home and every day after that, I called to check on my mother's health. I hated being so far away. Fitz recommended hiring a private nurse to visit my mother weekly. It was a great idea, and I thanked him in every possible position.

Some days I worried about my mother more than other days and it showed in the bedroom. Sex was the farthest thing on my mind. Fitz noticed, but instead of harboring ill feelings by my inactivity, he showed a compassion I had never seen before.

One night while lying in bed, he cuddled up beside me, caressing my face with soft kisses. "Riley," he whispered, "you are doing everything possible for your mother that you can do from here. She has the best care Sherman's money can buy, and the best doctors taking care of her. I see the wheels turning in there," he tapped my temple, "and you are tearing yourself apart wondering what more you can do. Am I right?"

I merely nodded but refused to look at him. I'm sure he noticed the single tear that escaped the corner of my eye.

He had mentioned, *Sherman's money*. It was true. When Sherman discovered—through Meredith, not me—about my mother's condition, he had called me and offered to help. Since it cost a pretty penny to hire a nurse on a weekly basis, I asked if he would foot that bill. Without hesitation, he agreed. That was genuinely nice of my husband.

When I finally turned my head toward Fitz, the remaining tears spilled from my eyes and fell onto my favorite silk pillowcase where they disappeared into the soft fabric.

He wrapped his arms around my shaking form and drew me into the curve of his body, stroking my back. "Shhh, now. I understand your pain. Lean on me. Cry all you want. Scream. Whatever you choose, I'm here to support you."

I clung to him as if my life depended on his strength. Mine had vanished. He told me to cry; I didn't want to. He told me to scream; I chose not to. What I really wanted was for Fitz to make me forget my worries, my trepidations, my fear.

He did.

Four months had passed when I received the dreaded call that my mother had taken a downturn in her health and was in the hospital. Fighting back tears while informing Coral of this news, I received her blessing to forget work and tend to my mother. Not that I needed her permission, but I sought it anyway. Leaving Kat with Meredith for what could be days or weeks, I made the journey to my mother's bedside.

My mother's illness was more severe than I thought; death hovered nearby. It broke my heart. Disintegrating on the inside, I tried to stay strong on the outside to keep her spirits up.

But who would boost mine through this ordeal? This would have been a good time to have a caring husband to help shoulder the pain, but I didn't have one. A husband, yes, a caring one, no. I knew I could rely on Hazel's shoulder to cry on over a phone receiver. She was always there for me when I needed her. I should have asked her to come with me, and she would have, but I didn't think it appropriate in this circumstance. I didn't know how long I'd be there or what to expect from day to day.

During one visit, my mother began speaking nonsensical sentences. Her gaze focused upward; her eyes opened wide. "Oh," her voice quivered, "you must be careful if you are going to play up there. Don't fall."

I followed her line of sight. "Mother, what are you looking at?"

"Children playing," she used her index finger to point up.

She had hallucinated people on the ceiling. Tears blurred my vision, but my mother's eyes seemed alert and bright as she followed these fanciful images scurrying here and there across an imaginary playground.

On a different day, she surprised me again. "Mama, Papa," she mumbled, smiling, "meet your new grandchild." No sooner had she verbalized this her eyes filled with tears. Her next words came out garbled to the point I understood little of what she said. There was some man and a baby; that's all I got from it. Putting two and two together, I assumed she meant her husband as the man, and I was the baby. Her crying made me think they were happy tears at my adoption. It warmed my heart.

Okay, so that explained the man and baby part. But for the other; I never knew my grandmother or grandfather because they had died before I was even born. So why would my mother introduce her parents to me who did not even exist yet? It took me a moment, but then it dawned on me that in her delirium, my mother visualized something she wished could have happened. She had wanted her mother and father to meet me and introduced me in spirit to them.

I brought her fragile hand to my lips, kissed it, then rested it against my cheek and cried with her. She never saw my tears, for she had fallen asleep.

During one of her more lucid days, I reminisced about Kat's second birthday and showed her pictures I had taken. There was one image she loved the most; the one where my daughter tried to blow out the candles on her cake. Kat's little cheeks looked as if she had a mouthful of nuts as she blew. My mother took the picture from me and placed it on her chest, covering it with her hand. Closing her eyes, she patted the picture and whispered Kat's name over and over.

I had to leave the room to prevent losing control. I ran down the hospital corridor, around the corner and into a woman's bathroom where I fell to my knees and openly wept. That day would haunt me forever as the day I saw the depth of my mother's love for a grandchild she rarely saw, and it was my fault, my selfishness, my stubborn streak that kept them apart.

As the days flew by, I offered words of encouragement and acts of support as she lay helpless in her hospital bed, visibly suffering. When she complained of a dry mouth, I placed ice chips on her tongue. Seeing how dry her lips became, I spread lip balm over them. If she had trouble taking in air, I added more pillows to raise her head. When she slept, I sat next to her bed and hummed a tune or softly sang "Rock of Ages," one of her favorite church songs. I never made it passed the first verse before my voice cracked and my throat swelled with emotion. Then, when she slept too long, I awakened her for no other reason than to assure myself she was still with me.

This routine continued until two weeks later, she slipped into the final state of unconsciousness. No matter how much I prayed for God to stop this, my mother was losing her battle against this devastating disease, which meant I was losing my mother.

When her wheezing became irregular and noisy, the doctor said it was just a matter of time. I couldn't bear hearing those words. My mother couldn't leave me; not now. Kat could not lose her grandmother so soon. My daughter would never experience what a wonderful woman her grandmother was. How loving. How compassionate. How wise. And I...I needed more time to right the wrongs when constantly disregarding my mother's advice and her wishes. I wished there were do-overs because I would do so many things differently in a multitude of ways.

All too soon, the day came when she took her last breath—my hand clutching hers. "Mother," I begged, "please don't go! Don't leave me! Please mother! I need you! What will I do without you! You can't go! You just can't! Please, please, please!" My whole being shook. I couldn't see through flowing tears. "God, why did you take her?!"

A nurse came in and put her hand on my shoulder. "Mrs. O'Keefe," her voice was soft and sympathetic, "I'm so sorry. Your mother was a lovely lady, and you can rest assured she's in a comforting place now. You can stay until the doctor arrives, but then, I'm sorry, you'll have to go."

Go? Go where? What do I do now? Grief clouded any reason I may have had.

Leaving the hospital, I went back to my parents' house and sat in one of the ugly owl chairs where I felt my mother's spirit beside me, her arm around my shoulder, pouring comfort over me. Of course, her presence had to make its appearance in that chair. A chair I hated to look at, but one she loved, and because she did, it became my favorite ugly thing in the world.

Sitting among the pink owls, I inhaled deeply, realizing I had arrangements to make.

Standing yet again at a parental gravesite, I bid a final farewell to my beloved mother who had joined my father in the heavenly Kingdom of God. Laying a single, red rose on top of her casket, I watched the workers lower the box that held the remains of the precious woman into the ground. After throwing a handful of blessed dirt into the grave, I walked away.

Both my parents were gone now. I was an orphan once more.

It took two weeks to settle my mother's estate and get the house on the market for sale. Before saying my final goodbye to this part of my past, I took several mementos to remember my mother and father—not that I could ever forget them. Of my father's, I took a set of cufflinks, his old coins, and a top hat he wore to a party with my mother once. Silly thing, but he loved it. So, did I. I remembered wearing it as a child and playing dress-up on several occasions. No one saw me, but the image in the mirror—my head swallowed up inside the large hat—will always be with me.

Of my mother's belongings, I took larger items: her cedar chest where she kept sweaters out of the mouths of moths, and the set of wing-back owl chairs. But, the most precious thing I took, but did not read at the time, was her old, fragile diary that looked well used. I would give it more attention when I got home, so I nestled it among a few of the sweaters I decided would look good on me. The rest of my parents' household goods went to charity. Someone would cherish these treasures as much as my parents did.

I priced the house to sell, and it wasn't long before I saw the "SOLD" sticker plastered across the "FOR SALE" sign in the front yard. It tore me apart to lock the door for the last time.

Standing on the front sidewalk, I stared back at the house and its surroundings. My throat swelled once more in knowing this would be the last time coming to this place. Accepting that, I left there with the memory of how everything looked right then. No matter who owned it, it would always be my parents' home.

Chapter Twenty-Nine

*H*azel sobbed her condolences when she came over bearing a still-piping hot chicken casserole covered with foil and holding it with oven mitts. I led the way to the kitchen where she put the dish on a couple of potholders I placed on the counter. She explained it was her best recipe, and I deserved nothing but the best. I gave her a bear hug and thanked her for the delicious gesture.

The next day, Coral came by with a flower arrangement to show her compassion. A perfect bunch of green grapes lay front and center of yellow daffodils, roses, and tulips. I touched the grapes to determine if they were real or plastic. They were definitely edible. Fruit with flowers in a lovely English glazed vase? Only an out-of-the-ordinary person like Coral would think of an out-of-the-ordinary combination. It made me smile. Something I hadn't done in a while.

Coral spent an hour with me, sharing my grief and prompting me to tell her some funny stories about my parents to lighten the heavy quality of the room.

I liked that.

Before leaving, she told me I could come back to work when ready. I told her I'd be there Monday. Offering Coral a hug and a wave goodbye as she left, I turned to my daughter and embraced her.

Fitz called me on the telephone and asked to come over, but I told him, no. My emotions were too raw yet to receive Fitz's manner of consolation. The one man I did allow over, though, was my husband. Sherman found out about my mother's death, again through Meredith, and he called to offer his sympathy.

Why did I allow him to occupy my space? Because he liked both my mother and father, and they in turn had loved him and enjoyed his company. All of us—Sherman, my parents and I—had a history together, and I wanted to speak to that history. Who better to wander down memory lane with than the man who shared my life for these past years, albeit separated now?

I didn't have the energy to hate Sherman anymore for what he had done and said to me those many months ago. Some anger remained, but not hate. His generous offer to pay for my mother's nurse, and his considerate condolences now, softened my heart. Perhaps my mother's death had something to do with it.

Strangely enough, it pleased me to see Sherman again. He must have been out in the sun a lot since we broke up because a beautiful, bronze tan covered his face and neck. He had to have joined a gym and worked out *hard* as his shoulders seemed broader and his arms more muscular. His potbelly had vanished, replaced by a tighter abdominal structure obvious through the brown, pullover tweed sweater he wore. Gone were his frumpy, black-rimmed glasses, replaced by an updated pair of burgundy horn-rimmed frames. He looked as if he stepped out of an issue of Gentlemen's Quarterly.

I liked what I saw.

We talked a while, he played "horsey" with Kat, then he offered to take us out to dinner. I accepted the invitation. Conversation and a good meal would go far in easing the rollercoaster of emotions inhabiting my soul.

During our evening together, Sherman did not dredge up anything from his and my ugly past. I appreciated that. He and I laughed about old times; the ones that brought smiles to light, not the hurtful ones that would end our conversation. He also informed me on how his and his office team's efforts brought Unified Automobile Company back on top in the car manufacturing business. He received my congratulations.

When he took Kat and me home, we all lingered at the front door under the illumination of the single bulb on the front porch. "I still have your favorite bourbon in the cabinet," I timidly said while holding Kat's hand in mine. "Would you like to come in for an after-dinner highball?"

"Not that I don't want to, I do. As God is my witness, I do, Riley," he muttered, "but I don't want to overstay my welcome. Besides, you look tired…"

His eyes widened, and his mouth fell open. He didn't offend me, though by the blush on his face along with his expression, he thought he had. I *was* tired and being with Sherman again emotionally drained me.

Poor man, he shifted from one foot to the other like a child having to go to the bathroom. No doubt nerves got to him. My nerves were on edge as well. "I mean, you look great," he added, "it's just that…" he ran his fingers through the stubbles of his hair.

"Sherman, I get it, so don't implode."

He smiled and took a deep breath. "Do you suppose…I mean, would it be all right if…oh, hell," the blood drained from his face. He reached out and placed his hands over Kat's ears. "Riley, I didn't mean to cuss in front of Kat, I'm sorry." He smoothed our daughter's hair and looked her in the eye. "Daddy said a bad word, honey," he said in a higher pitch and pursed his lips. "I'm sorry. Do you forgive me?"

"Bad daddy," Kat replied with a giant grin and slapped his hand.

Sherman furrowed his brow in looking up at me.

"Bad daddy, indeed," I stated with soft amusement. "You were saying?"

He straightened his posture. "May I see you again? You and Kat, again, that is?" He hesitated. "Or…just you?"

I simply nodded.

"Thank you, Riley, and thank you for giving me tonight." He bent down on one knee and kissed Kat on the cheek. "Goodnight my little Kat, daddy loves you."

Kat wrapped her arms around his neck and squeezed hard. "Daddy."

What in tarnation did I do with this new situation? What did this one night imply? Did Sherman want to get back together? Did I? Was I willing to give up the piping hot iron I had in my fire for a second chance with my husband? Did I want to think about this right now? No. In the words of Scarlett O'Hara, *"After all, tomorrow is another day."*

Fitz had phoned me every day until I determined life had to go on. In other words, my eagerness for sex had been lacking for a while, and it was time to get back in the swing of things. Besides, I missed being with him. He was a choice I had to keep, at least until I got my head straight and decided what my future looked like. I didn't have a future with Fitz…just sex. Was that enough for me? For now, yes.

When he rang my doorbell on Friday night, he embraced me hard and long. He professed his sympathy, but never once did he ask what took so long for me to allow him over. We sat in the living room on the same couch where we had our first sexual tryst months ago, and one or five after that. I never counted.

The mood changed though. For the longest time, we held each other and talked…verbally…to each other. It was good to smell him again, touch him, and have his arms around me. I quickly sank into that all too familiar state of euphoria, even though up to this point, he had not touched me sexually.

Unexpectedly, I leaned over and kissed him. It surprised him to find me the aggressor and allowed me to take the lead. Where I led him was to my bedroom to pick up where we left off, but with a twist.

I stood him against the side of the bed covered with a peach chenille spread, and seductively unfastened his buttons. It was *I* who meticulously relieved him of all his clothing. It was *I* who started feather kissing his body and allowed my hands to caress, yes, every part of him. It was *I* who pushed him onto the bed. It was *not* I, however, who straddled him. He took the dominant position on top of me.

The power of his arms and legs amazed me as he lifted himself above me, teasingly rubbing his penis against my stomach. He kept plunging its head into my belly button, making me laugh. Then he started doing push-ups over me. More laughter. With every down movement, he kissed me, then raised himself up again. Ten times. Ten push-ups. Ten kisses before he lowered his pelvis, lined himself up and entered me. He slipped in with no problem. I said I had been without sex for a while, so my *woohoo* slathered his penis with hot, vaginal *yeeha*.

"Keep your legs down, Riley," he quietly ordered.

Doing that one thing allowed me to tighten my inner thighs around him. I had not experienced this before. It was glorious.

With every slow movement of his penis entering, he matched the speed as he pulled out, but not all the way. He stopped just as the head touched the outer folds of my vagina, then bam! A hard thrust in and out, then back to slow and steady. He varied the pace and rhythms, so I had no idea what to expect next. Keeping me off balance made it hard for me to come, but then perhaps that was the whole idea. At his manipulation, I reached my peak and cried out his name. At last I came down, exhausted and sated. Only then did he reach his climax by his own hand. It took less than a minute.

In a spooning position with this man, relaxed and weary, I experienced a gnawing at the back of my mind. I couldn't put my finger on it. I just wanted it to go away. It did when I fell asleep.

As usual, Fitz had to leave—some things never changed—meaning I spent my night in bed alone with my thoughts; my thoughts that drifted to, of all people, Sherman.

*Ahh, so **that** is what harped on my brain.*

I shook my head to rid myself of the vision. Sherman and I were…hell, I had no idea what we were, or even if there *was* a "we."

The following Friday, I gave Meredith the night off from babysitting. Kat and I had a date with Sherman and the new Walt Disney movie, "One Hundred and One Dalmatians." Earlier in the week, I prepared Kat by buying her a stuffed Dalmatian dog. We called it Pongo after one of the main characters in the story. She loved it, though not able to pronounce the character's name well, she called it Paggo.

Fitz called in relation to our standing Friday night engagement schedule and asked if I wanted to stay in or go out. He did not expect or approve of my answer.

"What do you mean you already have plans?" Fitz's tone lowered with a rising frustration laced in. "With whom?"

"Sherman, actually," I stated. I still wore a wedding ring on my finger, so it's not like I was cheating on Fitz with my husband. I was cheating on Sherman with Fitz.

"You don't say. And when were you going to tell me this bit of information, Riley?"

I hadn't thought about when or how, or even *if* I would tell him. But I suppose I had to at some point. "I, well, um, to be honest—"

"Honest?" His voice raised a notch in aggravation. "Honesty comes with consideration, and it seems you had planned to keep me in the dark about your little excursion with your husband."

"No, I was going to let you know—"

"When?!" His voice turned angry, which made me bristle.

"When I saw fit, Fitz." How dare he raise his voice to me. Who did he think he was? My father? No. He was my LOVER.

My lover broke off the call.

Well, I'll be damned!

I sat there and thought about an important question: Fitz and I were lovers, but did I love him? We had a great time together in and out of the bedroom, but was there enough substance between us for me to love him?

I searched my soul for an answer.

What soul. I sold it to Lucifer when putting my passion where it doesn't belong.

Then I asked myself this question: *would I give up my life to save his?* Not a chance in hell. As a result, Fitz was not my love; just someone with whom I had amazing sex. As my friend Hazel would say, *"Well now, isn't that just a barrel of sour pickles?"* Indeed. I have most certainly found myself in a pickle.

After the movie on Friday, Sherman took us to a pizzeria, then we came back to my house. I put Kat to bed, poured two glasses of wine, then he and I talked on separate ends of that same goddamned couch.

I have got to buy a different one if Sherman plans to sit on it. Putting my husband's and my clothed butts right where my lover and I put our naked ones does not for a good conversation make!

When the mutual discussion ebbed, I felt his eyes on me. "Riley," he began, then took a sip of his beverage, out of what looked to me like nervous tension, "I've been an ass—"

"Yes, you have." I, too, took a draw of my wine for the same reason.

He slid closer.

Placing his glass on the coffee table, he faced me. "I was wondering," his tone softened as did his eyes, "if you can ever forgive me for the despicable things I did and said to you. I was angry, and when people get angry, they say stupid things to hurt the other. I didn't mean any of it. That's the God's truth."

My husband begged for mercy. I was guilty of the same transgression, but he would never find out. He cheated; I cheated. Nothing would change that.

I placed my glass next to his on the table. "Are you still involved with Mayzelle," my tone was not as temperate as the one he used, "because she and Gene continue to live together. Were you aware of that piece of information?"

He nodded and sighed deeply. "Yes. After the whole mess came out, I ended it. After losing you, something changed inside of me and life was never the same. I saw how much I lost when I left the house that night."

I rebuffed his remark with a visible smirk. "Well, *that's* reassuring."

He took my hands in his and squeezed. "Riley, I never meant to hurt you, I really didn't. It's just that—"

"Yes, you did, and it hurt more than anyone on this earth has *ever* hurt me. Angry or not, your words cut me to the quick. Your actions did too. Not believing me about the malicious phone calls made me feel like a fool. But your dismissal about the sabotage of my car was inexcusable. I could have been killed, and you would not have cared."

"That's not true, Riley! It was just hard for me to believe anyone would be so mean and spiteful to do that to you. In my mind it had to be a mistake. Thank God nothing bad happened. If any harm had come to you, I would have never forgiven myself. It was stupid of me, plain and simple. Please try and forgive my thoughtlessness, Riley. It will never happen again, I promise."

"It took a long time to get over how cruel you were to me, Sherman. As my husband you should have felt an obligation, if nothing else, to believe what I tell you, and above all, to remain monogamous with me. Isn't that why we took a vow?" My speech should have worked both ways, but I put the guilt solely on him. I would not lose this battle.

He kissed the back of my hand. "Yes," his voice turned urgent, "it is, and I destroyed that vow, but hopefully not beyond repair."

Repair? He wants to repair our marriage? He had my ear. "And how do you intend to fix this broken mess?"

"By showing you what a changed man I am. You can already tell I've begun my physical transformation with this new look," he grinned and brushed his hands over his torso. "I wanted to improve my body *and* my attitude to win you back, Riley." He lowered his head. "When I realized what a fool I had been, I went into a deep depression. It took professional counseling to bring me back to the point of wanting to make you see me in a new light. Let me prove to you that I am worth a second chance. I miss you." He captured my gaze. "I miss *us*, Riley. You, me, and Kat. Our lives as a family."

He scooted even closer and enclosed my hands again. "Riley, I've never stopped loving you and never will. Please," he petitioned, "allow me to make it up to you and our daughter." His eyes softened even more. "I need you back in my life, and I can only hope you need me. I promise you, Riley," he straightened his posture and took possession of the unfaltering tone I knew so well, "I will never break your heart again. I swear." He searched my eyes for a glimpse of forgiveness and found it.

How could my resolve not crumble at Sherman's sincere plea? Did he and I have a prayer at starting over? He *did* break our marriage vows (but then so did I). He said horrible things to me and made even worse accusations that weren't true (yet). *Was* it worth my giving it another go? Did I go the route my mother took with my father and forgive (but never forget)?

And what about Fitz who still held a spot in the picture, well, I thought he did. Could I soothe Fitz's ruffled feathers? Did I want to? This dilemma required a different kind of soul-searching. "I need time to think about this," I told Sherman.

With a ray of hope in his voice, he pounced on my reply. "Yes, of course you do. I know in my heart you will make the right choice for all of us."

He pressed his lips to my hands, which sent a flutter of excitement down my spine.

"I'd better go," his expression was soft and sincere as he rose from his seat. "I don't want to overstay my welcome. Wait, I've said that already."

I returned the expression. "Thank you for tonight. I enjoyed strolling down memory lane."

He nodded in agreement. "Me, too. Okay, then." He walked toward the front door. "I'll wait to hear from you." He wrapped his arms around me in a dignified embrace which I returned with more strength. The memory of his hugs flooded my mind, and I wanted to remain within his arms a bit longer, but he stepped back. Kissing my cheek, he left me at the door.

The following Thursday, Fitz called, all lovey-dovey, but I squashed his idea of coupling up on Friday night. Sherman had reserved that spot once again. The conversation began the same as the last one Fitz and I had over Sherman dominating my time, but it ended differently. Soon after hanging up, Fitz showed up at my door.

"Fitz, I didn't know you were coming over."

"Neither did I, but we need to sort something out here and now."

"Oh? And what would that be?"

"May I come in?"

I stood aside. "Yes, of course." I did not offer him a drink or anything else for that matter. "What did you want to talk about?"

"Our relationship."

Our relationship. Did we have one, or just have a good time in the sack. The latter, and I needed to tell him it was over.

"Fitz, I think our time together has run its course. I've enjoyed being with you these past months. You've made me feel like a whole woman again, a beautiful and desirable woman, and for that, I thank you. But I'm in a place now where I need more than one day a week.

I want seven days a week, and you can't give me that. Sherman can. He's Kat's father and she needs him; I need him." I stared at the floor. "I'm sorry, Fitz, but I can't see you anymore." I raised my eyes to his; he deserved that much. "I'm going back to Sherman, so," I heavily sighed, "this is goodbye."

He stood there, rigid and eyes narrowed. He nodded slowly. "So that's it? Just like that you decide you've had enough of me? What about what I want, Riley?"

I didn't expect that, but I stayed with my resolve. "It doesn't matter, Fitz. You have a lot of women to share your bed. I was just one of many, and I am taking myself out of the harem. All I want from you now is to accept my wishes and not contact me again. My future is with Sherman." I had nothing else left to say.

"All right, Riley. I will honor your request and walk away. But I want you to know that you meant more to me than any woman other than Coral. You were special." In silence, he turned and walked out my door.

I watched him go. My eyes misted, and my lip quivered.

Goodbye, Fitz.

It was over. It wasn't a happy ending with Fitz, but a necessary one. Carrying out that sadness I threw myself on the couch and wept until a little hand reached up and touched my shoulder. "Bird?" I heard Kat say. My low spirit raised a notch when Kat held up a stuffed airplane she had swiped from Coral's house when her son, Beau, and Kat played together. Wiping the wetness off my face, I drug her up on the couch with me and hugged her close. I then attacked her neck with snuggle kisses while tickling her. Squeals of laughter filled the air. Thanks to my daughter, I started the process of shoving those awesomely wonderful, breath-taking sexual moments with my boss's husband to the recesses of my mind. A better future lay ahead.

Chapter Thirty

"Stop a minute," I gasped, pressing my palms against his bare chest. "You have to let me catch my breath before we do it again."

Sherman caressed my face with trails of light kisses that briefly halted on my lips before moving lower. "I love you so much, sweetheart," he purred, "so much." Still winded from our last encounter, he pressed more kisses on my shoulders and took his sweet time on my breasts.

By his swollen member digging into my pubic bone, I could tell he waited for me. Jesus Christ, he was a beast! But his voracity for having sex with me turned me on something awful.

"Okay," I panted, which took his current attention away from my belly button, "ready, set, let's go!"

This time I took the lead with a certain goal in mind—to conquer my sexual phobia. Asking my husband to roll over on his back, I straddled his legs and stared at his thick and elongated penis. I remembered how he had accused me of only being on the receiving end of oral sex and never reciprocating it. In the past, the mere idea of putting my lips on his pee-thing sent shivers through me and left a bad taste in my brain. I didn't value the importance of giving a man a blowjob, but maybe it was time to learn the proper way to do it so I didn't feel nauseous in the attempt.

Staying silent, I looked at the top of his penis and into the slit of what I saw as an eye. I placed my fingertips on either side of the tip and gently drew the eye open. Ha! It now resembled a mouth I could manipulate with the slightest pull. Giggling, I "made it talk" by opening and closing it! How fun!

Sherman looked perplexed as I played with his aroused shaft. "Riley, what are you doing?"

"Making your penis talk."

"Do what?"

I stopped my antics and got back to the business of overcoming my phobia. With my new mindset, I swallowed what spit I had and forced myself to place my lips on the tip of this body part.

My mouth to penis mouth! Stop now, Riley. Concentrate.

Thinking back to my wedding day and the previous lesson in how to execute this procedure, I slowly began the movement of lowering my mouth and sliding up and down, using my saliva to lubricate the shaft.

His skin is softer against my lips than I thought it would be.

My actions not only surprised but shocked him as evidenced by his gasp. About to engage in a conversation about my choice, he quickly became lost in the sensation and forgot about the urge to speak. Instead, he leaned his head back and groaned as he grabbed my head and manipulated it at the pace he wanted me to take.

I bit him.

"Hey, what did you do that for?"

"Your penis, my pace. I'm learning here Sherman. Leave me alone until I get used to doing this. Patience, please."

He sighed and leaned back.

It wasn't so torturous after all. The more I stroked with my mouth, the more times he hissed out my name in ecstasy. I had complete control. Lips on skin turned to teeth on skin, which made him squirm. This became a game for me. How many times could I make him scream out my name and groan with satisfaction? The answer was a lot!

When coming close to ejaculation, he lifted my head away and allowed his flow to discharge without my having to take it in my mouth. If that had happened, I would have erupted in a more violent way than he ever could: from my gut!

It still baffled me how Sherman and I got back to a sexual place so quickly. Two weeks ago, he had kissed me on the cheek, and this week, we were having unbelievably gratifying sex. Was it the romantic picnic that swept us away on a passionate journey? Or could it have been the enchanted scenery? Towering pines surrounded us as we sat on a blanket nestled within luscious green grass. A moss-covered bridge that looked as if it came out of the sixteenth century spanned a small, gurgling stream dancing over rocks and fallen tree limbs. Songbirds serenaded us with spiritual melodies, making me long to take flight and join them. Breathing the air, pure as freshly washed linen, rejuvenated the soul and ministered the heart.

Yes, all of these reignited our interrupted love affair. It took one piercing look, one stimulating touch, one sweep of lips on lips to catapult us to the level of primal desire. We lay sexually gorged, flesh to flesh, goosebumps and all, but they did not form from the coolness of the air. No. My skin "orgasmed" from Sherman's love. I belonged to my husband once more, lock, stock, and barrel.

In my mind, the time I spent with Fitz was nothing more than a long-term fling—fulfilling, yes; long-lasting, no. Destiny dictated that he would take up my time until I reunited with my one true love. The kind of love where I *would* give up my life to save Sherman's.

～

That following month, my period did not come on schedule. Pacing the floor and nearly squeezing the colors out of a dishcloth by twisting it in my hands did not soothe my frazzled nerves. I called my obstetrician and made an appointment.

"Congratulations, Mrs. O'Keefe. You are definitely with child!" exclaimed the same doctor who told me I was pregnant with Kat.

A moment crossed my mind in wondering if Fitz could be the father of my child, but then I felt relieved and confident that while he and I were having sex that last time, he pulled out before coming. That eased my mind on that front.

This news should have thrilled me, except for one more thing. How would Sherman take the news of expanding our family of three to four? He and I never talked about having another child.

That night I began with a nervous twitch in the corner of my mouth, "Sherman, I need to tell you something."

He wrapped his arms around my shoulders and kissed my ear. "Anything sweetheart. You can tell me anything your heart desires."

I pressed my lips together and widened my nostrils as the surrounding air became harder to breathe. After swallowing the thickened saliva that had accumulated in my mouth, I cleared my throat and swallowed again. "You and I are…we're…" I took a deep breath and released it. Without moving away from his embrace, I spit it out. "I'm pregnant!"

I didn't move.

He didn't move.

Why isn't he saying anything?

Then he drew back, his face a plateful of emotion. He creased his brows, then he raised them. He cocked his head one way then the other.

"Sherman, say something, please. This is unexpected, but—"

He grabbed me, twirling me around the room with pleasure.

When he placed my feet back on the floor, he took my head and kissed every part starting from forehead to chin, saving my lips for last. "Sweetheart," he whispered, looking me square in the eyes, "that is the best news you could have told me."

What I expected to be another manic meshing of carnal appetites when we went to bed later that night, ended up being a tender weave of affection. Each of us whispered words of adoration and devotion while loving hands caressed parts of our bodies other than those that previously brought us to a climactic conclusion.

It was a glorious moment, and one I'll never forget.

Chapter Thirty-One

This time at six months pregnant, I did something different. I resigned my position as Office Manager-slash-Receptionist at "Employment Opportunities for Tomorrow." Coral tearfully moaned at learning I had found a new direction for my life. Her using colorful phrases like, "I need you, and what am I going to do without you?" made it twice as hard to keep strong. Once I bid farewell to my friends, I walked out of the glass-walled office one last time and never looked back.

Giving up my status as a working mother was a difficult choice to make. But being pregnant this time brought about an enlightenment. My aspiration to have it all—marriage, a career, and children—reduced into something more impressive. Maybe the maternal instinct took over. Maybe my mother tapped into my unconscious. Whatever it was, working outside the home seemed unimportant now. I missed too many firsts with Kat, and come hell or high water, I was not about to miss a single one with this baby. I had a new position in this next phase of my life: that of mother and wife. Period.

While Kat napped, I grabbed the opportunity to start reading my mother's diary. It made me wish I had written an organized record of my life experiences like she did. Up to now, I jotted down my memorable events on whatever I had within my reach at the time, and haphazardly stashed them in some dark corner in the house.

It was strange holding it in my hands. The book, with the words A LINE A DAY boldly printed in gold letters across the top, was old and worn. The strap on the back of the overly stuffed and tattered book no longer fastened into its companion lock on the front. The pages lay liberated to reveal the essence of the woman who faithfully wrote on them over many years. A frayed satin ribbon stuck out like a beacon. It still shined in the light, and curiosity begged me to start my reading at that point to discover what the ribbon signified. But I resisted and started at the beginning.

I carefully opened the fragile cover of the book, paying attention to the flimsy felt material that had separated from the cotton webbing on the spine. It did my heart good to see my mother's handwriting again. It surprised me to discover how small she could write. At the top and bottom of most every page, I saw sentences squeezed in as if she remembered something later and felt compelled to add it. I needed a magnifying glass to read them.

There were scripture passages and poetry verses scattered throughout the book. Her poems reflected honest and profound expressions of love that displayed her inner-most sentiments. I peeled back the tough layers she portrayed to the outside world and unearthed a tender heart with an avid propensity for passion.

It took several weeks to pore over my mother's diary because life had a way of intruding on my progress. Finally, coming to the page where the satin ribbon lay, I almost stopped reading to gather the ingredients for the evening meal. However, it became very clear as to the significance of the ribbon's placement. I came across something in the diary that made me want to probe further.

It seemed when only sixteen years old, my mother had quite the illicit affair. A man had recently moved to her town and stayed with relatives while he searched for a job. He and my mother met at a nearby grocery store. A glancing exchange and a timid smile started the whole shebang.

Why, mother dear, does God know about this?

I mentally laughed at thinking my mother had flaws like the rest of us mortals. Forgetting about dinner, the story about this man who captured her heart kept me reading.

The narrative my mother entered about her multiple romantic rendezvous with him surprised the hell out of me. It was like reading a romance novel—no, more intense than that. No romance I'd ever read depicted this much sexual activity. My face flushed at some entries, and others made me downright embarrassed.

This was my mother, for Christ's sake. Why did she include so much detailed information, but then again, who would read it but her? Thinking about this further, it angered me to know she knew *a lot* about sex. But did she ever share with me the ins and outs of what to do, when to do it, or how it's done when I asked her about it? No. Never.

Turning the page, I came across a verse she had written:

"Divine bodies revolve in Heaven in a flurry of
    celebrated praise.
For you and I are in love, my sweet gem, never to
    part in this lifetime.
Forever is what you promised me, and forever is
    what I believed.
I offered my body, my heart, my soul, and you
    received each with gratitude.
Now you have abandoned me in my greatest hour,
    for I bear your seed.

You have discarded our future to seek pleasure in
your own light.
The celestial bodies are mourning the loss of our
love.
No longer will the moon and star feel the touch
beneath my fingers.
Never will you return to these arms that have loved
you so."

I stopped because the tears from the sadness this poem outlined, blurred my vision. My mother was pregnant? But who fathered her child? Nowhere did she disclose the man's name. I thought back and remembered her telling me one day that she hadn't met my adoptive father until much later in her life. I had to read on.

Once my eyesight cleared, I continued reading the entry, only to have the third shock crash down and rock my core.

My mother continued with the description of her child at birth:

"He's a healthy boy, with a cry to match. A tiny pink and wrinkly babe with dark hair and piercing eyes the color of cobalt. He is perfect, down to the same mark of his lineage. Though I no longer have the man I deeply cherish to share this blessing, I find solace in knowing the image imprinted on my son will forever remain a symbol of my perpetual love for his father."

I stopped again with the realization that my mother had born a son. She never told me any of this, *ever*. If this were true, what happened to the baby? I had no brother when my parents adopted me.

With questions flying around in my brain, I kept reading. Nearing the middle of the writing, the story took on a happy note, thank God. It clarified that right after my mother had given birth to her son on June 6, 1928, the child's father *did* return, which threw my mother into a fit of joy. He apologized to my mother for having been a fool and leaving her when he should have been by her side. My mother forgave his proclaimed weakness.

What we women do for our men.

The next entry went on to say that the morning of her release from the hospital, my mother joined her lover in cooing over their son until the nurse came to take the baby for his last feeding within the hospital walls. The child's father placed an impassioned kiss upon my mother's lips, told her he loved her *over the moon*, then said he was going to the nursery and watch his son take a bottle. After that, he'd be back by her side once more and never leave her again. Another kiss, and he left.

But this time, he did not return.

Nor did he leave empty-handed.

Under the noses of the nursery attendants, he kidnapped his and my mother's son. When told, my mother once again fell into a desolate state of mind with the all too familiar heartbreak.

Though her parents had money and could have hired an investigator to find the child, they convinced my mother this turn of events was for her own good. They thought my mother was too young to manage on her own, and they had no intention of raising another child. Grieving at the strong possibility of never seeing her son again, she vowed never again to speak the names of her son or his father.

My heart broke for my mother. But then again, reading about her in this new light made me realize how strong she had been in keeping such a dark secret all her adult life.

But then a memory struck me like a lightning bolt. A man and a baby. When my mother cried on her death bed that fateful day, she wasn't crying joyful tears about her and my father adopting me like I thought. No. Her tears meant something else entirely. When she was sixteen years old, her lover—the man—stole her newborn son—the baby. It had nothing at all to do with me. She kept this buried all these years until she verbalized it like a confession.

Wiping a run-away tear from my cheek, I turned the next page to discover the biggest shock yet. Who could have known what my mother had written in 1928, would reveal an unbelievable truth that reached all the way to 1961? For sketched with a pencil by my mother's own hand, was an image of a person's shoulder. Upon that shoulder, she had drawn a crescent moon with a star at its point.

I focused the magnifying glass on the statement beneath the drawing. Holding the book in one hand, I read the sentence my mother wrote:

"The love of my heart has left me with nothing more than a representation to remind me that the moon belonged to him and the star belonged to the son he stole from me."

This was the shoulder of my mother's lover.

At once, the air grew frigid. Chills covered me like tiny shards of glass piercing my skin. My body trembled, and the blood drained from my face. I had seen that symbol before. It was the night my co-workers and I went to The Midnight Lounge. The night my sex drive had gotten the best of me and I dragged Fitz into my house where he satisfied my craving from top to bottom. The night I saw his tattoo that he explained was a birthmark.

I gained the acute awareness that the man with whom my mother had an affair, bore the mark I had seen on Fitz's shoulder. That meant Fitz…Shudders rattled my body. Fitz had to be my adoptive mother's long-lost son.

"Oh, my God," I quietly exclaimed to myself.

According to her diary, she never saw her son or his father again.

I turned back a few pages to view this entry's recorded date: June 30, 1928—three weeks after her son's birth. I flipped forward all the way to the end of the book, scanning for more information.

"What the hell, mom! Where's the rest of the story?"

I found no other diaries at my mother's house when getting it ready for sale. Did she keep her word to herself and stop recording about this tragedy after it happened? That had to be the case.

Now what? Did I approach Fitz and ask him about it? If I did, would he believe me or tell me to mind my own business.

"Shit. What do I do with this information?"

I bit my lower lip as I drew my hand over the diary's cover. Maybe rubbing it like a genie's lamp would conjure up an idea. After a few seconds it came to me. *Yay, genie!* Who other than a wife would know her husband inside and out? Yes, asking Coral was my answer.

Chapter Thirty-Two

I heard Coral's excitement over the telephone. She thought I'd changed my mind and would return as her Office Manager after my baby was born. It only took a moment to disappoint her. However, her crestfallen tone didn't last long when I spoke about needing her advice on something. Now *that* piqued her interest. From experience I knew how much she delighted in providing me with her worldly pearls of wisdom.

I didn't go into detail over the phone, but she and I scheduled a lunch date at the end of the week to talk about a delicate matter. I needed those few days to determine how to spring this topic on her.

Coral got to the restaurant before I did and was sitting at the table when I walked up. "You've kept me teetering on the edge of curiosity long enough, Riley," she jokingly smirked when greeting me with a hug and cheek kiss. "I love a good mystery and can't wait to hear what you have to tell me, so out with it, pretty lady."

I slid into the seat across the table from her, forced a smile, and kept my purse on my lap instead of placing it on the empty seat beside me. My fingers clutched the top of the handbag as if to keep the contents inside from jumping out.

Looking at the sparkle dancing in her green eyes, and the excited lines creasing the edges of her mouth should have given me a sense of calm. It did not. In fact, just the opposite.

I felt a sudden chill in the air.

Am I doing the right thing by showing her my mother's diary and the image?

My hands are freezing.

Will she believe me, or tell me it's a story invented by a jilted woman? I don't want to hear my mother degraded in any way.

What degree does this restaurant keep its thermostat...thirty-two?

I swallowed the last bit of spit in my mouth as I stared at Coral. This unnerved her. "Does a cat have your tongue, Riley?"

I cleared my throat. "No, Coral, but I have something here that might entice that cat to grab yours."

Really, Riley? Humor at a time like this?

Coral leaned forward and placed her hands against the edge of the table as if ready to pounce on me at any moment. "If you don't tell me what this is all about, you little minx, I swear, I will throttle you right here in front of God and everybody." She leaned back. "You stated you need my advice, and I am more than ready to dig deep into my treasure trove and assist you. But the only way I can do that is if you spill the beans, so spill."

I unzipped my purse and slowly, so as not to snag it on the zipper, withdrew the tattered book. Placing it in front of me, I stared at it and remained silent.

Coral stared at it, too. "It's a diary, Riley."

I hated to see the disappointment on her face.

Then she leaned in again and cocked her head, a new lively twinkle in her eye. She pointed at the well-loved book with worn edges. "It looks ancient. Is it yours?" She gasped with ardent interest. "Are you going to share one of your best-kept secrets with me? Is it torrid, and you need my advice to fix the dastardly mess you've gotten into?" Her posture straightened and her tone of formality arose. "If so, I will do my utmost to find a way out for you, my dear."

"It's not mine, Coral. It's my mother's diary."

Coral squinted her eyes and allowed her shoulders to drop. "Oh. All right, so why are your mother's school-day crushes and stories about men and her risqué escapades with them so important that we are having lunch over it?"

I narrowed my brows at her. "What makes you think that kind of information is in here?"

She rested her elbows on the table, interlacing her fingers. "All women put that kind of thing in their diaries. It's like a bible of our misdeeds and unsavory thoughts that nobody knows but us." She then crossed her arms and rested them on the table "You should know, Riley, dear. Surely you have one of your own." With a devilish grin and a single raised brow, she giggled. "I can imagine all sorts of activities you jotted down to keep secret."

"I *did* start one, it's just that the writings are on separate pieces of paper strewn about who knows where in my house."

"What a shame. You should find the pieces and put them together some day, because they are," her eyes sparkled with amusement, "pieces of your life!" Her laughter rang out, but after joining her in a short version of her sunny spirit, I brought it back to its darker position.

"Coral," I began, "this book holds more than menial infatuations. There is a truth in this that shocked me to the core." It was my turn to raise one brow. "I bet you will have the same reaction when I tell you what I found in it."

"Then tell me already!"

I had marked the entry by drawing the attached, narrow, white satin ribbon across the page. Taking the exposed end of the ribbon, I carefully pulled the diary open. The words on the page stared back at me, and I forgot the speech I had practiced. Instead, I pushed the book across the table to her. "Read the entry of June 30, 1928," I instructed.

Coral eyed me, then turned the book around and read in silence.

A middle-aged gentleman with a white cloth draped over his arm came up to our table to take our lunch order. I didn't want to break Coral's concentration. "We are not ready yet," I whispered to him, "could you please come back in fifteen minutes?" With a smile, the waiter nodded and turned to wait on another table.

A few minutes passed when I heard a gasp leave Coral's throat. I knew she reached my mother's description of the baby boy. With eyes wide and hair practically standing on end, Coral gaped at me. "Riley," she whispered, "is this revealing what I think it is?"

I licked the corner of my mouth with a dry tongue. "That your husband is my adopted mother's son whose father had kidnapped him at birth?" I nodded and cleared my throat. "I believe that is the case, Coral."

She stared at the drawing of the birthmark. "This is a striking resemblance to the birthmark Fitz has, so it has to be true." She sighed. "Beau has the same mark, just lower on his arm."

The waiter came back, his pad and pencil in hand. Coral reached into her handbag and withdrew a cream-colored, lacey handkerchief to wipe away a falling tear. Composed once again, she directed her attention to the gentleman waiting patiently. "Please bring a bottle of chardonnay and two glasses. Thank you."

When the waiter left, Coral's shoulders slumped from her perfect posture position. "Oh, my God, Riley."

"It's incredible, isn't it? And that's why I wanted you to see this. Does Fitz know about his mother? About who his **real** mother is?"

Coral took a deep breath. "Everything about his family history I learned from him, but *this* version never came up. Fitz is aware of only one mother and it's not the one in this diary."

"So, I take it Fitz's father's name is Beauregard Fitzgerald Kingston the first. Is he still alive?"

"Yes, he lives in France with his wife; the woman Fitz considers his true mother. Oh, Riley, this is awful. I feel so bad for your mother. Did she perchance write a sequel?"

A sequel? Really Coral? A sequel? What is this, a romance novel?

I shook my head and shrugged. "I never came across a second diary. As far as a verbal version, she never breathed a word of this to me. I found out by reading it in there." I pointed at the open book.

Coral became stoic and silent. I could tell she wanted to ask the all-important question, so I relieved her of the responsibility. "Coral, I'm not sure what to do with this information. Do I tell Fitz or let this dead dog lie?"

She nibbled her thumbnail, which I had never seen her even attempt to do before. "Let me mull this over a while, Riley. This is too big to make any rash decisions." She took a sip of the wine the waiter had previously poured into each of our glasses when he brought the bottle. "Yes, let me think on this."

A week later, Coral called me with her opinion on what to do about my telling or not telling Fitz about his birth mother.

"This is a very painful decision I've made, here, Riley," she confessed, "because secrets are not part of my husband's and my relationship. Being that as it may," she breathed heavily, "I feel both you and I should keep the evidence in your mother's diary between us. Fitz's father has never confessed to his having had an affair that produced a son out of wedlock. Besides, what good could come from revealing the truth now? It would produce nothing but resentment and outrage on Fitz's part and even perhaps a division between his father and him. No," she sounded downtrodden, "say nothing...please. For everyone's sake, it's best left where it lies in your mother's diary...in the past."

I appreciated her candor and agreed with her reasoning.

When I hung up the phone, I ran to my bedroom, opened my mother's cedar chest at the bed's footboard, pushed aside the winter clothing, and buried the diary at the very bottom. It would be safe there. Sherman had no reason to poke his nose in it unless he wanted to wear one of my glamorous wool sweaters. It seemed a fitting place to hide the diary since it was my mother's, as was the cedar chest. Now both lay silently together, harboring secrets.

~

Three months later, I found myself in the hospital about to give birth. My joy gave way to nurses poking and prodding *where the sun don't shine*. As payback for their intrusive, albeit necessary actions, I spent the next four hours screaming bloody murder. Forget twilight sleep—they administered medication to send me into lights out!

When I woke, nothing around me looked familiar. It didn't take long to realize I was in the hospital's recovery room. Once the nurses acknowledged I had my faculties about me, they brought me a little bundle of joy swaddled in a soft blanket. They handed me the baby boy, and I cradled my love-bug in the crook of my arm. He was as beautiful as my daughter, Kat, when she came into the world. A boy and a girl. One of each.

How lovely.

After leaving recovery and entering my hospital room, Sherman greeted me with a broad smile and a bouquet sporting three large roses with a filler of daisies. He later explained that two of the roses stood for our two children, and the third embodied the love that created them. It lifted my spirits in knowing something so small, yet meaningful, cemented my belief we belonged together.

Soon, a nurse brought in our new baby—Peter Scott O'Keefe. Sherman joined me in crying over the newest addition to our happy little family.

And baby made four.

All too soon, that same nurse came in to take my son back to the nursery for his feeding. I asked if I could give him his bottle instead. Allowing my request, the nurse left the baby in my arms where he clamped down on that bottle's nipple. What a sucker; the good kind, not the fool kind.

The next day, we sponge-bathed our baby for the first time. Sherman wanted to take a more active role in this new child, and as Peter's father, he had first honor at bathing his son.

Standing over Peter in a bassinet, Sherman freed our tiny burrito from his blanket but left the cloth diaper on. I remained in bed and out of the way. When scooping up our baby to lower him into the towel-draped tub—minus any water—Sherman kept his attention on his son's face but aware of the crusty umbilical cord.

Once Peter's delicate skin touched the cooler temperature of the room, he loudly protested. Acting like a stick-pin doll, he threw out his arms, closed his eyes and tightened every limb. Though Sherman blocked my view of Peter, I leaned toward the tub and spoke soothing words to our son.

When Sherman introduced warm water on a washcloth against Peter's skin, the crying softened until it subsided completely. Our baby relaxed into the comfort of his father's hands and the softness of my voice. Sherman took to the task with great finesse and gentleness, allowing me to fall back onto the pillows of my bed.

"He's got your eyes, Riley. But his are a much darker blue than yours."

"The color is always deeper at birth, Sherman. They will lighten as he gets older. Mine did."

"That's my boy," Sherman cooed over our son. "See, daddy's good at giving you a bath, isn't he?" All I heard as a response was Peter grunting his appreciation of his father's efforts. "You are so handsome, Peter," he continued. "Oh, and looky here," Sherman got excited, "God loves you so much, He kissed your shoulder."

What did you say? God kissed our son's shoulder? What does that mean?

I slowly got out of bed and gingerly walked around to stand at the base of the bathtub and stared at Peter's left shoulder. Instantly, my wits left me as did the blood from my head.

Sherman quickly observed my face turn pasty white. "Hey, hey, now, sweetheart," he soothed, "don't look so concerned. It's just a birthmark. Don't get all discombobulated. It's nothing, really. Get back in bed before you fall over."

Oh, my dear husband, you are so wrong. It isn't, nothing...it's everything! How could this have happened? Oh, stupid woman, you know exactly how it happened.

I crawled on top of the sheets and lay there. Counting back nine months, I recalled having sex with both men within a three-week period of each other. Fitz fell out of my life when Sherman made his re-entry.

I saw my life crumble before my eyes. It seemed my original concern when first discovering I was pregnant came back to haunt me. During Fitz's and my last bout of having sex, he had not pulled out fast enough. One little swimmer had found its destination. My brain paused. Not even a cuss word formed in my head.

Ugh...that explains the deep blue eyes. He doesn't have mine; he has Fitz's!

Now, what did I do? Confess to Sherman about my adulterous affair that resulted in Fitz being Peter's real father? No, that would destroy my rekindled marriage.

Another even worse thought came to mind. Custody of Peter. It could be in jeopardy should Fitz claim his paternal right to my son. That was a possibility that made me want to do what my mother's lover did—kidnap the child and disappear.

I worried about it for days until remembering what I read in my mother's diary about the information of her own affair. She never spoke about it to anyone and took the secret to her grave.

Like mother like daughter.

My lips remained sealed.

Epilogue

*A*lone in my apartment, I sit in one of the whimsical wing-backed chairs covered in pink owl upholstery. In the quiet lull when the halls are sparse of residents shuffling up and down on their walkers or in their wheelchairs, I think of my husband.

Sherman crosses my mind more at times like this. The silence makes the heart grow not fonder, but lonelier. I can't believe it's been seven years since his death.

I long for those laughable conversations with him. I would even relive the more contentious ones. Now *that's* missing someone.

I reflect a moment. My nose gives that prickly sensation you get right before a flood of tears are about to spill. With a deep breath, as deep as my old, withered lungs can manage, I keep the moisture from falling. I hate to cry. It shows weakness, and I have tried my level best throughout my life to live strong and love strong.

Sherman excelled in those, too. With and without me. He and I also fought strong…well, not in our early days of marriage anyway, or the latter days. Only in between when I forwent my mother's advice of, "if you go to work, Riley, nothing good will come of it."

My mother was only half right. I had a lovely career as an office manager for Coral Kingston who was a great boss and friend. But then, Fitz entered my life. It was he who held the title of the *nothing good* that my mother spoke about. My mistake with Fitz will forever change my life and that of my family.

Secrets rarely stay hidden. I continue to thank my female God that Sherman never learned of my indiscretion with Fitz. Indiscretion, hell. I dove into the infidelity pool and nearly drowned.

No, I will not relive that. It hurts too much. Besides, Sherman might hear my thoughts from Heaven and come back to haunt me.

"Sherman, my sweet, sweet love, you don't have to invade my soul with ghostly rebukes. There's no more room since I have taken all the space with my own self-condemnations."

My gnarly hands grow cold.

I cross my skeleton-thin arms, remembering his embrace. "It won't be long until I feel your arms around me again." I close my eyes and draw the tips of my deformed fingers down my cheek and across my mouth. "Your fingers lightly stroking my skin, and the way your lips brushed against mine, then pressed with a hunger I knew so well." My lungs cannot draw a deep breath any more than my eyes can keep the welling tears from cascading down my hollowed cheek burdened with deep wrinkles. "To feel the warmth of your body next to mine as we spooned before falling asleep. My possessive arm draped over your chest, reinforcing that I was yours, and you would always be mine."

"The Price Is Right" comes on the television interrupting my melancholy. It takes only minutes before I smile again and place my past where it belongs. Well, that is until the next time the residents remain in their rooms and the halls grow silent once more.

About the Author

SHERLYNN A. MUCKELROY is a born and raised Texan. Many years ago, when her two boys were young, she tried her hand at storytelling and wrote a children's book to entertain them. To this day, it is still unpublished and lost somewhere in her home. Years later, she took up the pen again, writing a five-book Romance/Science Fiction series. Sherlynn also has two YouTube Channels. One where she reads classic tales to all ages. The other is an audible podcast where she "interviews her protagonist, Riley O'Keefe," and also reads the first ten chapters of this novel. She currently lives in New Mexico.

You can learn more at her website:

www.sherlynnmuckelroy.com

Facebook.com/AQuestoftheAges

Twitter.com/sherlynnmuckelr

YouTube Channels:

TRADITIONAL CLASSIC TALES Read by Sherlynn

https://www.youtube.com/channel/UCBddGQ9v4D4UuPMBa64-bJg

ROMANTIC ROMPS

https://www.youtube.com/channel/UC9W9WfkQneAMkgNVDhKfKsA

Thank you for reading! If you enjoyed this book, I would appreciate an honest review on the site from which you bought it.

Made in USA - Kendallville, IN
1200342_9798551065166
11.25.2020 1036